MURDER AT HATFIELD HOUSE

Center Point
Large Print

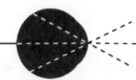

**This Large Print Book carries the
Seal of Approval of N.A.V.H.**

MURDER AT HATFIELD HOUSE

AN ELIZABETHAN MYSTERY

AMANDA CARMACK

CENTER POINT LARGE PRINT
THORNDIKE, MAINE

This Center Point Large Print edition
is published in the year 2014 by arrangement with
NAL Signet, a member of Penguin Group (USA) LLC,
a Penguin Random House Company.

The text of this Large Print edition is unabridged.
In other aspects, this book may vary
from the original edition.
Printed in the United States of America
on permanent paper.
Set in 16-point Times New Roman type.

ISBN: 978-1-62899-203-8

Library of Congress Cataloging-in-Publication Data

Carmack, Amanda.
Murder at Hatfield House : an Elizabethan mystery / Amanda Carmack.
— Center Point Large Print edition.
pages ; cm
ISBN 978-1-62899-203-8 (library binding : alk. paper)
1. Elizabeth I, Queen of England, 1533–1603—Fiction.
    2. Great Britain—History—Tudors, 1485–1603—Fiction.
    3. Murder—Investigation—Fiction. 4. Large type books. I. Title.
PS3603.A75373M87 2014
813´.6—dc23

                                                    2014018928

For Anne, who shared my obsession
with all things Tudor!

I miss you every day and wish
you could see this book now.

"A friend is one that knows you as you are,
understands where you have been, accepts
what you have become, and still, gently
allows you to grow."
—Shakespeare

MURDER AT HATFIELD HOUSE

PROLOGUE

"My lute awake! Perform the last
Labor that thou and I shall waste,
And end that I have now begun;
For when this song is sung and past,
My lute be still, for I have done."
— Sir Thomas Wyatt

February 11, 1554

It was a frozen gray day. The sun hid behind roiling banks of clouds and sent not even a ray of reassuring light to the earth below, which was eerily silent. There were no shouts in the streets, no cries from merchants selling hot cider or roasted almonds, no quarrels or laughter. The river was empty of boats, and the crowds on London Bridge scurried on their business with their muffled heads down.

The whole vast city seemed to hold its breath, and for a moment the ebb and flow of daily life, the stink and striving and heave of it all, had grown still.

Suddenly the bells of the Tower church and All Hallows Barking rang out in a slow, rhythmic, solemn song and the city lurched back to life. The door of the Tower lieutenant's house opened and a lady appeared there, soft and quiet as a ghost.

She was small and pale, and shockingly young. The crowd gathered outside gasped in surprise at the sight of her, so tiny in her stark black gown and furred cape, her oval freckled face framed by a fine French hood trimmed with jet beads. She clutched an open prayer book in her hands, which were steady and still.

She did not cry or tremble, but the two black-clad ladies who followed in her train sobbed. Lieutenant Feckenham and his men, Queen Mary's priest, and other grim officials joined the small procession, and they made their way slowly across Tower Green. The gathered crowd made room for them. No one said a word, overcome with sadness at the girl's youth and composure. Not even the Tower's ravens cawed or flapped their vast black wings.

The girl's lips moved in silent prayer as they came closer to the scaffold built near the chapel. As she glimpsed the church's open doors, where her young husband had been buried only that morning, she faltered for an instant.

"Oh, Guildford," she whispered. But then her calm composure returned, and she mounted the steps to the scaffold. A hooded, red-clad executioner waited there near the scarred black hulk of the block, his ax hidden from her view in the straw scattered at its base.

The girl stepped to the edge of the wooden planks and said in a clear, steady voice, "I pray you, all good Christian people, to bear me witness that I died a true Christian woman, and that I do look to be saved by no other means, but only by the mercy of God, in the merits of his only son, Jesus Christ. Now, good people, while I am alive, I pray you to assist me with your prayers."

While I am alive. Even at the threshold of death, she was staunchly Protestant, defying Queen Mary's Catholic ways and the priest who stood behind her. Prayers for the dead were futile, according to the new learning. The dead were beyond help.

She gave her gloves and handkerchief to her two sobbing ladies and her prayer book to Thomas Brydges, who had assisted her in the long, dull months of her imprisonment. The ladies removed her headdress and her black gown. Clad in her white chemise, she seemed even younger, purer—more vulnerable. Her waving red-gold hair fell over her shoulders.

She glanced at the executioner, who stepped forward. To him she said, "I pray you, dispatch me quickly." And as she knelt, she added in the first quavering hint of any anxiety, "Will you take it off before I lay me down?"

"No, madam," he answered.

She swallowed hard and nodded. In one quick motion, she tossed her hair forward and tied on a white blindfold. But then she lost her bearings in that darkness and grasped desperately for the block, her hands fluttering in the air. Her cool composure finally cracked, and she cried out, "What shall I do? Where is it?"

A shudder heaved through the crowd, a wave of revulsion at what was happening to this pale, frightened young girl. At last one of the guards gently led her to the block and laid her hands on it, and she rested her head in its hollow.

"Lord, into thy hands I commend my spirit," she whispered, and flung her arms out to the sides. The executioner, a skilled, experienced man at his profession, swung his ax high and brought it down only once—and it was done.

Jane Grey, sixteen years old and once Queen of England for nine days, was dead.

Her hysterical ladies were carried back to the lieutenant's house, where they had spent all the months of imprisonment with Lady Jane, and the silent crowds dispersed, their witness done. Jane's small body remained there in the bloody straw for hours until it could be officially collected and laid next to her husband and her traitorous father under the floor of the chapel.

Only the ravens watched over her, along with a cloaked and hooded figure lurking in the shadows of Beauchamp Tower. Alone and silent, this figure stayed with her like a guardian angel until she was carted away and the gory straw swept up and burned. The block was hidden and the Tower peaceful again—for a time.

CHAPTER 1

Autumn 1558

The horses' hooves pounded like thunder on the rutted road as the two riders dashed under the low-hanging trees, still heavy from that morning's rain. The storm had left the lane muddy and pitted, and it was late for travelers. The night was gathering in fast, and all sensible country folk were safe by their own hearths. The wind whipped cold and quick through the branches—winter was not so far off now.

But the riders took no heed of the chill. They had important tasks to perform, for very important people indeed, and they were already delayed. They had to reach Hatfield House by that night, which was why the lead rider traveled with only one servant and had ordered the rest to follow the next day.

"God's wounds, but this is a foul place!" Lord Braceton cursed as his horse slid on the wet ground. No one should have to live in such a forsaken spot as the damned countryside. It smelled of fresh, cold air and wet leaves, of cows and pigs and peasants, and the night sounds of hooting owls seemed ominous to a man used to the constant shouts and curses of London, the pungent, heavy air of the city.

The forest to either side of the narrow road was thick, full of shifting shadows and sudden sounds. It obscured the pale, chalky moonlight overhead and hid the few houses and cottages from view. A man could be lost in such a rural thicket and never be seen again.

Aye, Braceton thought grimly as he pulled hard at his horse's reins, making the beast whinny in shrill protest. The countryside was a godforsaken place, fit only for animals and traitors. It was no wonder so many of them gathered here, like a filthy, buzzing hive around their whorish queen.

The only solution to such a dirty, dangerous place was to destroy it and clean it out. That was why he was here. To crush out the treason—and get back to the civilization of London as fast as he could.

He glanced over his shoulder at his manservant. Wat slumped in his saddle, his hood drawn close over his head. The man had been more of a nuisance than an aid on this journey, whining and miserable every step of the way. But he was from a good, loyal Catholic family, servants to Queen Mary for a long time, and that was essential to Braceton's task. Plus, Wat was young and strong, able to carry all the baggage.

"Sit up straight, man!" Braceton shouted. "The faster we ride, the sooner we'll be safe by a fire with a pitcher of ale."

"If you can call it safe, your lordship," Wat

shouted back. "There's been no safe place this whole journey. One cesspit after the other."

And Wat had failed at his task in almost every "cesspit"—he had been told to make friends with the servants and listen to their gossip. Braceton himself had gotten nowhere with the stony-eyed landowners; no threats or promises could move them to do their duty to the queen. But servants were chattier, freer with their words, and they saw everything that happened in their houses. They could have been an excellent source of information, if Wat hadn't behaved like such a pouting fool.

But Braceton couldn't argue with Wat's assessment of those houses. Dark cesspits of stinking treason, all of them.

And now he was on his way to the greatest pit of all. Hatfield House, the lair of the heretic serpent Princess Elizabeth.

"You'd better be of more use to me in this pit," Braceton shouted above the wind. "Or the queen herself will hear of your piss-poor behavior."

The horses swung around a sharp curve in the road, and in the distance Braceton could see the faint flicker of golden lamplight, the dark outline of a roof and chimneys beyond. The gates of Hatfield at last.

But suddenly a sharp, high buzzing sound cut the silence of the night. Braceton twisted around in his saddle just in time to see an arrow arc out of the forest. It glinted silver in the darkness, like a shooting star.

With a cry, Braceton yanked his horse to the side and the creature reared up in the air with a terrified scream. It stumbled in one of the deep ruts and sent Braceton flying off into the mud.

There was a thud on the ground, not far from where he lay in a stunned state, and he pushed himself up. His head was spinning from the fall, and bright spots danced in front of his eyes, but he could see clearly enough to make out the body of Wat sprawled in the road. The servant's horse was galloping back the way they had just come.

The arrow had landed squarely in Wat's chest. His eyes were wide and shocked, glowing glassily in the moonlight, and his mouth was wide-open in a silent scream. He had died before he could make any sound at all.

Braceton's horse followed Wat's down the lane, leaving him alone with the dead body—and with whoever lurked in the woods. Two more arrows flew out from the cover of the trees, landing in the tree trunk over Braceton's head and vibrating with the force of the impact.

They could very well have landed in his chest, Braceton realized with horror. And then fury swept over his fear. He was an agent of the queen, curse it! He was here to root out the evils of treason and heresy, and those filthy beasts dared attack him for it!

He lurched to his feet and barreled into the woods as he drew his short sword. He could only see by the moonlight filtering through the branches, and it seemed as if laughing creatures lurked behind every tree and boulder. He slashed out at them, catching only leaves with his blade. Birds took flight from the treetops with terrified shrieks.

At last he saw a flash in the darkness, a whirl of a cloak as someone ran silently away. Braceton ran after that flicker of movement, crashing through the underbrush.

By the time he reached the jagged line where the trees gave way to the park of Hatfield, silent and serene beyond the low rock wall, the person had vanished. If it *was* a person, and not a demon or a ghost. Braceton's bearded face stung with sweat, blood dripped from the tiny cuts inflicted by the branches, and his lungs felt close to bursting with the labor of his breath. Golden light shimmered in the mullioned windows of the distant house, as if to mock him.

But he caught a glimpse of something shining stuck on the rough edge of the wall. He snatched at it and found it was the torn, feathered bits of an arrow's fletching. Whoever had shot at him had fled to Hatfield.

Braceton crushed the feather in his gauntleted fist. That witch Princess Elizabeth would pay for this—and pay very dearly.

CHAPTER 2

Curses on it all, Kate! This leg is going to be the death of me."

Kate Haywood smiled at her father as she helped him lower himself into his favorite chair by the fire. The red-gold flames crackled and snapped merrily, valiantly trying to drive the chill away from the small rooms at the back of Hatfield House. The wind moaned outside the window and stirred at the faded tapestries on the wall, and the ghostlike sound of it made her shiver.

"Poor Father," she said as she tucked a blanket around his legs. "Is your gout horrible tonight? I shouldn't wonder, with this damp, cold weather."

"It's bothersome all the time now, rain or shine," Matthew Haywood answered. "Ah, Kate, it is a terrible thing to be old. Enjoy being eighteen, my dear, before your youth is done and aches and pains beset you. I am falling to pieces."

Kate laughed and kissed her father's gray-bearded cheek. "You are not very old, I vow. You just claim you are so you can sit here by the fire and work on your musical compositions with no one to interrupt you."

"Would that were so."

"It *is* so. You cannot fool me." Kate turned to the sideboard, where their meager plate was stored, and poured out a goblet of rich red wine. "Here, Father, this will soon warm you. The princess sent it to you herself. She says the physicians claim it will strengthen the blood."

"Mustn't refuse the princess, then," Matthew said. He took the wine from her hand and swallowed a long sip. "It's quite good. You should have some, too. We all need strong blood to survive the winter."

"We need more than that, I fear," Kate murmured. She thought of four years before, when Princess Elizabeth and several members of her household were dragged away from Hatfield and tossed in the Tower on suspicion of treason in Wyatt's Rebellion against the queen. Matthew and Kate had fled and taken refuge at a friend's house, waiting in daily fear for word of Elizabeth's fate. Matthew was only the princess's chief musician, but everyone associated with her was always in danger. The queen hated her young half sister, the Protestant daughter of Anne Boleyn, and would do anything to see her downfall.

But at last there could be no evidence found, and so Elizabeth was released to come home, under the strict watch of Queen Mary's gaoler, Sir Thomas Pope, and his lemon-faced wife. Matthew and Kate came back to serve her, to bring what merriment they could to the silent house. But every day felt fraught with peril, as if they all waited with their breaths held to see what would happen next.

"What did you say, my dear?" Matthew asked.

Kate gave him her brightest smile, which felt tight and false on her face, and went to kneel beside his chair. Her father had enough to trouble him without knowing *she* worried too.

"I said I won't have some wine before I go to bed," she said. "It makes me sleepy, and I want to work on the new madrigal before I retire."

Matthew gently patted her cheek. "You work much too hard, Kate."

"On the contrary, Father." Kate carefully lifted his leg onto a cushioned stool and slid the slipper from his swollen foot. She reached for the basket that held clean bandages and the jar of herbal salve. It sometimes helped the ache. "I have to find things to do to distract me. Otherwise I am too idle."

"It is very quiet here, I know," Matthew said sadly. He groaned as Kate unwound the old bandages, but he let her do her nursing task. "Most unlike when you were a child and we were with Queen Catherine Parr. But we must not draw attention to ourselves. God willing, very soon . . ."

Very soon they would once again be part of a *queen's* household, that of Queen Elizabeth, and life would be extremely busy indeed. But those dangerous words could not be spoken aloud, despite the rumors that sometimes flew to them from London. Queen Mary was ill—her pregnancy had proved to be a phantom one, with no child but a tumor swelling her belly—and her Spanish husband, the hated King Philip, had left her again to war with France. Her people were angry with all the persecutions and burnings, the bad harvests and lack of work and food.

But Mary was still the monarch, and she would love nothing more than to see the end of her troublesome half sister. Kate's father was right—they had to be quiet and stay out of sight. For now.

"The princess will surely want some sort of revel for Christmas," Kate said. "We could all use some holiday cheer, even if it must be of a small nature." Elizabeth's allowance had been curtailed so much, she could barely feed and clothe her small household, let alone order elaborate masques. "I want to have the new madrigals done before then, and you must finish the church music you are working on."

"I'm sure Her Grace will appreciate the music very much," Matthew said. "But you still need your sleep."

"I will sleep, Father. I promise."

"Good. Now, are you quite done torturing me?"

Kate laughed and tied off the ends of the fresh bandage. "I am. You can drink your wine in peace."

She kissed his cheek and noted the gray that

flecked his beard and his dark brown hair, the same color as her own thick, heavy tresses. He had lost weight of late, and his face was pale and creased; his green eyes, also like hers in color, were rimmed with dark circles.

He *did* grow older in their exile, and it pained her to see that. Her mother, Eleanor, had died when she was born, and for all Kate's life it had been only her father and herself, a cozy little family. He had worked as a court musician ever since he was a boy, and when Kate was young he was appointed to the household of King Henry's last wife, Catherine Parr, a high and prestigious position where he also came to know Princess Elizabeth.

Matthew had taught Kate his art and trade, and she loved music with all her heart. When she sat down to create a new song, the sounds in her head drove away the fears and dangers of the real world and lifted her up into her own, secret place. One where she was free.

But there were some things even music could not banish.

The wind suddenly rattled violently at the window, making Kate jump. She hurried over to secure the latch on the old glass, and a cold gust swept between the cracks and tugged at her loose hair. For an instant, she saw her own reflection there, her round face and wide green eyes fractured and wavering, ghostly in appearance.

Kate laughed at her silly fancy and reached for the old velvet drapery to drag it closed. But then she saw something else, a flash in the kitchen gardens outside. It was very late—surely no one had any errand out there now? The cook and her maids would be asleep now. Kate peered closer but could see nothing.

There was a knock at the door, and Kate yanked the draperies shut to close out the night and all its dangers. She had enough to concern her inside the house without imagining garden ghosts.

"What can it be at this hour?" her father grumbled. He reached for his walking stick, but Kate hurried over to press him back down into his chair.

"I will go see what it is, Father," she said. "You finish your wine."

It was Peg, one of Princess Elizabeth's serving maids, who stood outside the door. Like Kate, Peg was still fully dressed, a shawl wrapped warmly over her gray wool dress and her silvery hair straggling from its cap.

"Begging your pardon, Mistress Haywood, but Her Grace cannot sleep."

Kate nodded with a sigh. This had been happening ever since the princess returned from the Tower. Sleepless nights and bad dreams. Only music seemed to help soothe her.

"I will go," Matthew said. Kate looked back to find him struggling to rise from his chair.

"No, Father," she cried, and hurried over to press him back down again. "I can go tonight. You need to stay off your feet and rest."

Matthew looked as if he was going to protest, but Kate grabbed up her faded and mended cloak and her precious lute, which had once belonged to her mother, and followed Peg into the corridor before he could say a word. She needed the cloak whenever she wandered away from the fire at Hatfield—the old halls were narrow and chilly. Wind whistled through the windows and along the wooden floors.

At least it was better than Woodstock, Kate thought as she and Peg dashed up the stairs. That house, the first prison Queen Mary sent Elizabeth to after the Tower, had literally been falling down around their ears. Chunks of the roof would land at their feet as they walked in the garden and rain would leak through into the rooms. Hatfield was a smaller, more comfortable manor house of pretty red brick and many chimneys, but it was still cold and lonely.

And the shadows that seemed to lurk in the corners were just as fearsome. Torches and candles were expensive and to be used sparingly. Nights were dark and quiet.

But the princess's bedchamber glowed with light. Candles were set on every table and atop every clothes chest, and lined up on the fireplace mantel. A fire roared in the grate, and the draperies were drawn back to let in the night's meager moonlight. No shadows were allowed to lurk there.

The bed, set up on a dais and draped in faded red hangings, was turned back to reveal the pale sheets and bolsters, but it was not occupied. Princess Elizabeth paced back and forth in front of the fireplace, the furred hem of her robe stirring the rushes scattered on the floor with every turn. Her red-gold hair spilled down her back, and she held a book in her long, elegant white hands, though it wasn't open. Even study couldn't distract her tonight.

Two of her ladies sat in the recessed window seat, also wearing bed robes over their chemises, with their heads bent over sewing. One was Lady Pope, the gaoler's wife and the new Mistress of the Robes since Elizabeth's faithful Kat Ashley, companion from her childhood, had been banished. The Popes were the queen's lackeys through and through, always watching, watching, waiting for any small, fatal misstep. Lady Pope looked most harried to be kept awake so late again.

The other was Kate's best friend at Hatfield, the young widow Penelope Bassett. She glanced up from her sewing and gave Kate a quick, conspiratorial smile. Her pretty, fashionably slanted, distinctive violet-blue eyes seemed to laugh at some secret, as they always did, but she sat quietly and decorously. She tucked a stray lock of blond hair back in her cap and went on with her embroidery.

Princess Elizabeth swung toward Kate and Peg as the door clicked shut behind them. Her dark eyes glittered in her pale pointed face, as if from some fever, and Kate knew it would be a long night. The princess's vast energy always burned bright, even pent up here in her rooms, and she could outlast everyone.

"Kate, by God's wounds, but I am glad you are here," Elizabeth said. "This wind is driving me mad. I need your music to drown out its moans and soothe me to sleep."

"Of course, Your Grace," Kate said. Her music was all she had to offer Elizabeth for everything the princess had done for the Haywoods. It was certainly little enough, but Kate was glad if she could help at all.

Even if it meant she got little sleep.

Elizabeth sat down in the carved cross-backed chair close to the fire and drew the heavy folds of her robe around her slender body. She gestured Kate to a stool across from her, and Peg came to take the book from her hands. Elizabeth tapped her long fingers on the wooden chair arms, a light, constant pattering rhythm like rain. Her ring, a ruby surrounded by pearls said to have once been her mother's, flashed in the firelight.

Kate tuned her lute, her head bent low over the strings. "What would you like to hear tonight, Your Highness? A lively volta or pavane to lift the spirits?"

"Nay," Elizabeth answered. "I am in no dancing mood tonight. An old ballad, I think. Something sweet and sad. Aye, that would suit the mood."

Kate feared "sweet and sad" was the last thing they all needed on such a night. The cold darkness seemed full of memories and longings, and old fears just lurking around every corner.

But her music was the princess's to command. Kate lightly strummed a chord and launched into one of the old songs of King Henry's day, a tune her father said had once been a favorite of Kate's mother.

Was I never yet of your love grieved,
Nor never shall while that my life doth
    last;
But of hating myself, that day is past,
And tears continual sore have me wearied.

As she sang, Kate fell down into the music, and it was like diving deep into a summer pool. All other sound was completely closed away. She didn't hear the wind or the whispers of the other ladies. Even her own worries were gone. She knew only the song.

I will not yet in my grave be buried;
Nor on my tomb your name fixed fast,
As cruel cause that did the spirit soon
   haste from the unhappy bones,
By great sighs stirred . . .

Kate glanced up to see Princess Elizabeth had ceased tapping on the chair. She sat perfectly still, her head turned to stare into the fire. Her white profile was sharply etched against the bright flames. One corner of her thin pink lips quirked in a slight smile. The music worked its magic again, and peace slowly descended on Hatfield House like a soft gray cloud obscuring the ugly world outside.

Until a crashing sound in the corridor outside tore that fragile peace asunder.

Kate's fingers faltered on the lute strings and the princess sat up straight in her chair. Her hands tightened on the chair arms, and she looked to the door like a tense bird ready to take flight. A woman screamed, and Penelope dropped her sewing to the floor.

A thunder of footsteps rang on the wooden floor outside and someone pounded on the door. Even Lady Pope turned pale.

"Lady Elizabeth!" a man shouted hoarsely. "Open this door at once."

"Her Grace has retired for the night," a maid-servant's nervous voice said.

"I care naught for that!" the man answered, still shouting despite the quiet of the house. "I come from the queen, and I will see the Lady Elizabeth at once, even if she's naked in her bed."

The queen! Kate clutched at her lute, feeling her hands shake and turn suddenly icy cold. This could mean only ill.

Elizabeth slowly rose to her feet. Her face had gone even whiter, but she was as still and calm as a statue.

"Peg, would you open the door, please?" she said softly.

"Are you sure, Your Grace?" Peg asked. "It is very late."

"You heard the man. We must not keep my sister's emissary waiting," Elizabeth said, as the barrage of knocks went on sounding at the door. "No matter how unexpected he might be."

Peg swallowed hard and nodded. Kate saw that she shook as if in a hard wind as she made her way slowly to the door. Peg drew it open and a giant of a man in a swirling black travel cloak pushed past her. He glared at them above his tangled black beard, taking in the warm domestic scene with one contemptuous glance. Mud and wet leaves trailed onto the floor in his wake, making Lady Pope, always a careful housekeeper, wince.

But Elizabeth refused to back away. She glared in return, equally contemptuous of such rude behavior. "I trust my sister is well?" she said. "Surely there is not some crisis in London that requires my attention at such an ungodly late hour, sir. I fear we are little accustomed to receiving guests and are ill-prepared."

The man gave a snort. He tugged off his dirty black leather gauntlets and slapped them against his palm. The loud sound made Kate flinch, but Elizabeth moved not at all.

"I am Lord Braceton, sent by Her Majesty to examine this household," he said. "I was greeted in your lane by a murderous villain, whose cowardly attack has left my manservant dead."

CHAPTER 3

G od's blood, but what is the meaning of this?" The sudden shouting, ringing through the wood-paneled corridors of Hatfield, made Kate gasp and jump. The pile of clean, neatly folded linen in her arms went flying to the floor in a flurry of white. From somewhere below, the shouting—which she recognized as coming from Princess Elizabeth—was followed by the crash of broken crockery, a dull thud, and a man's low, angry rumble along with the sound of scurrying footsteps.

Kate's heart was pounding. She could hear the blood rushing in her ears, drowning out everything else. After Lord Braceton's dramatic appearance last night with his wild accusations of murder and treason, Kate hadn't been able to sleep at all. Even though Elizabeth had kept her icy calm about her like a cloak, never betraying so much as a flicker of fear or any emotion but annoyance, Kate had seen the tiny, split-second flash in her dark eyes, which said the princess knew very well the danger they were in.

It had been the same on that terrible day when they had only hours' warning that Queen Mary's agents were coming to take Elizabeth to the Tower for questioning about Wyatt's Rebellion. The Tower—that terrible fortress that had swallowed up Elizabeth's mother, her young stepmother, and even her scholarly cousin, Jane Grey. The Tower, which always lurked there by the river like a great stone spider.

It was thus the same that day. For the merest instant, raw fear flashed through Elizabeth's eyes and her long, elegant white fingers clutched convulsively at her skirts. Then she launched quickly and coldly into action. Everyone set to work burning papers, even the most innocuous of letters and tradesmen's bills, for no one knew what could be held against her. Then Elizabeth pressed a purse of coins into Kate's hands, wrapped one of her own fine cloaks over Kate's shoulders, and whispered fiercely, "Take your dear father and go now, while you still can."

For one terrible instant last night, Kate was sure they would have to flee again. Run out into the cold, muddy darkness, even though her father could hardly even walk out of their chamber. But Elizabeth had merely ordered everyone but the Popes to leave her and faced Braceton with her chin tilted high, offering loud protests about his rude disruption of their household routine.

Kate had hurried from the room with the other ladies, all of them silent and white-faced. She barely had time to exchange glances with her friend Penelope before she rushed off to warn her father of what had happened, still clutching her lute tightly against her, as if it were a weapon.

She'd managed to persuade her father to take some more wine and go to his bed, but sleep had eluded her completely. She lay awake, listening to the rumble of thunder sound ominously in the distance. Waiting on a sword's edge for the moment the door would be flung open and they would be dragged away.

But mercifully, that moment never came, and eventually the light of morning crept through her window. She'd gotten up as she always did, washed, pinned up her unruly brown hair, dressed, and gone to fetch her father's breakfast from the kitchens.

Cora, the old cook, was kneading the day's bread while the maids scurried around, just as they did every morning in the Hatfield kitchens.

And yet things were not the same at all. No one spoke, not even a whisper. Cora didn't shout and scold the maids as she usually did. She didn't even look up at Kate, who piled a tray with bread, cheese, and a pitcher of small beer.

One of the maids whispered hastily that the princess was closeted with Lord Braceton and Sir Thomas Pope, and had left orders not to be disturbed, and that was all.

The whole house seemed poised on the rocky, fragile edge of a cliff, in that last breathless instant before it all tumbled down into the roiling sea.

Kate had managed to get her father settled with his new compositions, but she couldn't focus on the Christmas madrigals at all. The flowing melodies, the tumble of notes that usually filled her mind when she worked, kept tangling up and flying away. Last night's events kept coming back to her to take their place—Lord Braceton's furious face, his poisonous words of murder on the road.

His accusations of heresy and treason, which Queen Mary had sent him to root out.

Finally she'd given up and put her lute aside to go in search of some chore that needed to be taken care of. The house had still been quiet, all the servants scurrying about their work with their heads down, but one of the maids had stopped for a moment to chat with her.

"They do say more men are on the way to

Hatfield," the maid had whispered, wide-eyed. "That Lord Braceton is so infuriated by the death of his servant he has sent for an army to back him up here."

"I am sure it cannot be so large as an army," Kate murmured, but inside she was just as unsure as the maid. It was impossible to predict what such a man would do. Many men had come from the queen in the past, trying to break the princess and her household, trying to get them all to conform to the queen's changes, but so far none had been able. But Braceton seemed different. Higher ranking, closer to Queen Mary. Determined as steel to get his way.

And murder had accompanied his arrival. It had everyone most unsettled, including Kate.

"Even if it is only a few more men such as him, we will surely be in trouble, Mistress Haywood," the maid whispered. "I did hear tell that he—"

"What are you two whispering about there?" the cook shouted from the kitchens, irritation and a thread of fear in her voice. "Get to work right now. There is much to do today, no time for idle gossip."

The maid had shoved into Kate's arms the stack of newly mended, laundered linen to take to Lady Pope and run away, her head down.

Now the clean laundry lay scattered across the floor. Kate knelt down and tried to gather it, but she found her hands were shaking.

"My sister, the queen, has no more loyal subject than I," she heard Elizabeth cry, above the brittle sound of more shattering crockery. "I am sure Her Majesty would never countenance the peace of my home being so vilely disturbed."

"My orders, madam, are to search every corner of this house, nay, of this whole foul county, until this heresy is rooted out," Lord Braceton answered, his voice full of bitter anger. "I explained all this most thoroughly last night. The very fact that I was attacked so near to Hatfield proves I am close to some treason. I will search every room and box in this place—"

"And I say you shall not!" Elizabeth shouted, her Tudor temper obviously slipping free of her iron control. "My people are as loyal subjects to the queen as I am. They have been searched and questioned over and over, and no guilt has ever been found of them. I will not allow their peace to be so disturbed again."

"You will find, madam, that your previous questioners were not as thorough as I am. I will not be swayed by clever or pretty words. The queen and her husband, the honorable King of Spain, are bringing this country back to the true church, and I will assist her in that holy work however I can. And no Boleyn whore's daughter will stop it."

"How dare you!" Elizabeth cried, only to have her words drowned out by a thunderous crashing sound that shook the wooden planks of the floor under Kate.

Kate dropped the few linens she had managed to pick up, her hands suddenly gone cold and numb. She felt the same anger at Braceton's crude words as Elizabeth, the same fear wrapped up in fury. How dare such a man say such vile things! How dared he disturb their peace! Even the men who had come to interrogate Elizabeth after Wyatt's Rebellion never said such things. The maidservant who gave Kate the laundry was right—there was something different about Braceton. Something they all had to be wary of.

She felt a touch on her arm, gentle and fleeting as bird's wings, and it made her jump, her heart pounding all over again.

She spun around to see it was Ned, the mute kitchen boy. But he was actually no longer a boy; now he was a tall, gangly teenager, but still with a young mind, trapped in his own strange world. He watched her from under the shaggy fall of his hair, his brown eyes wide. He held out his hands from beneath his frayed, overlong sleeves and shook his head.

Kate pressed her hand over her still-racing heart and made herself take a deep breath. Ned never meant any harm. He gave some of the maids the shivers, they claimed, with the way he always watched and watched and never spoke. He slipped around the house like a shadow, doing chores no one else wanted to do. But the cook said he worked hard, and he seemed to enjoy listening to Kate and her father play their music. He would hover in the doorway of their room, refusing to come in but swaying back and forth in time to the tune.

Now he helped her gather up the scattered linen, still silent as she muttered words of thanks. Once Kate rose to her feet, he gestured that he would take the laundry to Lady Pope, and then he vanished again as silently as he had arrived.

Kate hurried on her way, now with no chore at all. She could still hear the sounds of a bitter quarrel from downstairs, and her mind was racing. Ned moved around Hatfield unnoticed all the time; what had he seen or heard since Braceton arrived? Could she possibly find a way to do the same? She well knew the value of being quiet and unobtrusive, and she also knew the value of information. Of knowing what might happen next.

Something seemed not quite right about Braceton's sudden arrival in their midst. Something beyond the obvious terror of any visit from one of Queen Mary's men. Why had he appeared so abruptly, after weeks of tense silence from London? Why this man, and not the usual inquisitors the queen sent? Those had been queen's men too, but also courtiers, smooth and polite, careful in the knowledge that one day the woman they interrogated might be their queen and they would be dependent on her for their places. Braceton seemed to care for none of that. What was happening Kate could not quite fathom, not yet. She had been too isolated at Hatfield of late.

The murder of Braceton's servant on the road had changed all that, dragged her into the tangle of politics and the courtly world, whether she wanted to be or not. What would have happened if Braceton had died instead of his servant, as it seemed sure the assassin's intention had been? The maidservant had said it was whispered Braceton had sent for an "army" to back him up. Would even worse have descended on them if the master and not the servant had died?

Or maybe, just maybe, it was the servant in truth who was the target. She knew nothing of him beyond the fact that he served Braceton. Maybe he was a courtier in his own right, with enemies himself. She fairly burned to know what had really happened on that dark, rainy road. Her curiosity would always get her into trouble, she feared.

"Psst! Kate."

She twirled around at the sound of the sudden, hissing whisper, which seemed to come out of the very air.

"Kate! Over here."

Then she recognized the voice. It was Penelope

Bassett. There was a creaking sound, quickly cut off, and a hand in a frilled white cuff emerged from a crack in the dark paneling, between two tapestries.

"Come quickly," Penelope said, and Kate rushed through the opening before it slid shut behind her.

She found herself in one of the old, narrow passageways tucked behind the plastered walls and wood panels. She'd been in them before once or twice. The servants still sometimes used them. A few trunks and crates were stored there, so thickly crusted with dust they were surely left from when Hatfield was old King Harry's hunting lodge. But the passages were mostly abandoned, being dim and musty, and inconvenient for such a small household.

They were no less musty and dusty today, as well as damp from the cold rain outside, but Kate couldn't help feeling a small, dark thrill at suddenly finding herself closed in its secret space. There was still danger, but there was also a measure of control. And Princess Elizabeth always said one must do what one had to do to stay safe.

"Penelope, what are you doing here?" she whispered, even though there was surely no one there to hear them.

Penelope laughed and held her candle higher to cast a gold circle around the narrow passageway with its dingy plastered walls. Her blond hair was swept up atop her head, and her violet-blue eyes sparkled on her heart-shaped, catlike face as if she also felt a dangerous thrill at being there.

"I was tired of being trapped listening to Lady Pope's sermons," Penelope said. "I wanted to know what was going on out there today. Aren't you simply dying of the suspense, too, Kate?"

"Aye," Kate admitted. "I keep wondering when we shall need to flee all over again."

A frown flickered over Penelope's brow, a fleeting dark shadow, and she nodded. "We have had to face doom far too many times, haven't we? All the more reason I had to escape Lady P's clutches for a while. I said I had desperate need for the necessary, and came here to hear what was happening in the hall. It took me a while to find the entrance, though."

"What have you discovered?" Kate asked, intrigued.

"Naught as of yet. I found myself quite lost in here. Then I heard you talking to Ned, and I thought perhaps we could find out together."

Kate nodded. Having a task to accomplish, a way to cease feeling quite so helpless, infused her with a new energy. Of course Penelope would find a way to more excitement. Life at Hatfield had been far less lonely since she had arrived there to wait on Princess Elizabeth after her return from the Tower. She was Kate's first friend of her own age. "We should hurry. I have the feeling that Braceton is not a man who will let the princess argue with him for long."

"Indeed not, the brute," Penelope agreed. "Just like a man." Still holding the candle high in one hand, she took Kate's arm with the other and they made their way through the maze of corridors and twisting staircases.

It was so narrow they could only walk single file, and the walls were so thin Kate could hear the occasional footstep or murmured word from the house beyond. It was all strange and muffled, the darkness thick beyond the small circle of Penelope's candle. Chests and boxes were also piled up, stored there out of the way. Most of them were plain pine bound with iron, but one was a prettily painted blue chest decorated with twining vines. Penelope shoved it out of their path.

At last they emerged through another small crack in the wall, and Kate found herself tumbled into the light of the gallery that ran the length of the house above the great hall. Tapestries and paintings hung on the walls, hiding the water stains and cracked paneling beneath. Beyond the carved balustrade that curved to the grand staircase, far below, was the entrance hall. The booming echo of voices told her that was where Braceton and Elizabeth were arguing.

They stopped next to the wall and Kate

watched, fascinated, as Penelope carefully felt around the edges of the rough plasterwork.

"It must be here somewhere," Penelope muttered.

"How do you know about this place?" Kate asked.

Penelope laughed. "Not all of us are buried in musical scores, Kate. Lady Pope keeps us running from day to night on errands. It's good to find faster ways to get about. Ah, here we are."

There was a small click and the seemingly solid wall eased open a crack. The muffled voices grew louder, clearer, and Penelope and Kate hastened into this next passage and down the secret stairs.

". . . you have read the letters I brought, madam, and surely you know you cannot hinder me in my task," Braceton was saying. His voice was thick with impatience, as if he had said those words before and his control would soon snap if he had to say them again.

Kate pressed her hand to her lips to hide a laugh. Many of Queen Mary's men had come to Hatfield in the last months, and none of them had sounded thus. They were too courtly, too cautious of their places, in a way Braceton was not. But Elizabeth had perfected the needle-fine art of hearing only what she wanted to hear, of replying with a swirl of artful words while her meaning became less and less clear the more she spoke. It had driven men twice her age and with multitudes more power to shout with rage. Shout—and then do what she wanted, which was leave her alone.

But even though Braceton shouted, he showed no signs of giving up and leaving. Those other emissaries had tempered their bullying from the knowledge that one day Elizabeth might be their queen, but not Braceton.

Kate carefully eased the secret door a little farther open and peered out into the entrance hall. Several trunks stood open on the flagstone floor, their contents spilling out in a jumble of clothes and papers, cloth and parchment all tangled together. Books were tumbled hither and yon, bindings cracked, their pages ripped.

Shards of broken pottery, carelessly spun out of their wrappings from the trunks, were crunched underfoot as men in dark doublets and brimmed caps marched past carrying more cases. Hatfield was being thoroughly searched—again.

Braceton stood with his back to Kate's hiding place. All she could see was his quilted velvet robe and grizzled hair straggling from beneath his fine pearl-sewn cap. His shoulders were slumped, his fists planted on his hips. Last night Kate had been overwhelmed by all that happened—the stormy night, Braceton's sudden, violent appearance. All she could think was how like an enraged bear at a baiting the man was.

She saw now how bearlike he was in appearance—a huge, hairy, lumbering bear—especially next to the princess's delicate figure.

She came only to his shoulder, small and slight in her plain black-and-white gown, her bright hair drawn tightly back from her pointed face. Her hands were folded demurely at her waist, but she would not back down from the man who loomed before her. She stared up at him steadily with her burning dark eyes, ignoring the other men rushing around her, destroying her house.

"I have read your letters, Lord Braceton, and I will of course obey the queen in all things," she said in a steady, cold voice. "But no treason has ever been proven of me or any in my household. That you dare violate our personal possessions thus—"

"Any of your household, madam?" Braceton roared. Kate flinched, and she felt Penelope stiffen beside her, but Elizabeth was as still as a statue. "What of your head lady, Mistress Ashley? Many heretical tracts and forbidden books were found in her possession and she confessed to her wrongdoings in the Tower. She was a poor guardian for you, as her behavior with Thomas Seymour proved."

Kate saw Elizabeth's lip tremble at the mention of Kat Ashley, who had been her governess and lady-in-waiting almost since birth, a second mother to her. Kat Ashley, who had let Elizabeth nearly be seduced by her stepfather, Thomas Seymour, and almost led them both to disaster. But Elizabeth quickly bit her lip and did not move at all.

"I am forbidden to contact Mistress Ashley by the queen's order, and I have not. None of my present ladies were involved in any such doings, and my chief lady is Sir Thomas Pope's own wife. I told you, Lord Braceton, we live here quietly and calmly."

"So quietly that I was almost murdered just outside your own gates," Braceton said in a cold tone far more frightening than his angry bluster. "My own servant was killed. A sure sign that wickedness lurks in this house, and I will find it and be rid of it once and for all."

"I can't help it if highwaymen and villains lurk on the roads at night," Elizabeth said. "I have no power to secure this kingdom."

"The murderer escaped into *your* garden!" Braceton said. He gestured to his men, the armed group who had arrived just as the maidservant said they would, and added, "Enough here. I am going to speak to your ladies now. They had all best be where they are meant to be—minding their embroidery as ladies should."

The man stalked off, lumbering up the stairs with his servants hurrying behind him.

Kate felt Penelope gently touch her arm. "I must be away, then," she whispered.

"Aye," Kate whispered back. "Heaven forfend we be doing anything but sitting over our embroidery."

As Penelope rushed away, Kate watched Elizabeth moving through the now-deserted hall. The princess picked up a book and gently smoothed its bent cover.

"You can come out now, Kate," she called softly. "He should be occupied for some time."

Kate gasped at the unexpected words, but knew she should have realized Elizabeth would know she was there. Her life—all their lives—depended on being aware and wary at every moment.

Kate slipped out of the passage and let it close behind her. She nudged an askew tapestry into place to cover it. "Forgive me, Your Grace. I am a poor spy indeed."

"On the contrary—you are an excellent spy. I would not have thought of the passages. Foolish of me to forget." Elizabeth turned the book over in her hands, her ruby ring catching the dull light from the high windows. "Braceton knows nothing of them, I think. But we must all be very careful in the future. How does your father today?"

"A little better, I think, Your Grace." Kate picked up a few gowns from the floor, unsure what else to do. She shook them out and folded them. "The wine you sent eases some of the ache in his joints."

"I'm glad. Your music, and that of your father, gives me much comfort in these uncertain days. I have so little to offer my friends except wine now. Your talent is great, Kate, greater than you know. Perhaps you should seek other employment where it could shine."

Other employment, away from the princess? From everything she had ever known? "Oh, nay, Your Grace! I am happy here. I only wish to make my music for you, and to remember—remember . . ."

Kate shook her head, not knowing what to say. What words could express what working for Elizabeth, being with her, meant for herself and her father. It was the glories of the past and the hope of the future bound up all together.

"You were a child when we all lived with my stepmother, Queen Catherine," Elizabeth said.

"I was young, true, but I do remember that time well," Kate said.

"Queen Catherine's household was a place of great learning, of art and music and fashion," Elizabeth said quietly, her hand slowly smoothing over the book as if she was far away, back in Queen Catherine's rooms, where there were always books and conversation, music and dancing. Beautiful gowns, laughter, friendship.

Aye, it had been a place of great learning—*Protestant* learning. A place where a new, enlightened world seemed possible.

Kate had been young then, just learning to play the lute and the virginals, yet she remembered it all.

"It was a very good time, Your Grace," she said simply.

"And one that was long ago," Elizabeth said. She sighed and tucked the book into one of the trunks. "Ah, Kate, I feel so old sometimes, though I am only twenty-four. So weary."

"Weary, Your Grace?" Kate cried, astonished. Elizabeth was always such a whirlwind of bright energy.

"That is why I'm glad to have your music, Kate. To remind me of those days. Even though it would be better for you if you went to another household."

Kate gave a wry smile. "No one else would hire a mere female to play music, Your Grace. And as I am helpless at embroidery, I must stay here."

Elizabeth laughed. "Then we have that in common. I can do naught with a needle too, though so many of my stepmothers tried to teach me." She reached into the purse hanging at her waist and drew out a few coins. "Here, Kate. I need you to go into the village and fetch some spices. I think some mulled wine would do us all good tonight. I feel a headache coming on and I must retire to rest for a time."

"Of course, Your Grace." Kate tucked away the coins and watched as Elizabeth unfolded a cloak and handed it to her. She recognized it as the same red velvet, satin-lined and fur-trimmed cloak she'd worn the night she and her father fled ahead of the queen's soldiers.

"And if you happen to hear any bits of gossip . . ." Elizabeth said with a wink.

Kate tugged the hood of the cloak over her head to cover her laugh.

CHAPTER 4

Mistress Haywood! It has been some time since we saw you here. I fear the new lute strings have not arrived from London yet."

Kate turned to find Master Smythson, who ran the largest of the village shops, hurrying toward her along the lane. Or hurrying as fast as the muddy ruts would let him. The hem of his cloak was as flecked with dirt as hers was, his round, lined face red as if he had walked a long distance. His breath was labored as he rushed to join her.

For an instant she wondered what he could have been doing outside on such a chilly gray day, a fair distance from the village. But then she shook her head, feeling foolish. The dark atmosphere at Hatfield had infected her with suspicion of everyone. Master Smythson was merely an aging widower who had run his shop well and efficiently for many years, with nary a whisper against his honesty or loyalty.

But loyalty to whom? In these complicated days, it was impossible to tell.

"Master Smythson," she said. "It is good to see you again. I fear things have been so busy at Hatfield I've had no time for outings. I can wait for the new strings. The last ones you so kindly procured for me are of such fine quality they still sound most excellent."

"I am glad to hear it, Mistress Haywood. With this foul weather we've had few deliveries from London." Master Smythson shook his head. "I fear we shall see yet another bad harvest if the rains do not cease."

"I fear you may be right." Together they turned toward the village, picking their way between the deepest of the puddles. "We must hope for better days soon."

"Indeed we must." Master Smythson studied her carefully from under the brim of his hat, but Kate had learned her lessons well from Princess Elizabeth. She merely smiled at him blandly. "So if not for the strings, what brings you to the village today, Mistress Haywood?"

"Princess Elizabeth has sent me on a few small errands," Kate answered. Then, because she knew how quickly gossip spread through the neighborhood, she added, "We have visitors from London, emissaries of the queen."

"Ah." Master Smythson's bushy brows rose and he nodded. "We did hear tell of riders late last night. Old Mistress Regan was out to deliver a baby and claims they nearly ran her down on the road as she walked home. A strange business. Were they not expected, then?"

"The princess has many people who call on her with court business," was all Kate could say. She thought it best not to mention the murdered manservant, but to wait and see if the villagers knew something of it she did not yet know.

But Master Smythson said nothing of the murder, or of the attacker who had escaped into the woods. "Indeed, indeed. We all remember when the queen herself came to Hatfield."

Kate remembered that visit too. It was the spring after Elizabeth had been released from house imprisonment at Woodstock and returned to live at Hatfield. Queen Mary had determined to make a show of how the sisters were reconciled, and had arrived with a large, gaily dressed retinue amid blue skies and brilliant sunshine. There had been a grand banquet in the gardens, exchanges of gifts and embraces. Kate and her father were kept busy playing dances and madrigals.

But that seemed long ago, and that elaborate rapprochement had turned quickly sour, as did the weather, ruining harvests and spreading disease and despair.

"I remember that as well," Kate said. "But the

queen was not able to come herself this time."

"Her health does not permit Her Majesty to travel?" Master Smythson said.

"It is a difficult time of year for journeys," Kate answered carefully. It was always dangerous to openly speculate about Queen Mary's delicate health. "But we are in need of provisions for her emissaries."

"Will the princess be wanting supplies for a banquet?"

"I don't think so. I believe this will be a short visit." Please God, let it be *very* short, Kate added silently. Braceton's roughness would wear them all down soon, and all their unwary words would go straight to the queen. Braceton had made it clear he was Mary's servant and no other's, and that he had no interest in treating Elizabeth carefully in hopes of future preferment.

"That is a shame," Master Smythson said as he unlatched the gate set in a low, rough stone wall and held it open for her. "We should all so love to hear your playing again. It is so cheering."

"Thank you, Master Smythson. I do enjoy seeing people dance to my songs. Perhaps for Christmas."

"May it be a merrier Yuletide than last, I say!"

Just beyond the wall they found themselves in the village proper. It was not a large settlement, merely one long main street with a few lanes leading off it, lined with double-story, half-timbered shops and thatched-roof cottages set in small gardens. The largest structure was the church, a square, squat building of faded stone built centuries ago, surrounded by a churchyard crowded with tilted, time-worn stones and new crosses. A vicarage was tucked away in the back, shuttered and empty at the moment because no Catholic priest had yet been sent to replace the ousted Protestant minister.

As they passed the wall around the churchyard, Kate peered up at the old bell tower. When Edward became king, his men had come to break out the stained glass windows and whitewash over the fresco of the Last Judgment that had looked down on worshipers for decades. The screen was torn down and the altar replaced with a linen-draped stone table.

Kate hadn't been there to see it, as she had been a child still, living in Catherine Parr's household at Chelsea, but she could imagine it. She had seen such scenes enacted all over London. She had attended Queen Catherine's own Protestant funeral at Sudeley when that remarkable woman died too young in childbirth.

Then Mary became queen, and it all reversed. The screens and statues and vestments were all coming back, but slowly. Scaffolding had gone up around this village church and workers had been there for months, but the windows remained blank. It was silent, empty—watching and waiting.

But the village wasn't silent. Kate had half expected everyone to be hiding in their houses, as if Braceton and his accusations had infected everything for miles around. Yet it seemed all wished to take advantage of the rain ceasing. The lanes were still rutted and thick with churned-up mud, but the doors to the shops were propped open, their meager wares laid out in the windows. People were hurrying in and out, their arms filled with packages, their cloaks and skirts tied up out of the mud.

Kate noticed several people whispering together on the rough plank walkways. They broke off as she came near, watching her approach with curious eyes. Though they gave her polite greetings, they didn't press her to stay and talk more, didn't ask questions.

So the seemingly normal, bustling day in the village wasn't quite all it appeared—just like everything else. Surely more was known about Lord Braceton than the fact that he had almost run down the midwife in the road. Did they know of his servant's murder? Did they know who had done it—and why? The servant's death had infuriated Braceton even more than he already was, and yet everyone seemed intent on ignoring it, on keeping their secrets.

Would they let Princess Elizabeth bear the blame for it?

Kate smiled and bowed at their bland greetings,

wishing with all her might that she could see past all the careful masks, all the heavy mist that seemed to hang over everything, and realize what was really going on.

She followed Master Smythson into his shop and gave him the list of spices they needed at Hatfield. While he filled the order, she examined a display of fabric near the bow window. Her father's winter robes were wearing out, like all their garments, and he needed sturdier clothes to keep the chill away or she feared his joints would pain him even more. Even though her sewing skills were mediocre at best, she could make new robes—if they could only afford the finely woven wool.

"Kate! Is it really you?"

Kate spun around at the sound of the familiar voice, her heart suddenly lighter. "Anthony! I'm most glad to see you today. I was going to walk very slowly past Master Hardy's rooms and see if I could wave to you through the windows."

"No need. I have a day's holiday while Master Hardy attends to business elsewhere." Anthony's handsome face was even more attractive when he was smiling, as he was now. It was a teasing grin, and he took her hand and bowed over it in an elaborate courtly gesture.

Kate laughed. Despite the worries that plagued her mind, the dark clouds that hovered over Hatfield, she felt her heart lighten even more.

She had become friends with Anthony Elias, a lawyer's apprentice the same age as herself, as soon as she met him at a musical party at Hatfield.

She'd never seen anyone quite as handsome as he—with his black hair and jewel-bright green eyes, his tall, lean figure—even at court, where there were dozens of handsome, peacock-clad men. When he'd come to sit next to her and asked her about the lute she played, for long moments she'd been frozen, tongue-tied. Men seldom paid attention to her like that; she was too young, too thin, too wrapped up in her music. Too insignificant in the complex web of the Tudor court.

She'd read sonnets, listened to other girls giggle about their suitors, but until she saw Anthony, she was mystified by what it all meant. When he smiled at her, she knew.

But she'd soon found there was much more to him than his green eyes and fine legs. He could make her laugh when she felt too solemn. He talked to her not as a mere girl, a child, but as an equal who could argue and discuss and understand any concept or idea. He told her about the law, about philosophy, and she talked to him of music and poetry.

But they met very seldom. Kate's place was with her father and the princess, and for now that meant living quietly at Hatfield. Anthony's time as apprentice in the law office of Master Hardy would soon be over, and he would have to go to one of the Inns of Court in London to finish his studies. His father, another lawyer, had died many years before, and Anthony had to work hard to take care of himself and his mother.

When they did have occasion to meet, Kate tried to make the most of it, to talk and listen and laugh and not waste a moment. She had so few friends; she wouldn't take one for granted.

"How have you been keeping, Anthony?" she asked as they strolled together through the shelf-lined aisles of the shop. "It has been too long since we've seen you."

"Since Princess Elizabeth's last-of-summer banquet, I think," Anthony said. The last party held at Hatfield, more than two months ago. "Master Hardy still speaks often of her generosity and kind spirit. But we have been kept busy with all the new heresy laws that are being passed in London."

Kate shivered at the very mention of that word, "heresy." She'd heard it too much that day in the furious voice of Lord Braceton. "There are no pending heresy cases here, I trust?"

Anthony hesitated, and Kate thought she saw a strange shadow flicker through his green eyes. "Not as yet."

There was some darkness in those three words that made her freeze. She started to reach for his arm. "Anthony—"

"Here are your spices, Mistress Haywood," Master Smythson said, interrupting her.

Kate's hand dropped to her side, and she turned to take the parcel from the shopkeeper. She gave him what she hoped was a genuine-seeming smile, not too strained or fearful.

"Thank you, Master Smythson," she said. "The princess will be most grateful for some mulled wine on these cold nights."

She started to take the coins from her pocket, but Master Smythson shook his head. "It is a gift to the princess. Tell her we pray here for her good health."

Kate's throat suddenly felt tight at his simple, kind words. So often it seemed they were alone at Hatfield, buffeted by storms from every direction. But Elizabeth was not forgotten in the wider world. "Thank you, Master Smythson. I shall tell her."

She drew up her hood again and followed Anthony out of the shop. The wind was brisker, sharp around the edges as it swept down the lane, but the sun still tried weakly to light the day overhead.

"Shall we walk for a while?" Anthony said. "Or are you needed back at Hatfield?"

Kate thought of the chaos of Lord Braceton and his men sweeping through the house, of shouts and breaking glass, scurrying maids. The fear and hiding. She needed to breathe, to clear her mind before she plunged back into that.

"I can stay for a while," she said.

Villagers still hurried by on errands, stopping to greet her and Anthony. To be somewhat alone, they walked to the church and turned through the rickety, rusty gate to stroll amid the jumble of stones.

"So you have a visitor at Hatfield?" Anthony said once they were alone. The only sound nearby was the rustle of the wind through the old towering, twisting trees, pushing the leaves in a thick fall to the ground.

Kate leaned against the cold, rough stone of an old crypt. "How do you know of that?"

Anthony shrugged, his plain black doublet rippling over his lean shoulders. "This is a small place where not much actually happens but much is always rumored. Word spreads quickly. And Master Hardy heard an emissary of the queen was coming, which is why he left to consult with some of his colleagues on how best to deal with such people."

Kate sighed. "His name is Lord Braceton, and he does come from the queen," she said. "He arrived last night. He says he was attacked on the road by an unseen assailant, his servant killed by an arrow. He is utterly furious."

"Does he say what his business is from the queen?"

"The usual when such people arrive. He is investigating word of treason and heresy in the princess's household, and he must search and question us all. But he seems even angrier, more determined, than those who have come before."

Anthony nodded, frowning. "Word of the murder did reach us here."

So the village had heard of the servant's death, yet they expressed no curiosity to her about how it had happened, asked her no questions, told her nothing of what they knew. It was so strange, and infuriating, coming from a place she knew loved to gossip. What could it all mean? What did they know? She was determined to find out. "Have you heard anything else?" Kate asked. "Is it known who did it?"

"If anyone does know, they aren't saying," Anthony said. "But Hatfield isn't Braceton's first destination in the neighborhood."

"What do you mean? Where else has he been?"

"You know Sir Nicholas Bacon? At Gorhambury House?"

"Aye, Sir Nicholas is the brother-in-law of the princess's surveyor, Master Cecil. He sometimes comes to supper at Hatfield, but we haven't seen him in a while. Braceton was at his house?" The man had said nothing of any other destinations.

"Investigating reports of heresy, of course. Bacon and his family were great supporters of Lady Jane Grey, and now they are closely associated with Princess Elizabeth."

"They've been questioned before and nothing

was found," Kate said, puzzled. "And they've lived such quiet lives since then. What would make the queen suspect them again now?"

Anthony leaned closer, his palm braced to the stone crypt next to her as he whispered in her ear. "Rumor from London says Queen Mary is not at all well since King Philip left her to go back to war in France. They say she is in such pain and has such terrible swellings that she cannot even walk. That she merely stays in her chamber weeping and praying, begging God to heal her and give her a child so Elizabeth will not sit on the throne."

"But twice she thought she was with child and twice she was wrong," Kate murmured. She remembered those long, tense, hot days when the queen had gone into confinement and Elizabeth waited to hear if a new Catholic prince had supplanted her, taken away what little power she had . . . if they were all doomed. But it all came to naught and Elizabeth went on as before, the heir—but not declared as such.

That was when the burnings increased.

"No one now believes the queen will ever have a child, not even her husband," Anthony said. "That is why he has gone, washed his hands of this whole English mess."

"A mess he himself helped create!" Kate said, angry at the haughty prince who had tried to bring Spanish ways to England. Yet even she knew it was not truly King Philip's fault. He'd prevailed on his wife to have Elizabeth released from the Tower and sent back to her own house, even if it was only because he wanted Elizabeth wed to his Savoyard kinsman and England thus tied closer to Spain. It was the queen who had hated Elizabeth and all she stood for ever since she was born.

It was the queen who, ill or not, had the power to destroy them all. And Braceton, her devoted officer and bully-man, had been sweeping through the houses of Elizabeth's allies. But why the Bacons, why now? And why go to Gorhambury before Hatfield? Where else had he been?

Kate had the feeling she needed to find these answers before she could discover who had killed Braceton's servant and thus exonerate the princess and her household. Perhaps whoever had killed the man had done it in a misguided effort to help Princess Elizabeth. Or perhaps it was all a ruse to cast even more suspicion on her.

"Even if Mary is ill, she is still queen," Kate said. "The burnings still go on."

"More every day," Anthony said gravely. "The latest was five people in Ipswich, including two women."

Kate shuddered at the images his words painted in her mind. If evidence of heresy *was* found at Hatfield, Elizabeth wouldn't burn—she would face the ax, like her mother and her cousin Jane Grey. But her servants could go to the stake.

Servants such as Kate, her father, Penelope Bassett, even the poor mute kitchen boy.

Nay! She would not let that happen. England had one hope for the future, and that was Elizabeth. And a raging bully like Braceton could not be allowed to bring that down.

The problem was that Braceton was a *powerful* bully, and Kate a mere young musician. But she had her life and the life of those she loved to fight for.

"Can you find out more about what happened at Bacon's house?" she asked Anthony.

A wry smile touched the corners of his mouth. "You think you can discover what this Lord Braceton is about?"

"I can try. Somehow I have the feeling he is up to more than merely searching for heretical books or letters about any planned uprisings. I can't do anything against him unless I know what is really going on."

"I will help you however I can, of course. I'll always help you, Kate. I hope you know that," he said softly. Then, to her shock, he took her hand and raised it to his lips for a kiss.

Unlike his salute in the shop, this was no mere mock courtly gesture, but a gentle, lingering touch of his mouth on her skin. Kate stared at his dark head bent over her hand, astonished, amazed . . .

Delighted? She hardly had time to try to

decipher her jumbled feelings when a shout split the cold air.

"Fornicators!" The stark, explosive word sent birds from the trees in a burst of wings and squawks.

Anthony dropped her hand and spun around, his body protectively blocking Kate's. She went up on tiptoe to peer past his shoulder, her stomach in knots.

The figure that greeted her sight was surely like something out of that vanished Last Judgment painting. Tall, thin to the point of being skeletal, with pale waxy-white skin stretched taut over sharp bones and burning water blue eyes, all draped in dusty old black robes. The specter pointed one long, shaking finger at them.

"Fornicators!" the phantom shouted again, a voice shockingly loud and booming for such an ethereal figure. "How dare you defile God's house in such a way?"

"Master Payne, I assure you we were doing no such thing in, er, God's house," Anthony said calmly. He held his hands up in a peaceable gesture, but he still sheltered Kate with his body. "We were merely walking through the churchyard."

Kate recognized the man then. It was no ghost, though in truth it might as well have been. For it was Master Payne, who had been the Protestant minister of the church under King Edward. He had been turned out unceremoniously when Mary became queen.

Master Payne had been of a distinctly Puritan bent and, it was said, had preached extreme, almost Lutheran ways in his sermons, railing against ornament and merriment of all sorts, tossing Catholic prayer books and vestments onto bonfires. It was said most of the townspeople were relieved to not listen to him from the pulpit any longer.

Not that Master Payne was completely silenced. When he had been tossed out of the parsonage, he refused to go live quietly with his family in the next county or to flee abroad as so many other ardent Protestants did, including Elizabeth's own Carey-Boleyn cousins. Instead he found an old sheepherder's hut in the woods and took up residence there, as hermits did in centuries past.

He sometimes emerged from the woods to stagger around the village, exhorting people to mend their sinful ways, to embrace martyrdom and defy the demon Papist queen. How he had not been seized and burned long ago was a wonder. Most people merely thought him quite unhinged and rather harmless, easily batted away. Kate herself had only glimpsed him once or twice, darting around the empty church that had been his domain.

But was he really so very harmless? She

couldn't think so now, as she stared at him, her mouth dry with startlement.

He was so very large, the arm revealed under his fallen-back sleeve surprisingly muscled. And his eyes were glowing with an inner, furious fire she'd only seen on Queen Mary's most Catholic ministers, who came periodically to harangue Elizabeth.

Just like Lord Braceton.

"I have been watching you—all of you!" Master Payne shouted with a sweep of his torn sleeve. "You come to this place to do your foul deeds. England has become a sinful place, and we shall all be destroyed by it. All except the righteous, who have a duty to fight back. I see everything."

"Everything, Master Payne?" Kate said, finding her voice again. Master Payne did indeed have a way of lurking around, unseen by everyone because they did not want to see him. Didn't want to acknowledge madness in their midst, as they tried to keep their heads down quietly and survive. Perhaps he had seen who attacked Braceton.

Perhaps he had even done it himself, "fought back" against the Papists. Surely attacking the queen's man was an act of madness.

Kate eased around Anthony, still afraid as Master Payne turned his wild stare on her. But she was calm, knowing they were still within shouting distance of the street, and remembering her promise to Elizabeth that she would find out all she could. Master Payne, for all his shouting of fire and sin, might be able to shed a tiny bit of light on the confusing tangle of Braceton.

"Did you happen to see anything last night, Master Payne?" she asked quietly.

"Kate . . ." Anthony said. He moved to take her arm, to push her behind him again, but she held him off.

"I see many things," Payne said. "God has given me the gift of seeing into men's hearts, and most of them are black with sin. But they shall be punished in the fullness of time."

"Indeed, sinners shall be punished," Kate said, as if what he preached was the most logical thing in the world. "God has chosen you as His instrument, has He not? He knows you are a faithful servant."

Payne's gaze shifted, as if a flicker of uncertainty passed over him. "I am His faithful servant. I will do anything to bring God's favor back to this land."

Anything—even kill? "Then we must all be grateful to you, Master Payne, for your great work and sacrifice," she said. "Were you out doing God's work last night?"

"I do His work in every moment. It leads me to see shameful things. I could tell you much, young lady, but I will not sully you with further knowledge of such sins. You should not go out at night. Evil lurks on these very roads. But one day soon the evil will be purged. I will see it done."

Kate swallowed hard and nodded. She wanted to shout with impatience, as Princess Elizabeth sometimes did, to grab Master Payne by his meager hair and demand he tell her what he'd seen or done on the road last night. But, aside from the fact that he was much taller than she and could swat her off in an instant, she knew that was no way to find out what she wanted.

"You have seen more Catholics come into the neighborhood of late," she said.

"Kate, we should go," Anthony whispered to her. She nodded, her gaze never leaving Payne, whose skeletal face hardened.

"They are polluting the very air," he said. "But one has paid. The others will soon."

"What do you mean?" Kate demanded. Payne gave her a smug smile, but before he could answer, a shout came from the churchyard gate, a man passing by trying to shoo Payne away as if he were an errant pig broken loose among the tombstones.

Payne whirled around and fled at the noise, vanishing behind the church in a flurry of black robes.

"God's blood," Kate whispered, using Elizabeth's favorite curse. Surely she'd been close to finding out something! Payne seemed mad, but there had to be a kind of truth in his words.

"You shouldn't speak to him at all, Kate," Anthony said as they walked out of the church-yard. He held the gate open for her, making sure no one still lurked on the walkway. "There is no knowing what a madman like that will do when provoked."

"Everyone says he is quite harmless," she murmured, turning over Payne's few words in her mind as she searched for a kernel of a clue.

"As long as he stays in the woods, perhaps. But we have all seen the lengths people in the grip of religious fervor will go to," Anthony said quietly, solemnly. "These are dangerous days for everyone. We must walk very carefully."

"Somebody refused to 'walk carefully' last night, and it has put us all in danger," Kate said. "But you are very right about religion—it can be such a force for good, but it can also make people unhinged. Payne is surely as fanatical a Protestant as Braceton is a Catholic. Do you think then it was Payne who tried to kill the man?"

"Payne?" Anthony said, his voice full of surprised consideration. "Perhaps so. He surely wouldn't consider murdering a queen's man, a Catholic, to be a sin. In his mind he would be ridding the land of one more dirty, sinning fornicator."

Kate laughed at the word "fornicator," shouted

at them so furiously by Payne in the churchyard. And so ridiculous—Anthony had never so much as kissed her cheek. "He would consider it his duty as God's instrument. And he is strong enough, though it doesn't take enormous strength to wield a bow like that."

"But he also wouldn't scruple to admit it. The man cares naught for what happens to him."

"Nay. I think he would welcome the stake. I just need to get him to talk longer, to admit it if he is the culprit. Perhaps there is some link between Master Payne and Lord Braceton? Mayhap Braceton is responsible for the deaths of some of Payne's reformist friends. Or maybe . . ."

"Kate." Anthony suddenly took her hand, swinging her around to face him. "You must not speak to him again. It would be too dangerous."

She felt a sudden flash of warm anger flare through her at his stern words. She was not his wife—she was no man's wife, and no one's to command except her father's. And he never tried to command her, which had given her a sense of her own mind. What right had Anthony to tell her she "must not" do something—especially when Payne seemed her only hope to find out what had happened on that dark road?

But then she saw the concern in his eyes, his beautiful green eyes, as he looked down at her, and her anger softened. She didn't want to analyze why his concern, his protectiveness, moved her.

Not now. Braceton's attack was a thorny enough problem. How much more complex would a heart's hidden desire be?

"I know you speak as my friend, Anthony," she said as they walked on, side by side but not touching. She still remembered that shout of "Fornicators!" and wanted to attract no more gossip to Hatfield. "And I thank you for it. But I must help Princess Elizabeth if I can; she has been so kind to my father and me. And I am quite sure Master Payne knows something that would exonerate her of this attack."

"Something that has already gotten one man killed," Anthony muttered.

Kate swallowed hard. "I know that very well, and I shall always be careful. But as you said, these are dark days. We must all be prepared to defend what we believe in or all shall be lost."

And she believed Elizabeth was the future. A future that was so near it seemed to shimmer just on the horizon—but it was not there yet. It could still all be snatched away.

"Then promise me one thing—as my friend," he said.

"What is that?"

"That if you insist on finding Payne again, you will let me go with you."

"I can't let you put yourself in danger, not now when you are so close to going to London!"

"Then I will just follow you in secret. I won't let you put yourself in harm's way if I can help, Kate."

She smiled at his words, and nodded. "Then I would be most grateful, truly, both for your sword-arm and your lawyer's mind. I think it will take every ounce of both to wring a coherent answer from Master Payne."

Anthony gave a wry laugh. "You have more than a touch of the lawyer's mind yourself, Kate. You could certainly outstubborn any jury."

"I shall take that as a compliment," she said happily.

"And so you should, for I meant it as one," Anthony said as they reached the edge of the village.

The road back to Hatfield stretched before them, the trees crowding thickly on either side as their leaves drifted down. "There is no one quite like you, Kate." He squeezed her hand as they parted and gave her a dazzling smile.

At his words, Kate's steps felt strangely lighter as she turned toward home. A faint ray of sunlight broke through the slate-colored clouds, casting shifting panels of pale yellow light on the muddy ground. Kate paused to let some of its watery, elusive warmth touch her skin. She would be shut up behind cold walls again soon enough, with Braceton and his men restricting everyone's movements at Hatfield. Surely, for a few minutes,

72

there was no need to hurry. She had so much to think about.

She sat down on a fallen log, tucking the folds of Elizabeth's red cloak around her as she remembered the events of the day. The whole village seemed determined to go on as normal, despite Braceton and the death of his manservant. Except for the usual fears they always lived under in these dark days, there appeared to be nothing out of the ordinary in the cobbled lanes and busy shops.

That was odd. News and gossip were usually vital to everyone in such a small place. Why were they minding their own business now?

Surely someone knew far more than they were telling. The truth had to be close by. And despite the fact that Kate knew very well indeed that she should follow their example, keep her head down and say nothing, she couldn't. Something inside of her, some spark of eager and dangerous curiosity that had been with her since she was a little girl, wouldn't let her. All that had happened since Braceton burst into Hatfield was swirling around in her mind and wouldn't be cast out.

They were all going to hell for their popish ways, she remembered Master Payne shouting, and when she closed her eyes she saw again his wild expression, the bony, trembling finger pointing at her. Mad he very well could be, just as everyone said. But mad people could sometimes see things others could not. And, even though Payne himself had been spared prison and the stake, surely many of his reformist friends had not. Maybe one of them was connected to Braceton. Maybe Payne thought God urged him to find revenge.

Before Kate could change her mind, she turned around and headed back the way she had come. But she didn't return to the village. They were too closemouthed there at the moment. She went the opposite direction at the turn of the lane and headed into the cold shadows of the woods.

As the light was blotted out above her head, she shivered and pulled the warm cloak closer around her. She never liked venturing into the woods alone. There was a strange feeling along its pathways, the eerie sense that something was always watching from under the cover of trees and underbrush. That feeling was even stronger now that murder had been done nearby.

Kate pushed away the fear. She had to find out all she could; there was no time to cower when so much was at stake. Holding the hem of her skirt above the damp ground, she hurried in the direction of where she knew Master Payne had been living since his church was taken from him. It was said that he wasn't there often, that he preferred to wander about shouting of sin and doom—which Kate could certainly attest to. Yet maybe she could find something there that would tell her if Master Payne knew more about what had happened to Braceton and his servant.

She found the old hut in a small clearing in the woods. It didn't look as if anyone could possibly live there; the walls were tilted so precariously and the thatched roof sagged. No smoke came from the crumbling chimney. Kate crouched behind a tree and carefully examined the scene, listening closely for any hint of sound. She heard only the whistle of the wind in the bare branches.

She tiptoed closer and knocked on the splintered door. "Master Payne?" she called, pushing down the nervousness inside her. "Are you there? I mean you no harm; I only wish to talk to you for a moment. To talk about—about salvation."

There was no answer. Kate tested the door latch and it turned under her hand. The door swung slowly open.

A terrible stench rolled out over her as she peered over the threshold, and she choked on it. But she forced herself to move forward against the smell and the darkness of the tiny space.

If Master Payne *was* hiding something, he had few enough places for it, Kate thought as her eyes adjusted to the gloom and she could see just how cramped, damp, and dusty it all was. A thin pallet was rolled up in a corner, and the fly-speckled remains of a meal sat on a rough-hewn table. The floor was hard-packed dirt, no room for a trapdoor. The only possible hiding place was a single old box in the corner.

Kate glanced back over her shoulder to the gray light of day beyond the door. Everything was silent and still out there, but surely it wouldn't be for long. Even if Master Payne had gone off to harangue someone else, fired up by thoughts of sin and fornication, he would have to come home sometime. To hide from Braceton and his men, who would surely find him soon enough. And Kate had to be back at Hatfield before dark if she didn't want to get into trouble herself.

She hurried over to pry open the lid of the box and peek inside. Another rolling wave of stink hit her in the face, and she pressed her sleeve to her nose. Through watery eyes, she saw the smell came from a pile of rusty old black clothes, a plain white surplice turned yellow from age. She quickly shoved the garments out of the way, and at the bottom of the box she found old books and papers.

Kate reached for the first one and turned it over in her hands. Tyndale's English Bible, the leather cover stained. Kate gasped when she saw it, for this was the very first on Queen Mary's list of forbidden books. A book that would get a person imprisoned, fined, even killed if he were caught with it. And Master Payne was hiding it almost in plain sight.

Except that no one dared come near him in his seeming madness. But how far would a madman go to protect such dangerous things?

Kate took a quick look at the other volumes and saw they were the same sort of thing. Foxe, Cranmer, all manner of German Protestant pamphlets. And one book she remembered Queen Catherine Parr and her ladies reading in the queen's chamber so many years ago. She carefully opened it and read over one of the pages. The parchment was a bit water-stained and the ink had run a bit, yet still she could read the words.

In the margin, a wavering hand had written in pencil: *Sinners must pay, the righteous avenged.*

Something suddenly clattered outside the door, breaking the brittle silence around her. Kate's breath caught in her throat at the shock, and the book tumbled from her hand. No one was there, but she knew they soon would be, and she dared no longer linger.

She hastily closed everything back in the box and ran out of the horrible little house, with all its darkness and secrets. She could see no one in the clearing, but she ran toward home anyway, still feeling the burning heat of who knew what in the woods.

Only when she was close to Hatfield's gates did she dare slow down and try to catch her breath. Master Payne's books were very dangerous, to be sure, but were they indeed some clue to Braceton's servant's death? Perhaps if she had more time to look at them—if she could bear to face the woods and the dank stench again, if Master Payne was gone for a time—she could find out more. Find if there was a connection between Payne and Braceton.

She was lost in her thoughts, but when she passed the gatehouse at Hatfield she glanced up at the blank gleam of the house's windows in the sunset light. The sun skittered away and the cold wind caught at her cloak. It felt horribly as if someone watched her, the sensation palpable and physical as her skin prickled. She turned in a slow circle, trying to see if anyone was there. But there was no one.

No one at all.

CHAPTER 5

*S*he was going to get them all killed.

The figure lurking behind the wall at Hatfield peered out at the courtyard, watching as the woman in the dark red cloak hurried toward the house. What was the foolish creature thinking to go sneaking about in the middle of the day? Princess or no, she was obviously losing her mind and dragging them all down with her.

Not that it would be such a terrible thing to

lose her. There was always a long line of eager claimants ready to leap on the throne, and at this point one was as good as another. But it wasn't time for this little adventure to end and Braceton to be gone. Not yet.

The lurking figure watched as the girl, the foolish princess in her pretty crimson cloak, stopped at the side door and glanced back over her shoulder as if to make sure she wasn't followed. The hood didn't fall back to show her red-gold hair, but who else would be running about in her fine cloak at that time of day? Elizabeth's tale of being confined to her chamber sick with a headache was patently false.

Just like all her lies, her craven prevarications. She wasn't worthy of her place, the position she had stolen.

She'd be sorry one day soon, the Boleyn bastard. All her vaunted cleverness couldn't save her. But for now, she had to stay. Plans would take longer to come to fruition than intended—that was all.

The watching figure curled its gloved hand into a tight fist as a wave of cold, bitter frustration washed over them. Once word came that it was Lord Braceton sent to question Elizabeth, Braceton who was lurking in the neighborhood, all seemed set to finally fall into place. Braceton was not the largest prey, but he was assuredly one of those who had to pay. And his downfall would set so many others in motion, like a carefully arranged set of dominoes. It had all seemed so very easy.

Until the arrow went astray in the darkness. A terrible miscalculation, but not one that would be made again.

The girl in the red cloak slipped into the house and the garden was empty again. The drapery swung into place and the figure turned away. Failure again was simply impossible.

Braceton had to go. And Elizabeth with him.

Kate heard the shouts and sobs as she ran up the back stairs, and she felt the fear that had vanished all too briefly return. It seemed that their once quiet, if ever watchful, house was being turned upside down all over again.

She took off the princess's cloak and draped it over the banister post as she listened carefully, trying to figure out where the noise was coming from and what might be going on. She heard Cora, the old cook, scream, "Not in my garden, you won't!"

Kate turned on the landing and hurried back down into the kitchen. The cavernous space, usually warm and humid with cooking fires and pots of boiling soup, was cold and empty. The smoldering remains of a fire in the vast grate, usually assiduously tended, were down to mere cinders. A pot of stew congealed on its stirring spoon. Lumps of bread dough were deserted on the table.

There was a flicker of movement in one corner, and Kate spun around to see it was Ned, the kitchen boy. He huddled on the floor, his arms flung protectively over his head as silent tears rolled off his chin. She started to go to him, but another cry from outside made her run out the half-open door to the walled-in kitchen garden.

She took in the scene with one darting glance, only half-aware that things had gone terribly quiet for such a large gathering. The small courtyard, which led via narrow gravel pathways to the neat beds of herbs and vegetables, was crowded. Braceton's men hurried by, piling up firewood in a hastily dug pit, while the man himself loomed in front of the cook and her cowering kitchen maids.

For a tiny woman of advancing years, Cora would not back down from the hulking man before her. She stared up at him, her fists planted on her bony hips, glaring.

"I have to prepare supper, which will never be ready in time now," she cried. "I can't have this nonsense in my garden."

"Do you call this *nonsense,* woman?" Braceton said coldly. He held up a ripped pamphlet, which Kate recognized as one smuggled out of Geneva in recent months and circulated among the countryside. "This filth was found in a cupboard in your own pantry."

"I can't help what others here might do—I have too much work at my hearth, which I need to be getting on with," Cora said. "And I don't call that nonsense, or anything at all, because I can't read a word, you dolt."

Suddenly, Braceton's large hand, shimmering with jeweled rings, shot out and slapped Cora hard across the face. With a sharp cry, the slight old woman tumbled backward, caught by two of her maids before she could fall onto the paving stones.

"I will not have such abuse in my house, Lord Braceton!" Elizabeth suddenly shouted. She hurried out from under the sheltering eaves of the roof, where she'd been standing half-hidden with Penelope behind her. Her pale cheeks were bright red, her eyes glittering with fury and pain. A shawl was wrapped hastily around her plain gown and her hair hung in loose red waves over her shoulders. She had obviously been rousted quickly from her sickbed.

"These are my servants," she said. "I will not allow you to treat them thusly."

"Madam, your servants—and anything else you have—are yours only by sufferance of the queen," Braceton answered, turning his back on the weeping cook. "And yet you repay her by allowing such treason in your midst."

"Not even Bedingfield dared to treat me thus," Elizabeth said with icy dignity, mentioning her most careful gentleman-gaoler from the terrible time at Woodstock. "The queen shall hear every detail of your deplorable behavior."

"Indeed she will, because I will tell her myself," Braceton answered. He tossed the pamphlet into a puddle. "You have been treated most mercifully by the queen, madam, and you have repaid her by sheltering vipers in your house. But no more. I am here to discover the truth and that I shall do, by whatever means necessary."

"The truth, Lord Braceton, is that my sister has no more loyal subject than myself," Elizabeth answered. "That is all you will discover in your brutality."

Braceton just laughed, and turned away as one of his men set a fire in the pit and others carried boxes into the courtyard. Penelope beckoned to Kate, and she hurried over to her friend's side. Penelope held tightly to her hand as they watched the flames crackle to life.

The fire recalled terrible images of burning Protestant heretics, brought by the clouds of acrid smoke stinging their eyes.

"What is happening?" Kate whispered.

"Braceton forced the princess to rise and come down here, along with these servants you see," Penelope whispered back. "For what purpose but to harangue us yet again, he has not said. But surely it can be nothing good. Even Pope and his ever-watchful wife have kept away, as you see."

Elizabeth stared, white-faced, as Braceton opened the boxes and tossed the contents out onto the wet paving stones, just as he had done in the entrance hall that morning. Some he threw back into the case, one or two he tucked away in his doublet. The minutes ticked past, horribly drawn out with uncertainty, the only sounds the booted footsteps of Braceton's servants and Cora's sobs.

A stack of letters tied up with a black ribbon landed in the dirt. Penelope's eyes widened when she saw them, and Elizabeth took a step forward.

Kate recognized the writing. They were missives from Elizabeth's cousins, Henry and Catherine Carey, children of her aunt Mary Boleyn, who had fled abroad to freely practice their Protestant faith.

"Those are no heretical tracts, sir," Elizabeth said. "They are merely letters from my family, which have been read over by my sister's people and which I have been given permission to receive."

Braceton gave a contemptuous snort. "Letters from Boleyn traitors."

"From my family," Elizabeth said simply, but there was a world of danger and pain in those three words. Elizabeth never mentioned her mother and very seldom her mother's family, but Kate knew she was very close to the Careys and missed them desperately. The few messages she was allowed to have from them were treasured.

Braceton tossed the letters onto the fire, where they immediately burst into flame and crumpled to ash. Elizabeth froze, her lips tight, white at the edges.

A small piece of embroidery sewn in faded colors in the pattern of Anne Boleyn's falcon badge followed into the fire, and a manuscript of Elizabeth's Latin translation of some writings of Catherine Parr. Somehow Braceton had found Elizabeth's smallest, most treasured keepsakes, and since they held no clues to treason, they were destroyed. It was as if the people whose memory they evoked were being snatched away all over again.

"Nay, you must bring that back, I say!" Kate suddenly heard her father cry. "I must have that back, it is not finished."

Her desperate gaze swung toward the open kitchen door just in time to see one of Braceton's men emerge with a sheaf of parchment in his hands. Matthew Haywood stumbled out after him, leaning heavily on his stick. Tears streaked his gaunt, lined face.

"Father, no!" Kate cried. She ran over to him, catching him as he tripped on the last step. When she'd left for the village, she had made sure he was warm by their own hearth, with a glass of the princess's good wine beside him and hard at work on his Christmas church music. He was having a good day, relatively free of pain.

Now here he was, barely able to walk, desperately lurching through the house, another victim of Braceton's mission.

"Father, you must go back to bed," Kate whispered urgently.

"He took my manuscript," Matthew said, pointing a shaking hand at the servant as the man handed the papers to Braceton. As Braceton carelessly flicked through them, Kate saw it was her father's Christmas church music, the work he had been laboring over all summer in hopes of cheering the princess's holidays. The composition that was his only distraction, his only passion.

"My father must have that back," she insisted. "It has naught to do with any treason. My father is only Her Grace's musician, and that is his livelihood."

"What is it, then?" Braceton said, frowning down at the notes as if he tried to decipher words in the Araby language.

"A Christmas service for Princess Elizabeth's chapel, that is all," Kate said. Her father's breath sounded strained and wheezing, and he leaned against her heavily. She feared he could not speak at all, that the exertion had only increased his illness.

"A Protestant service?" Braceton casually tossed the manuscript into the fire.

Matthew moaned and sagged against Kate's shoulder as his months of work, his art, burned away. Elizabeth rushed over to wrap her arm around him and help Kate hold him up.

"Be of good courage, Master Haywood," she whispered. "They can burn paper, or even flesh, but never what is in our hearts. Here, Kate, let us get him back to his chamber."

But as they started to turn away, worse was coming toward them. Another of Braceton's servants emerged from the house, and in his hands was Kate's own lute. The lute that had belonged to her mother, whose spirit seemed to be with her every time she touched the strings.

"I hear tell they sometimes hide messages in instruments, Lord Braceton," the man said. "This was near that manuscript."

"Indeed so," Braceton answered. "Good thinking, my lad. They do say that even that traitor Wyatt sent letters in a spinet. Let me see it."

As the man handed Braceton the instrument, Kate was so blinded by fury she strangled on the words crowding in her throat. But Elizabeth shouted, "That you shall not have!"

She gestured to Penelope, who hurried over to take her place holding up Matthew. Then Elizabeth strode forward and actually snatched the lute from Braceton's meaty hands. The hands that were defiling the delicate inlaid wood and precious strings. Kate had never felt such anger.

"How dare you, madam?" Braceton shouted. "I am under orders from the queen to search every inch of this snake pit. You shall not gainsay me."

"Search my own rooms to your petty heart's content," Elizabeth said. "But Mistress Haywood is a young, innocent lady who has done nothing to earn your abuse. This is her personal possession."

Braceton and Elizabeth stared at each other for one eternal moment. Finally, astonishingly, Braceton stepped away and went back to searching the boxes. All was silent, but Kate knew very well that a price would be paid later.

Elizabeth pressed the lute into Kate's hand. "We have little enough left of our mothers," she said quietly. "We must guard what we can. Take your father to bed now, Kate. Then wait on me in my chamber."

Fearing she might burst into tears if she spoke, Kate merely nodded. She would *never* cry in front of the likes of Braceton.

"Let me help you," Penelope said, and together they turned her father back to the house. He seemed to be in shock, sagging against their shoulders, muttering to himself. Kate's heart ached as they helped him up the stairs and into his bed. What would she do if his mind snapped over this sad business?

For a long time after Penelope left them and Kate wrapped her father up in their warmest blankets, he merely lay there, staring up at the bed curtains, plucking at the sheets with his callused fingers. Kate was so afraid; she had never seen her father like this. Even in his illness he always tried to be strong for her, her father and friend, her teacher, her only family.

Yet losing his work so suddenly and brutally, so casually, seemed to have broken something in him. She knew she had to be strong now for them both, but her anger toward Braceton threatened to overwhelm her.

She did the only thing she knew would calm her. She reached for her lute, the cherished instrument Princess Elizabeth saved, and started singing.

Hark! You shadows that in darkness dwell,
Learn to contemn light.
Happy, happy they that in hell feel not the
    world's despite . . .

"Eleanor," her father suddenly said, clearly and calmly, just her mother's name. "Eleanor."

"Nay, Father, 'tis me. Kate," she said, carefully laying aside the lute and leaning closer to smile at him. "Are you feeling better? Shall I fetch you something to eat?"

"Kate," he said, shaking his head as if he was emerging from a dream. If only she could make it a dream for him, erase that terrible afternoon. "I am only weary. You played that song so beautifully. It was one of your mother's favorites. She would play it for you before you were even born."

"I know, Father. I love to play it." It was the only thing that could take her out of herself, out of the fearful world they lived in now. It was her mother's gift to her, and she had so nearly lost it.

"You do look so much like her." He suddenly reached out to take her hand. "That man has brought evil into this house."

Kate swallowed hard. She had heard those words from the madman Payne already that day. "He will soon go, just as all the queen's men have. There is nothing for him to find here."

Matthew shook his head. "He is different somehow. Be careful of him, my Kate. Stay far away from him."

"That commandment I can happily obey," Kate said. She gently took her hand back and tucked the bedclothes closer around him. "Now you must rest, Father. We can start to re-create your Christmas music this evening after supper. I do remember quite a lot of it."

"Someone must do something about him," her father muttered as his eyes drifted shut. "He must be made to leave us alone. . . ."

"Ah, Kate, there you are." Elizabeth was pacing the length of the floor in her bedchamber, a book held tightly between her hands but unopened. Her hair was still loose. Penelope and Lady Pope sat in the window seat, watching her in silence. Penelope still looked a bit stunned by all that had happened that day, her blue eyes wide and distant.

The faint, sour scent of smoke drifted up through the partly opened window.

"How does your father do?" Elizabeth asked.

"He is resting now, Your Grace," Kate said. "I will help him to re-create his music, but he is—we both are—much comforted to still have my mother's lute. You have our greatest thanks."

Elizabeth waved the thanks away, and turned to pace back toward the chairs grouped around her fireplace. "I fear my friends suffer so much for their kind services to me. But be assured I will always help whenever I can. I do not forget loyalty."

Elizabeth sat down in the cushioned cross-backed chair farthest from the window and gestured for Kate to sit on the low stool beside her. "What news in the village?" she asked quietly.

"Little enough, I fear, Your Grace," Kate answered. She told her of the scraps of gossip she'd heard in the shop and from Anthony, and of seeing Master Payne in the churchyard and of what she found in his house. She wished she could have provided more news, that she could have found more.

"Could the parson have done this thing, do you think?" Elizabeth said, tapping her fingertips anxiously on the armrest.

"I am not sure, though I did try to find out. I

think perhaps he did see something—it is difficult to make sense of his ramblings. He ran away before I could question him further." She didn't mention the bit about fornicators.

"Aye, he has been sadly out of his right wits for some time, even when he was parson," Elizabeth said with a sigh. "It was brave of you to even try to question him; most people won't go near him. And you say Lord Braceton was at Bacon's house before he came here?"

"That is what I heard. No one could be sure what he was doing there, as none of the servants from Gorhambury have been to the village. I do wonder if perhaps he or the servant who was killed found out something there someone would go to extreme measures to conceal," Kate mused. "Shall I go out again tomorrow, Your Grace, and try to find out more? I could surely come up with some pretext to call on the local farms."

Elizabeth frowned and shook her head. "Not as yet, I think, Kate—especially if there is a matter someone would kill to protect. We mustn't call undue attention to Hatfield. I will write to Sir William Cecil, who is surveyor of my properties and thus has a fine excuse to visit us. He is Bacon's brother-in-law, and might very well know something."

Kate felt a touch of excitement at the thought that something could be discovered soon. They had been isolated at Hatfield for so long. "Surely

Lord Braceton will be gone soon, Your Grace, just as the others before him."

"I do hope so. But there is something overbold about Braceton, as if he knows something we don't—or thinks he knows something. He has some errand here, beyond merely finding heretical books, that I cannot yet see, and he is most determined to carry it out."

Elizabeth sat in silence for a long moment as she stared into the empty fireplace. Kate could hear Lady Pope shifting restlessly on the cushioned seat, but even she dared not try to tell Elizabeth what to do in that quiet tension. A rumble of thunder sounded in the distance, and the air felt heavy.

"Aye, I shall write to Cecil this very night," Elizabeth said, loudly enough for the other ladies to hear. "It is past time I looked over the accounts for my properties. You must go see to your father, Kate. I will have more wine sent to him."

"You should dine soon yourself, my lady," Lady Pope said. She was always particular about keeping to set mealtimes. "The hour grows late. Should I order the food served in the hall tonight?"

"I will have something in here," Elizabeth said. "My head still aches, and I doubt the kitchen staff is in any order to prepare a large meal after their treatment this afternoon. You and Sir Thomas may dine with our—guests, if you so choose."

As Lady Pope tried to argue with Elizabeth that

all due courtesy must be shown to the queen's emissary, Kate quickly curtsied and hurried out of the room. She wanted to find the quiet of her own small room, to try to make some sense of the strange day just passed. To try to piece together something from the scraps of information floating in her mind.

She met Peg hurrying up the stairs. The maid held a letter clutched tightly in her hand, the parchment carefully folded and sealed with scarlet wax wafers.

"This just came for Her Grace—from London," Peg whispered.

News from London was seldom good. "From Queen Mary?"

"I don't know. It was left by a messenger at the kitchen door just now, and then he rode off as quick as could be." Peg held the letter most carefully between her fingers, as if it could suddenly turn into a serpent and bite her.

As it very well could.

"Did Lord Braceton see it?" Kate asked. Surely not, or he would have snatched it away by now.

"No, Mistress Haywood. He is locked away in the library with some of his men, luckily. Old Cora is still furious."

"Good. Hopefully he will stay locked away privily all evening. You should get it to the princess at once."

Peg nodded and dashed up the rest of the stairs.

Kate went down and turned along the narrow, winding corridor that led to her rooms at the back of the house. She ached to know what could be in a letter from London, but she also didn't want to know at all. There had been nothing but a barrage of bad surprises in the last few hours. Any more news could surely wait. She had to make sure her father was recovering.

The corridor was dimly lit, the only light from one small window set high in the wall. It was too early yet for torches, but the clouds were rolling in again, casting the house in gloom. She was too far from the kitchens and the main stairs to hear anything but the ever-louder thunder.

Suddenly a door shut somewhere along the corridor behind her, the click of it unexpectedly loud in the gloom. Her nerves already on edge, Kate spun around just in time to see a fluttering shadow dart away.

"Who is there?" she called, but her only answer was the patter of running footsteps.

Surely anyone who had business there, Cora or one of the other servants, would answer her. There was nothing in this part of the house anyone would need at this hour, merely some of the princess's household's chambers and storage cupboards. Unless it was one of Braceton's spies, sent to find more things to burn.

Kate ran after the fading footsteps. She turned a corner, sliding on the wooden floor, just in time to see someone darting out of a side door that led toward the stable yard.

At first she feared she must be imagining things, for this looked like no spy of Braceton's, or anyone else she knew, for that matter. The figure resembled nothing so much as a ghost—a small, slender woman in a dark gray gown swathed in a filmy black veil that hid every hint of human features.

"Wait!" Kate called, and for an instant the woman glanced back. All Kate could see was that veil, matte black, and the effect was so very eerie it made her stumble.

She quickly righted herself, but her one false step gave the veiled figure the advantage. In a ripple of black and gray, the woman vanished through the door. Kate ran after her, only to find the gate from the stable yard open and no one around at all. A smell of violets hung in the air.

She dashed to the gate, but the lane was empty. Whoever it was had to have fled into the woods beyond, and darkness was gathering too fast for Kate to follow.

She pressed her hand to the stitch in her side just as the first cold drops of rain hit her skin. Reluctantly, she turned back to the house. There was no way she could track the veiled woman in the rain, and even if she did, what could she do if she found her? Tackle her into the mud and rip off her veil?

What if the woman was a ghost? Some strange imagining? The thought made Kate shiver even as she dismissed it. There was no such thing as ghosts, no matter what tales floated out of the Tower. And even if there were, surely ghosts made no audible footsteps.

Whoever was behind that veil, she was all too corporeal and would surely return soon to find whatever it was she came searching for at Hatfield. As Kate turned back to the house, she cursed the fact that she had not been fast enough. Next time she would not be caught off-guard.

As she stepped back through the door, she heard a low sound like a keening moan. She peered around the corner to find Ned the kitchen boy crouched on the floor, just as he had been earlier when Braceton rampaged around. Ned had his arms over his head, his thin shoulders shaking, his long legs tucked awkwardly beneath him.

"Ned," she said gently as she knelt beside him. She touched his arm and he flinched away from her. "Ned, it's me. Kate. Don't be afraid."

He peered up at her from behind his arm. His eyes were huge with fright.

"Did you see the woman in the veil run past?" she asked. She'd long felt that Ned saw much in the house that everyone else missed. He just didn't know how to tell them.

He shook his head wildly, shrinking back to the

wall again. He waved his hand in the air and made a wordless cry.

"Nay, she was surely no ghost," Kate said. "Only someone who had no business being here. If you saw something, Ned . . ."

He broke away from her and ran as fast as his thin legs could take him, disappearing up the stairs toward the kitchen. Kate sat back on her heels for a moment and closed her eyes as a wave of weariness washed over her. When would peace ever come back to Hatfield? She had to try to find that woman in the veil.

CHAPTER 6

You speak Spanish, do you not, Kate?" Elizabeth suddenly asked, breaking the brittle silence of her chamber.

Kate looked up from the musical score she was studying, startled. Elizabeth had been lost in her own studies all that gray morning, taking advantage of the moment of peace as Braceton and Sir Thomas Pope had gone to question some of the tenants on the estate. Penelope and Lady Pope were occupied with their sewing in the window seat, as usual.

"I— Yes, Your Grace. A little," Kate answered. "Many of the most fashionable songs come from Spain, and my father thought I should learn enough to read them. I cannot speak it nearly as well as you do." Everyone knew of Elizabeth's formidable scholarship, that she could read and speak Greek, Latin, Hebrew, Italian, French, and Spanish.

"I'm sure you speak it well enough to be understood," Elizabeth said. "I shall need you to accompany me this evening to Brocket Hall, to dine with my friend, Lady Clinton. I know you are concerned about your father, but we shall only be gone the one night and Peg can stay with him at all times. Penelope will go as well."

Penelope's face, set in distant, distracted lines since she sat down with her sewing, brightened. Penelope loved parties and merriment, and life at Hatfield had supplied little of either. Still Lady Pope frowned.

"Really, my lady, the weather is not conducive to visiting," she said. "And with such guests in the house . . ."

"All the more reason for an outing," Elizabeth said with one of her rare cajoling, charming smiles. "I have been friends with Lady Clinton since we were children, and I have not had the chance to see her in a long time. Surely Sir Thomas would not begrudge me the opportunity to call on the wife of the queen's own Lord Admiral? Besides, there is nothing to look forward to here since the colder weather has set in."

Lady Pope's lips tightened. Everyone knew

that Lord Clinton was one of Elizabeth's most ardent supporters on the council, yet Queen Mary kept him as Lord Admiral despite it. And Lady Clinton, a descendant of Queen Elizabeth Woodville and daughter of the Irish Earl of Kildare, was renowned for her great beauty and charm. Forbidding Elizabeth outright to call on them would be a great faux pas, but still Lady Pope shook her head.

"We should wait until my husband and Lord Braceton return," she said, stabbing at her linen with the shining needle.

"That could be many hours," Elizabeth argued. "And we will have to set out soon if we are to reach Brocket Hall in time for supper."

"The roads are not safe," Lady Pope said tightly. "If the queen's own man can be attacked there . . ."

"No one would dare attack *me,*" Elizabeth said. "And that is all the more reason to leave soon, while there is still much daylight. I will take some men-at-arms with me, as well as Penelope and Kate. Surely Sir Thomas cannot protest if I take guards with me?"

Kate bent her head over her music to hide a smile. With guards, Elizabeth could not flee abroad or foment a rebellion in the woods.

Lady Pope shook her head, but she said, "Very well. But you must be home by tomorrow morning, with a full report of your doings."

"Of course," Elizabeth said serenely. "Kate, you must bring your lute and play for us after we dine. Lady Clinton is so fond of those Spanish songs. . . ."

"My dearest lady!" Lady Clinton cried as Elizabeth stepped into the entrance hall of Brocket Hall, Kate and Penelope close behind her. "You are here at last. It has been too long since we saw you."

Kate glanced up as Lady Clinton hurried down the stairs, her blue satin skirts rustling and the dying daylight catching on her upswept golden hair. The poets had called her "the fair Geraldine" and her beauty hadn't faded with the years.

Neither had her seeming devotion to Elizabeth, her childhood playmate. The two of them embraced, exclaiming over the terrible weather.

"My husband will be so sorry not to have seen you," Lady Clinton said as she waved a servant over to take away their mist-dotted cloaks. "But he was summoned to London for a council meeting. These are such complicated days."

"Indeed they are," Elizabeth said. "Has your other guest yet arrived?"

"He has," Lady Clinton said with a conspiratorial smile. "You received the letter from London?"

Elizabeth nodded, and Kate remembered the missive Peg was delivering, with all its heavy seals. Perhaps the sudden visit to Brocket Hall made some sense after all. But Kate still didn't know why *she* was there—or who the letter came from.

"Come into the dining hall. You must be so hungry after your ride," Lady Clinton said. "I have some fine new wine my husband sent from the Continent on his last journey."

"I will certainly welcome one of your good meals, my dear friend," Elizabeth said as they turned toward the carved doors of the dining hall and passed through its dim splendor. "And I have brought Mistress Haywood with me. You enjoyed her music so much the last time you visited Hatfield."

"Of course," Lady Clinton said. "Welcome, Mistress Haywood. Your music is sure to cheer us all."

"I hope so, my lady," Kate said.

"And she speaks some Spanish," Elizabeth added quietly.

Lady Clinton laughed and threw open the doors to a smaller chamber off the empty grand dining hall. It was a more intimate space lit with a myriad of candles that cast a soft amber glow over the verdure tapestries on the walls and the round, polished table. Cushioned chairs were drawn close to the shimmer of silver plates and goblets scattered over the table, which also held heaps of fresh fruit and loaves of fine manchet bread.

A man seated there rose and gave a courtly

bow. The candlelight shone on his glossy black hair and neatly trimmed beard, and on the gold embroidery on his rich black velvet doublet. Next to Kate, Penelope stiffened as if in surprise, and Kate was sure she did the same. For the man was the Count de Feria, Philip of Spain's dearest friend and deputy. He had visited Princess Elizabeth at Hatfield before, bringing confidential messages from his master, but of late he had been in the Low Countries with Philip.

If he was suddenly back in England, surely something very important was about to shift. Now Kate could see why Elizabeth had asked if she spoke Spanish.

Not that Feria wasn't entirely fluent in English. He had been in England with the prince on and off ever since Philip arrived to marry the queen four years before, and Feria himself was betrothed to Jane Dormer, the queen's favorite lady-in-waiting.

"My lord de Feria," Elizabeth said with one of her brightest smiles, the smile Kate had seen soften the most prickly of foes. Like her parents, King Henry and Queen Anne, she could charm when she wished—then wield her sharp tongue as soon as she turned away. Elizabeth hurried forward, her hand held out for Feria to bow over. "What a delightful surprise to see you again."

"And you, my lady Elizabeth," he answered, "you have only grown more beautiful since I left England."

Elizabeth laughed merrily. "And you have been gone from our shores far too long. I hope you bring news that my sister's health has improved of late. We receive too little news of court here and I have been very anxious for her."

Feria rested his hand over his velvet-covered heart. "Alas, my Jane tells me that though Her Majesty seemed to rally in the cooler weather, she has tired again of late."

"I am quite sure the news you bring her of her husband will improve her spirits."

"They are enormously fond of each other, it is true," Feria said. "Their affection flows even across the sea."

"Indeed it does. An example of marital felicity for us all," Elizabeth said, with every appearance of sincerity. Though it was clear to everyone that while Queen Mary was devoted to her handsome young husband, Philip had other matters on his mind. "How do the plans for your own nuptials progress, my lord?"

"Too slowly for me, I confess," Feria said as Lady Clinton showed them all to their seats around the table. "The queen wishes to be well enough to attend the wedding, and it is my Jane's hope as well. Pray God that will be soon."

"Marriage is a most blessed state, is it not?" Lady Clinton said with a wink to Elizabeth, who Kate saw pressed her lips together to hold back a laugh. A maidservant poured some of the sweet

Canary wine into the goblets, and others brought in yet more platters of food—salmon pie, lamb stew with cinnamon and raisins, a dish of pears in honey syrup, and a salad of the last of the summer vegetables dressed in fragrant wine vinegar. Delicacies they couldn't often afford at Hatfield.

But Kate knew she couldn't be distracted by salmon, no matter how savory and delicious. Elizabeth's unspoken request had been that she watch and observe, to see what Feria might know of why Braceton was now at Hatfield and what the queen was thinking on her sickbed. So even as she sipped at the fine wine and nibbled at the pears, she surreptitiously watched Feria.

Not that the man gave anything away. He had been in the service of Philip of Spain for too long to easily let his mask slip. The expression on his handsome face was all that was pleasant and amiable as he waited for the servants to depart.

"Indeed, marriage is a most blessed state, my ladies," he said. "A gift that God has given us to enrich our lives here on earth."

"Only if one's chosen partner is agreeable to one's own heart and mind in every respect," Elizabeth said. She laughed, but Kate could hear the bitter tinge to those words. Most of the marriages Elizabeth had seen in her life had ended in disaster, even violent death. "All too often in this world such is not the case, and more misery ensues than a person would ever know if he remained in their single state. Though I am very sure you and Mistress Dormer will be most happy, my lord de Feria."

Unlike his master, King Philip, and Queen Mary. The unspoken words hung as heavy in the air as the scent of cinnamon sauce, but Feria merely nodded.

"And so we shall be," he said. "As have Lady Clinton and her husband. But I would most heartily wish the same happiness for you, Lady Elizabeth."

Elizabeth toyed with a bit of the fine white manchet bread, tearing it to crumbles between her fingers. "I have not yet found any man I could be so fond of, my lord."

"Truly?" Feria said with a teasing smile. "I have heard it said around court that you will surely soon wed the Earl of Arundel."

"What calumny!" Elizabeth cried. "The earl is forty-five if he is a day, and a blustery old fool with the draftiest of castles. Who says such a thing?"

"Why, the earl himself, of course," Feria said. "He is very detailed in his plans."

Elizabeth burst into merry laughter, Feria and Lady Clinton with her. "Ah, yes, Arundel is ever full of fantasy. I assure you, my lord de Feria, I shall never wed such a one as that."

Feria turned his goblet between his fingers, seemingly fascinated by the sparkle of the gems set around its base. "Then who would you wed, my lady?"

Elizabeth sat back in her chair and shook her head. "I would choose someone kind, of course, and educated. And well dressed! And a fine dancer. But my marriage is in the queen's hands, as I told the Swedish ambassador when he dared to approach me directly about a match with his king's brother."

"A match with Sweden would be a poor one indeed," Feria said. "But what of a greater match? With King Philip's own friend the Duke of Savoy? When that was proffered you turned it away as well, and yet there is accounted no greater or more chivalric knight in all Europe than Emmanuel Philibert of Savoy."

Elizabeth's face hardened as her laughter vanished. Lady Clinton folded her hands carefully atop the table, and Penelope looked down studiously at her lap, but Kate saw that Feria watched only Elizabeth. It was fascinating, like observing a closely matched chess game. One never knew which way the players would leap. She was learning so much from the princess.

"You know my hesitations about the Savoy marriage, my lord, as I am sure Philip confides all in you," Elizabeth said. Feria's glance flickered uncertainly toward Kate and Penelope, but Elizabeth waved away his doubts and switched her words smoothly into Spanish. "You can speak freely, senor. My ladies here speak only English." She turned to Kate and added, in English, "Perhaps you will play for us while we chat?"

Kate nodded and quickly went to fetch her lute. As she strummed a soft song, she listened to their conversation and found that, though her Spanish was a bit rusty, she understood their words well enough.

"I would be happy if the whole world understood my words," Feria said. "King Philip is at all times concerned with your well-being, my lady. He advanced the Savoy marriage only to help assure your place in the succession. If the queen your sister was assured you were well-married . . ."

"Yet the queen did not approve the marriage any more than I did," Elizabeth said, a thread of steel in her voice. "And I shall be honest, as we are in confidential conversation here, senor. I saw how my sister lost the good affection of the people, the most solid protection of any monarch, because she married a foreigner."

Feria's jaw tightened, but it was the only indication he reacted at all to her words. "Then who would you choose to marry, my lady?"

"I have no thoughts of marriage at all at present," Elizabeth answered. "And surely that question is of concern only to myself and the queen."

"Philip is also most concerned with your welfare, as you surely well know," Feria said.

"When the queen ordered you to the Tower, he worked most diligently to have you out again and invited back to court. He has only wanted to encourage cordial relations between yourself and your sister."

Elizabeth's eyes narrowed. "And I give my most sincere thanks to His Majesty for all his kind efforts on my behalf. They shall not be forgotten."

"It was only thanks to him, not Queen Mary or her council, that your rights of succession have been assured. . . ."

With those words, Kate saw that Feria went too far. Elizabeth slammed her palms down hard on the table, making the gilded plate clatter and wine slosh in the goblets. "My lord de Feria, we shall be clear about one thing. It was the people alone who have put me in my present position—the people and my birth. So it was with the queen herself. The people supported her rights and raised her to her correct place on the throne when the dukes of Northumberland and Suffolk would have snatched it from her and placed it into the hands of our cousin Jane Grey. Not Philip, nor any nobility of the realm, had any part in my place."

"My lady," Feria said, his hands held out as if to placate her. "I meant only that King Philip and the council shall always stand as your friends."

"My friends?" Elizabeth said. Even in the

candlelit dimness of the room her eyes blazed fire. "It was thanks to the kind offices of the council that I have been made a prisoner over and over again these past years. I hope I may know who my *true* friends are."

"I would offer you a warning, my lady, on letting such anger lead you to seek revenge when you are in a position to do so," said Feria. "Everyone has great hopes of finding that you are indeed the kind and good princess rumor holds you. Everyone would sacrifice much for such mercy."

Elizabeth's shoulders trembled as she drew in a deep breath, as if she tried to rein in her Tudor temper. "My sister was also reckoned to be full of feminine tender mercies when she became queen," she murmured. "But you may be assured, senor, that I only wish certain of the council members to realize how badly they have behaved toward me when I have been innocent of any wrongdoing. I would pardon all the rest. I do know who my friends are."

"And I hope you will not trust in heretics, my lady."

"Heretics?" Elizabeth said sharply.

"Men such as Lord Bedford, Carew, or Robert Dudley. The Dudleys have surely proved they are traitors over and over."

Elizabeth's eyes flickered at the mention of Robert Dudley's name. It had been a very long time since she had seen him, but they had been friends for many years. It was clear she remembered him well. "I shall trust my true friends," was all she said.

Feria seemed to sense he was defeated. He inclined his head, and asked Elizabeth in English how she fared at her properties with all the foul weather, if she had seen any crop yields at all. After the sweetmeats were served and Kate played more songs, Feria exclaimed at the lateness of the hour and rose to take his leave.

"King Philip wants very much to see you again, my lady, as soon as he is in England once more," Feria said as he bowed one last time over Elizabeth's hand.

"I do hope he may be here again soon," Elizabeth answered with a cool smile. "To see my sister, who I know misses him very much."

"Of course," Feria said. "But sadly, if that day does not come soon enough for Her Majesty, I hope you will summon me at once. I am under orders from my master to come to you as soon as may be."

"How kind King Philip is to think of me," Elizabeth said as Lady Clinton led them out to the drive, where Feria's servants waited with his horses to bear him back to Mary's court. "But I must beg you to wait for my summons. I fear the English people may come to resent any favor I show to foreigners."

"My lady!" Feria protested. "Surely my betrothal and my many years on these shores might mean I am considered English myself. But I will await your summons. Only remember that I, and my master, are your devoted servants."

"I will consider all you have said most carefully, my lord de Feria," Elizabeth answered.

As they waved the count and his party off, Lady Clinton said quietly, "You know he will be writing to Philip before daybreak, telling him how bold you have become in rejecting his overtures."

Elizabeth tapped her foot on the gravel drive. "Let him write. Philip, and everyone, must know I start as I mean to go on. I only hope it was not too soon to say so."

"Too soon?" Lady Clinton said. They made their way back into the house, closing the doors against the chilly night. "Whatever do you mean? The gossip has it that the queen is very ill. She never recovered from her false pregnancy, and the sicknesses of the summer hit her very hard."

"Ill perhaps, but still the monarch—and capable of sending her followers out among us," Elizabeth said. "Has a man named Lord Braceton called at Brocket Hall?"

"Nay, but we have heard tell of him," Lady Clinton answered. "Was he not at Bacon's house of late? I have not seen him here, though my husband has said he is accounted a rather obnoxious man at court. Queen Mary is inexplicably fond of him."

Elizabeth followed Lady Clinton up the stairs toward the bedchambers, Kate and Penelope trailing silently behind them. "But you have not heard tell of his errand at Bacon's house?"

"Not at all, but we have seen little of Sir Nicholas or his family since the troubles last year. I have been living quietly here while my husband is in London." Lady Clinton ushered them into a small but beautifully appointed bedchamber, where a fire crackled welcomingly in the grate and servants hurried about laying out the bed. "I hope this room will serve for the night, my dear?"

"Very well indeed," Elizabeth said. "I am weary from the journey, and quite looking forward to a night of sleep without worrying about who may burst in at any moment. Penelope can help me retire, I think."

She turned to Kate, her pale pointed face unreadable. "Kate, could you go to the kitchen and have them prepare a posset to help me sleep? I am sure you remember the recipe."

"Of course, Your Grace," Kate said, a bit confused. Kitchen matters had never been her expertise.

But then Elizabeth leaned closer and quickly whispered, "See what the servants are chattering about, Kate. I do remember the cook here was always accounted something of a gossip. I fear my dear friend Lady Clinton has not told us quite all she knows from her husband. . . ."

Of course—the posset was an excuse to spy, as Elizabeth herself could certainly not go marching into the kitchen to chat with the servants. Kate nodded, excited at being given a new errand to perform, and hurried away. One of the maids pointed her toward the kitchen.

CHAPTER 7

Unlike at Hatfield, where the kitchen was small for the size of the household and everyone was crowded in close as they worked, Brocket Hall's kitchen was overlarge, almost cavelike. Kate found Lady Clinton's cook sprawled in a chair by the fire in her stained apron, hair straggling from her cap. A scullery maid was rubbing her feet in their darned knit stockings.

"Not so hard, girl!" the cook groaned. "You will be the death of me."

Kate wasn't at all sure she could really get any gossip out of such a frazzled group. But then again, it always seemed a little sympathy could do wonders.

"Excuse me, mistress," she said. "I am terribly sorry to disturb you when it's time to retire, but the Princess Elizabeth begs for a posset to help her sleep."

The cook groaned, not opening her eyes. "Oh, she does, does she? It's not enough that we put together a grand feast on only two days' notice! That we must find cinnamon and almond milk where there is none to be had in the shops. My old bones are weary unto death!"

Kate wondered if this cook was related to old Cora at Hatfield. "I am terribly sorry," she said again, most contritely. "I can make it myself, if you will direct me to the herb pantry. It does help the princess to sleep."

"Well, if it is for the princess . . ." the cook grumbled. She pushed the scullery maid away and lumbered to her feet. "But I don't want any stranger rummaging in my pantry, disarranging everything. Hand me my clogs there, girl, and I will make it. But only for her. Not for any of those wretched Spaniards running about. So much to-ing and fro-ing here of late."

"That must be a tremendous amount of work for you," Kate said as she followed the cook into the small herb pantry. Bunches of fragrant greenery hung from the rafters over stone-topped tables, filling the air with their sweet scent. Bottles of fragrant oils were brewing on a ledge and baskets of fresh flowers sat on the floor. "But the princess did enjoy the meal so very much. She said she had never tasted such a prune tart before."

A reluctant smile broke across the cook's face. She plucked down some peppermint leaves and a sprig of lavender and dropped them into a mortar and pestle to grind them together. "Ah, well, I'm glad she liked it then. Appreciates good English cooking and hard work, I'm sure."

"Indeed she does," Kate said. "Has there been more work than usual here at Brocket Hall of late? We haven't been as quiet at Hatfield as we're accustomed to, either."

The cook shook her head, scowling again. "Usually when my lord is at court, it's only Lady Clinton to serve, and she gives us much notice if guests are coming. Lately it seems strangers are always thundering up the drive, demanding refreshments."

"Are they sent from Lord Clinton?"

The cook shrugged. She poured in a measure of sweet red wine and a splash of milk, stirring them vigorously with the herbs. "Who knows where they come from. Luckily they soon go galloping off again. But they are up to no good—that I can tell you."

"Are they not?" Kate asked in a shocked voice, hoping to encourage more confidences. "Why, mistress, is there something awry in the neighborhood? Some danger we should all be aware of?"

The cook peered at her with narrowed eyes. "You serve the princess, do you not? You are her lady?"

"Aye, I do serve her. As my parents did before me."

"And you were at the dinner with the Spaniard tonight."

"I was. But I heard nothing of any danger there. The count merely presented King Philip's compliments to his sister-in-law."

"Compliments!" the cook snorted. "Of course he would say naught of anything else. But my sister works at Gorhambury House. You know it?"

"Sir Nicholas Bacon's house," Kate said.

"That's the one. And a good, generous master he is, if a bit eccentric, what with all those books and stargazing and whatnots."

Kate nodded. Sir Nicholas was well-known for his studies of astronomy and astrology. "He is a good friend to the princess."

"Then you know how he came by his house."

"In the Dissolution of the Monasteries," Kate said. As so many noblemen's dwellings were these days, Bacon's home had once been a religious house.

"Aye." The cook studied Kate closely for a long, silent moment, as if she tried to gauge her trustworthiness just by looking. Finally, the old lady nodded. "My sister tells me Sir Nicholas had a visitor from the queen, a most unpleasant sort who tore the house nearly asunder. He claimed he was looking for heretical tracts and books."

"Lord Braceton," Kate said. "I fear he is at Hatfield now."

"Then you must tell the princess to have a great care in all her doings with him!"

"Princess Elizabeth knows nothing of heresy about her person."

"Perhaps not. But my sister at Gorhambury heard a most interesting bit of news about Lord Braceton from her friend at a house he visited in Kent in the summer."

Ah. Now she was getting somewhere. Elizabeth was quite right when she said the servants of great houses always knew what was really happening there. Kate nodded and leaned forward confidentially. "Indeed?"

"Indeed." The cook glanced around uncertainly. "I should not gossip, of a certes, not in these days. But we do all love the princess here, and she should know."

"I will tell only her. If she is in danger . . ."

"She is always in danger, is she not? And her friends with her. But Lord Braceton's errand involves property."

"Property?"

"Aye," the cook whispered. "My lord Clinton is on the queen's council, and word there has it that the queen seeks to return her own properties that were once seized from the church under her father. And she will urge her ministers to do the same."

Kate felt her jaw sag with astonishment. She had heard vague talk that Queen Mary sought to assist England's return to Rome by restoring the monasteries, but Kate had put little stock in it. None of her men, Catholic or not, would want to give up their own estates. But if the queen could order it . . .

Utter chaos would surely ensue. There was scarcely a noble family in the country who had not been enriched by the seizure and distribution of church property so long ago.

"Does Braceton survey the properties to be returned?" Kate asked, confused.

The cook shook her head. "He is surely as greedy as anyone else. But I have heard tell that if anyone can be proved to be a heretic, their property is forfeit to the Crown and the queen can return it to the Church or gift it to a Catholic subject. If they can seize them fast enough, perhaps they should not even have to be returned to the Church."

Kate nodded as the picture became a little clearer. The more Protestant estates that could be seized now, while Queen Mary was still alive, the better. Perhaps this meant that a nobleman in danger of losing his land or the relative of someone Braceton had already robbed was the link to the death of Braceton's servant on the road. So far the council had blocked Mary's efforts to requisition the estates of exiles like Elizabeth's Carey cousins, but what of proved heretics here at home? And the cook was right. If the estate could be seized now, while Mary was alive, and then claimed by a Catholic family, it would not have to be returned to the Church when Mary was gone.

"Who wants Bacon's house?" she mused aloud. "Braceton himself?"

The cook shrugged again. "How would I know? I am no gossip for certes. But we have seen a great deal of that Spaniard lately."

"Count de Feria?"

"Aye, he's the one." The cook gave Kate a long, shrewd glance. "And who is he to marry?"

"Jane Dormer," Kate said, disbelieving. She knew little of Mistress Dormer beyond her rumored beauty and kindness, and she did come from an old, ardently Catholic family. But Jane Dormer was one of the queen's favorite ladies and didn't lack for fortune. "She seeks to seize Protestant lands? But what use will she have of them when she is married to a Spanish count?"

"That I could not say, mistress. But if the queen is indeed not for the world much longer"—the cook hastily crossed herself, for predicting the monarch's death could be called treason— "Mistress Dormer and her Spaniard would have no more recourse here. But there are dozens besides her who would happily conspire to grab what's not theirs."

"That is all too true," Kate murmured. The lands had been the Church's, then the king's, now his noblemen's. They could easily change hands yet again. But did Braceton want them for himself? Or was he in the pay of someone else? How did bullying Elizabeth and her household help him with that?

Kate feared she was more confused than ever. But she was determined to see it all clear—no matter what she had to do.

CHAPTER 8

God's teeth, but you will never get the scene right! You lackwits!" The shouted words split the campfire-scented night air, and were punctuated by the sound of a boot kicking a cart wheel and a muffled curse of pain.

Rob Cartman glanced up from the script he was reading by firelight in the wooded clearing. He saw his uncle Edward Cartman, leader of the troupe of players known as Lord Ambrose's Men, go limping past from around the edge of the cart. The two young apprentices he was no doubt shouting at went fleeing into the night.

Edward's lean, lined face was so brilliantly red with fury that Rob had to laugh.

The sound of merriment made his uncle spin around toward him. He made as if to grab Rob by the throat, before he suddenly seemed to remember his nephew had outgrown him long ago. Instead,

Edward tugged his scarlet doublet into place with a great show of wounded dignity.

"And what do you laugh at, varlet?" Edward demanded. "You, who are meant to be getting on with your work, not lazing about."

Rob held up the sheaf of papers, smudged with crossed-out words. "I am learning the lines for the new play, Uncle. At least I am not wasting time shouting at the apprentices—again."

"Those bacon-brains! They are good for nothing at all except drinking and wenching in taverns!" Edward shouted. There was a furious rustling in the night-dark trees, as if the hapless boys were trying to run even farther. "If their apprenticeship contracts were not already signed . . ."

"And if we did not need someone to play the fair Lady Rosamund and her maidservant . . ."

Edward gave Rob a speculative glance, and Rob laughed. "Nay, Uncle, not I. In case you had not noticed, my beard came in a long time ago. My fair maiden days are behind me."

"Alas, aye. You were always a pretty maid indeed in your apprentice days," Edward said, scowling. "At least now all the ladies in the audience sigh over you as the ardent young lover."

"And pay good coin to see our plays over and over," Rob reminded him. Wenching was surely good for something, even if it was just receipts.

"There is that. If we're ever paid the coin for this . . ." Edward sat down heavily on the nearest props trunk and rubbed his hand wearily over his bearded face. "We would be doing well enough indeed. But I fear we won't see a farthing of it if we land in the Tower."

Rob sat up straight and studied his uncle with sudden concern. Edward had always been a temperamental man, filled with worries and complaints. It came with being an actor and leading a troupe of equally temperamental players in the very changeable fortunes of the theater world. Rob had seen it ever since he was a child, when his parents died of the sweating sickness and his uncle took him in and trained him in the actor's trade.

But of late there had been something more to his uncle's unpredictable temper. Ever since their sponsor Lord Ambrose left for France and tasked them with this tour of Hertfordshire, with all new plays to learn and country houses in which to perform them. They had been to the houses of Sir William Cecil and his brother-in-law Sir Nicholas Bacon lately, surely not two of the queen's favorite subjects. Edward's manners had been even rougher than usual, his temper shorter. He was even stricter about how lines were said, the blocking around the stage.

And in the last house where they performed, Edward had disappeared after the play and not reappeared for hours. Usually he was always watching what the men were doing.

"What is it about these plays that could fetch us into the Tower, Uncle?" he asked quietly. "If any of these new lines are treasonous in some way . . ." The Master of the Revels had been doubly strict since the queen returned the English Church to Rome. Plays were gone over not the once they were before, but thrice or more.

"There is no treason there, Rob," Edward snapped. "But we must follow Lord Ambrose's instructions before we can return to London."

Rob was even more confused. "Have we not done that? We are learning the new plays as quickly as we can. They will be better at the next house. At Gorhambury . . ."

"Gorhambury!" Edward spat. "Aye, we did poorly enough there, that gloomy pile. At our next stop all must go perfectly, just as instructed. Do you understand me, Robert?"

"Nay!" Rob shouted in complete bafflement. "Where is this next stop? What must we do there? What will *you* do there—disappear as you did at Gorhambury?"

Edward's face went white even in the firelight. He opened his mouth as if he would shout an answer, but then he just shook his head and pushed himself to his feet. "Never you mind that now. Just learn those lines and make sure those cursed apprentices learn theirs, too. We move out at first light. Pray God the rains don't start again to slow us down."

Rob watched his uncle stride away into the darkness, none of his questions answered. There had been something most odd about this tour from the beginning—and it grew more curious all the time.

"So the queen's loyal subjects are engaged in snatching lands, are they?" Elizabeth said as they rode down the lane from Brocket to Hatfield early the morning after their strange dinner.

"It would appear that something of the sort is indeed happening, Your Grace," Kate answered. She hadn't ridden for some time until this sudden trip, and was struggling to keep her mare from dashing off the road into the woods. But she had to tell the princess all she'd heard from the cook while they had a quiet moment. Penelope rode behind them, and the men-at-arms were ahead to make sure the road was clear.

Elizabeth laughed. "Of course they are. It is ever thus when an old regime is fading—everyone looks to themselves and their future. I saw it with my father and my brother both. But obviously Braceton had no success at Gorhambury, whatever he seeks there. How can he think he'll find it at Hatfield? We can have no secrets left after all this time."

"I am not sure," Kate said. "The cook had only those scraps of gossip from her sister at Gorhambury."

"You did well to get her to talk thus, Kate. So—our quiet neighborhood is not so very peaceful as it seems after all," Elizabeth mused. "I think we will see much coming and going down this road in days to come."

"By friends or by foes, Your Grace?"

"Who can know? Braceton is foe—that much is clear enough," Elizabeth said with a sigh. "Though who knows what he is really after. We have been searched so often for 'heretical books' he must know there is naught left to find."

"Or messages hidden in lutes," Kate said with a laugh.

Elizabeth smiled. "Or that. Braceton does hate me, I can tell, but who can say truly why? Feria—I do not know why he came here."

Kate thought she must know a bit. King Philip would soon lose what little he had gained in England and wanted Elizabeth's friendship for the future. Yet like everything else, it could not be simple or at all plainspoken.

Elizabeth peered out from under her cloak's hood, frowning as she studied the thick, dark line of trees at either side of the road. "I do wonder what lurks there, Kate. If someone points their arrows at us even now."

"Your Grace must not think thus!" Penelope cried at those words, her voice trembling as if with fear. "Surely there would be no such attack in daylight. Not on you. It must have been merely thieves who have now fled."

"Must it?" Elizabeth said quietly. "I used to think Hatfield was my haven, far from the prying eyes and lying tongues at court. But there can be no haven in life, not really."

Kate felt a chill chase over her skin as she looked into the woods, imagining eyes peering out from its dark cover. Suddenly there was a burst of noise, shouts, and the ringing of bells resounding from around the bend in the road just ahead. She cried out, and heard Penelope do the same behind her.

"Alas, Your Grace spoke true!" Penelope cried. "We shall all be killed now. Murdered on the road."

Kate wondered that Penelope, the same coolheaded friend who had led her through the Hatfield passageways, should be so panic-stricken now, but she certainly didn't blame her. The gloom and uncertainty of the past few days had put them all on a knife's edge. Everything was confusion as the guards surrounded the princess, their swords drawn and ready.

"Hush, Penelope," Elizabeth snapped. "What murderer announces their approach with drums and bells?"

As Kate tightened her grip on the reins to hold her restive mount still, her heart pounded. Yet surely Elizabeth was right—this was no sneak attack. Or if it was, it was a most incompetent one—hardly the work of the stealthy archer who had attacked Braceton and his servant.

As Kate sat on her horse behind the princess, she held her breath and listened to the cacophony grow closer.

An amazing sight came around the bend in the road. It looked like a market fair on the move, full of fluttering banners of bright red, yellow, and green carried by men in equally colorful doublets and hose. Tall plumes fluttered from their beaded caps, waving as if in time to the music. They were terribly out of tune, Kate thought with a laugh, but seldom had she heard anything played with such loud enthusiasm.

She watched them marching closer, and saw they were followed by a covered, red-painted cart, drawn by horses draped in matching red and driven by a boy in a saffron-colored doublet and short cape. She realized they must be a troupe of players, perhaps come all the way from London, and the gloomy day suddenly seemed brighter. It had been many months since they had seen a play.

Elizabeth seemed to agree, for she laughed and clapped her hands at the merry sight. She edged her horse around the guards as if to get a better view.

"Madam!" the captain cried. "You should not go nearer. . . ."

"Nonsense," Elizabeth answered. "It is merely

a group of play-actors. Anyone can see that their swords are pasteboard. I wish to find out where they are going."

"We should not dally," the guard insisted. "You are expected back at Hatfield, and we are late as it is."

Elizabeth ignored him. Kate watched as she drew up her horse, and the leader of the colorful band—a tall, whip-lean older man with a lush gray beard and blue-and-purple coat—approached her. He paused in the middle of the road and gave a flourishing bow. The music faded away.

"Good sir, you have already brightened this gray day considerably," Elizabeth said. "Are you going to play at the inn yard in the village?"

"I'm glad we have brought joy to such a beauteous lady's heart," the man said, bowing again. The bells on his tall walking stick sang out. "Have I the honor of addressing the most fair Lady Elizabeth?"

"I am Elizabeth Tudor, aye. And who, sir, are you?"

"My name is Edward Cartman, my lady, leader of this poor troupe of players and Your Grace's most devoted servant. We have actually come to seek you out, my lady."

"To seek me out?" Elizabeth said. The guardsman tried to interrupt her again, but she imperiously waved him away.

"We were lately at the home of Sir William

129

Cecil, my lady, presenting some of our poor plays. We have been traveling the roads since the summer, and he seemed to enjoy our frolics during our stay at his demesne. He hopes we may cheer my lady as well."

As he spoke, Kate studied the group arrayed behind him. She always enjoyed a good play, as did her father, and she had seen many productions, from elaborate court masques to crudely done morality plays in inn yards. She liked them all, liked getting lost in another world for a few hours. Such an escape would be especially welcome during these bleak days, but in Elizabeth's quest to lead a quiet, unobtrusive life of late, they hadn't seen a play in months.

But "quiet and unobtrusive" had availed them nothing except a queen's man like Braceton come to break their precious peace. Maybe this troupe, sent by Elizabeth's friend and surveyor, Cecil, could bring a bit of merriment again.

"Have you a license?" the guardsman demanded. "If not, we'll have you clapped in gaol as vagabonds."

"Of course we have a license," Master Cartman said indignantly. "We are the Lord Ambrose's Men. But as he has gone to France on an errand for the queen, he has no use of our services of late and has sent us to cheer the autumn months of his friends. We must make our coin where we can— but only legally, naturally."

As Master Cartman produced the all-important license and the guardsman snatched it up to study it closely, Kate watched the other players. Two women, one young and one older, peeked out of the cart, but the rest were men, of course, all clad in bright actors' garments, lazily twirling their banners as they watched the proceedings.

One caught her notice. He lounged against one of the wheels of the cart, idly swirling a beribboned staff between his hands. He was as tall as Master Cartman, but where the older man was thin, he had impressively muscled shoulders beneath a tight-fitting doublet. The bright satin hugged a narrow waist and hips, and multicolored hose and tall leather boots revealed equally impressive legs. He didn't wear a cap, and golden blond hair fell in a straight, shining tumble to his shoulders.

He was surely the most handsome man she had ever seen, a vision of some classical god like Apollo, and for a moment Kate could only stare at him in astonishment.

Then he caught her looking. He grinned, and gave her an insolent wink.

Kate sniffed and turned sharply away. *What an errant rogue!*

"Your Grace, may I present my nephew, Master Rob Cartman?" Master Cartman said, ushering the beautiful young man forward to give a graceful bow. "He is my late brother's son, and my most invaluable assistant."

Kate noticed that Elizabeth's pale cheeks turned the merest bit pink as she nodded to young Master Rob. For all her great dignity and scholarship, Kate had noticed that Elizabeth also had a good eye for beauty in all its forms—even the male. Her old friend Robert Dudley was accounted one of the most handsome men in England, just like all his accursed tribe of brothers. But even Sir Robert was not as dazzling as this namesake of his.

"We are pleased to welcome you all to our neighborhood," Elizabeth said. "I hope you will lodge with us at Hatfield for a few days and grace us with a few plays? We would be most grateful for the fine diversion."

"My lady," the guardsman sputtered. "Lord Braceton will never—"

"God's wounds, man!" Elizabeth snapped. "Is Hatfield not my own house? If I wish to have entertainment there, I will have it. Come, Master Cartman, be so kind as to follow us back to the house."

Elizabeth spurred her horse forward into a gallop, forcing everyone to scramble to follow her. As Kate rode past Master Rob, she glanced down at him—only to find him watching her in return.

CHAPTER 9

W hat is the meaning of this?" Braceton's roar rang through the house, sweeping up the stairs and down the corridor like a cold wind.

Kate's fingers fumbled on her lute strings, and Peg nearly dropped the linen she was mending. They both glanced anxiously toward the closed bedchamber door where her father slept. Fortunately he didn't seem to stir, even when Braceton shouted yet again.

Kate and Peg exchanged a quick look before they tiptoed together toward the half-open door to the corridor. Kate was far too curious to resist.

"He must have found those actors," Peg whispered.

Kate nodded. Lord Braceton had been gone when they arrived back at Hatfield and Elizabeth let the troupe set up their rehearsal in the long gallery. Kate had become absorbed in making sure her father ate a midday meal before putting him to rest again, and she hadn't heard Braceton return. But he was obviously there now.

"Do you mean to say, madam, that you found these vagabonds in the lane and brought them here with you, just like that? After I was kind enough to give you permission to travel?" Braceton blustered.

"They are hardly vagabonds," Elizabeth said coldly. "They have a license and Lord Ambrose is their sponsor. Does Lord Ambrose not serve the queen?"

"That is scarcely the point! Lord Ambrose is not here now. These—these people will only be in the way while I am trying to do the queen's business."

"What nonsense." There was a rustle of fabric and the patter of footsteps as Elizabeth came down the stairs.

Kate and Peg ducked behind the doorway, even though there wasn't any way she could see them from there. They heard Braceton thundering after her, but Elizabeth's light steps didn't slow.

"This is my own house, my lord, and I wish to watch a play in it," Elizabeth said. "I do not need to ask your leave for that, do I? I was under the impression Thomas Pope was still my guardian here."

"You have this house only by the queen's grace!" Braceton said. "And you should be very careful what you do in it."

"I have this house by the terms of my father's will," Elizabeth replied. "And my other properties, too. Queen Mary has no more loyal subject than myself, and my household has given you every cooperation—though you have given them little reason to. Watching a play surely cannot impede you."

"I would have a care if I were you, my lady," Braceton said, his sudden quiet calm far worse than any shouting. "If these so-called actors prove to be other than they appear . . ."

"And what else could they possibly be, my lord?"

"Come now. You cannot pretend to be so naive, madam, nor think I will be so," Braceton said. "These people have lately been at the home of the Cecil family."

"My surveyor—who thought I would enjoy a bit of their merriment in these cold days," Elizabeth said with a laugh. "Marry, my lord, but I think your suspicious nature has colored your view of all the world, which is a sad thing. A fine play will do you some good as well, I vow."

"My men will search them most thoroughly before they can be permitted to remain here."

"Of course, Lord Braceton. I would expect nothing less."

There was the echoing slam of the front door and a moment of deepest, reverberating silence. Then Kate heard Elizabeth's light steps coming closer.

Kate and Peg scrambled away from the door, back to their tasks. Just as Kate took up her lute again, the door opened and Elizabeth appeared there. She swept a quick glance over the room and smiled.

"Hard at work, I see," she said.

"Of course, Your Grace," Kate said. She jumped up to make a quick curtsy.

"Very good. Our—esteemed guest is hard at work as well, for Lord Braceton has gone to fetch his men to go through the players' belongings. Poor souls. I fear they will be sorry they came here."

"When shall they be allowed to perform, Your Grace?" Kate asked.

"Tomorrow evening, if all goes well. In the meantime, they have asked if you would be so kind as to assist them with some music, Kate. It seems their accompanist is indisposed."

"Of course, Your Grace," Kate said, feeling a tiny thrill of excitement at the thought of playing with other performers again, perhaps even learning a new song or two from London.

But she glanced back at her father's closed door. If he woke and she wasn't there . . .

Elizabeth seemed to sense her thoughts. "Peg and I will sit here with Master Haywood for a while," she said. "It is so quiet in the rooms back here, and I will enjoy an hour or two to read in peace."

"Thank you very much, Your Grace," Kate said.

"How does he today?" Elizabeth asked, sitting down in Kate's chair by the fire and arranging her plain dark blue skirts around her.

"A little better, I think," Kate said. "He took some broth earlier and is sleeping now. I hope he may work on his music later. Peg stayed with him last night while we were at Brocket, and she says he slept the night through with no bad dreams."

"Oh, aye, Your Grace. He was very quiet-like," Peg said.

"Very good," Elizabeth said with a nod. "I will do all I can to help him, as he did for me when I was young and living with my stepmother. But run along now and play your music, Kate. I will send for you if you are needed. And hopefully you can make sure Braceton's men do not do too much damage to the poor players' belongings."

Kate doubted she could stop Braceton from doing anything at all. But for the princess she would certainly try. By the time Kate had gathered up her music, Elizabeth had her book open and was reading, her pale sharp-chinned face seemingly serene. The house was quiet enough, everyone lying low, as they had ever since Braceton arrived.

Until she opened the door to the gallery where the players rehearsed. Noise and color burst out toward her, and she had to laugh at the sudden merriment of it all. Even Braceton's black-clad men sorting through trunks of costumes didn't seem to affect the actors.

An improvised stage had been hastily built at the far end of the long, narrow room, planks added to expand the dining dais Elizabeth rarely used, except on holidays, since she preferred eating privately in her chamber to dining in state. The two women Kate had seen earlier in the cart were hanging red velvet draperies around the edges of the stage, while two young apprentices unpacked cases of props. Others sat around the margins of the carved, dark-paneled walls, reading over lines or idly chatting, as Master Cartman dashed around shouting at them, red-faced with obvious and extreme anxiety.

The portraits hanging on the walls, of Elizabeth's larger-than-life father, her stepmother Catherine Parr in furs and velvets, and her brother, young Edward VI, stared down at the activity as if astounded to see it all.

And two men were sword-fighting down the makeshift aisle, the furious, metallic clash of the blunted blades ringing in the air. Their boots scuffed and pounded over the rush-covered wooden planks of the floor, as first one opponent, then the other was driven back.

As Kate watched, mesmerized, she recognized one of the swordsmen as the handsome young Master Rob Cartman. His golden hair was darkened with sweat, and he laughed as he fought, as if the effort was nothing to him.

Suddenly Rob drove his opponent back and back in a furious volley of blows. His blade flew so fast, so lightly, that it seemed to blur and flash in the air. The other man toppled to the floor and flung out his arms in surrender.

"Pax, Rob!" he cried. "I yield."

Rob Cartman laughed and tossed his sword down. He swiped his forearm over his sweat-dotted brow, and Kate saw that his white linen shirt was damp from the exercise, clinging to his strong shoulders and the lean line of his back.

"It must be done just thus in the play, Harry," he said. "With a slice here and an uppercut there, a wound, a shout, until the audience is breathless with suspense of what shall happen next."

He helped his opponent to his feet, and as he turned he caught Kate standing there watching. That roguish grin he'd given her earlier spread over his face again.

"Why, 'tis the fair Mistress Haywood!" he called, making several of the other actors, and even Lord Braceton's searching men, turn from their tasks to look at her curiously. "A most welcome distraction from our labors."

Kate felt her cheeks turn uncomfortably warm, and her tongue seemed suddenly tied in knots. She wasn't accustomed to feeling flustered, and she found she did not like it at all. She suddenly wondered why the Cartmans had been on the road at such a providential time. She should not be interested in someone who could very well be the murderer of Braceton's manservant. Really, they knew nothing yet of the actors.

Clutching her lute and the sheaf of music, she

strode into the gallery. She held her head high, as Elizabeth would, and looked neither right nor left, ignoring everyone.

"I was sent to aid you in your labors, Master Cartman, not to distract you from them," she said. "I was told you needed assistance with the music for your play."

Rob still smiled at her, as if he was amused by her brisk tone. But he led her to a pair of stools set in the corner with a trunk filled with sheets covered in scribbled musical notes.

"We are most grateful for any assistance you can give us, Mistress Haywood," he said. "Eli over there usually plays our accompaniment, but as you can see, he is no help at the moment."

Rob gestured toward a lanky bearded man who sat slumped by the wall, his right arm bound in a linen sling.

"My own skills with the lute are poor indeed," Rob added. "And I fear we must have songs for this particular play."

Kate took up the papers from the trunk and studied them. They were easy enough to learn, a simple melody and consonant harmony, as many love songs were. She instantly felt calmer as she went about the familiar task of learning a new song. The suspicions of Rob and his troupe were still there, lurking at the back of her mind, but there was music, too.

"What is the play you're to perform for the

princess?" she asked, strumming a few experimental chords on her lute.

Rob was silent for a long moment, and she looked up at him to see a flicker of uncertainty cross his chiseled face. Which was most odd, for from what she'd seen of Master Rob thus far, he did not lack for confidence.

"It is a new work—*The Tragical History of the Princess of Carthage*," he said. "Sir William Cecil asked especially if we could present it to the Lady Elizabeth, and we have been working on it every hour during our journey."

"I'm sure my lady will enjoy it very much."

"If we present it at all," he muttered.

"What do you mean? If Sir William requested it . . ."

"And my uncle agreed. But today he declares it would not be the best choice. We may have to do *The Fair Maid of Cheapstowe* instead."

"I have seen that one before, when the queen visited Hatfield. But I am sure we would all be distracted by any play in these dreary days," Kate said. "Yet if the princess's own surveyor declares she should see your *Princess of Carthage*, surely that is the best choice? He knows her taste exceedingly well."

"That is what I told my uncle. Sir William will not be happy if he hears we did not follow his request. But my uncle will seldom listen to me," Rob said wryly. "He has been in a most changeable mood of late. I vow I do not understand him."

"Families are something few of us understand—even when we are in the midst of them," Kate said. She played another line of the song, liking how it flowed so sweetly from one bar to the next. "How did you find Sir William and his family? Are they all well? We have not seen them since he last came to go over the princess's accounts in the early summer."

"They are all in good health, though feeling a bit dull, I think, so far from the doings at court."

"I am sure they must be. I do not know Sir William well myself, but surely he is a man accustomed to doing rather than sitting and watching," Kate said with a laugh. She had to find a way to ease more information from him. "Has your company played of late at court, Master Cartman?"

"Would you not call me Rob, fair Mistress Haywood?" he asked.

Surprised, Kate glanced up at him over her lute. She thought he would look flirtatious, teasing, ready to laugh at her. But instead he looked oddly—sad. Sincere. "I hardly know you well enough for such liberties."

"We needn't be so formal here in the country, surely," he said with a grin, that sadness vanishing in an instant. "But just as you like, mistress. I'm sure you will call me Rob soon enough. And, yes, we have performed at court, though it was before the king departed. Our sponsor, Lord Ambrose, is a favorite of the queen, or he once was. He has commissioned us to appear before the royal couple twice."

"But not this new play."

"Nay, not this one. It is apparently of too romantical a nature for the queen's taste."

"And sad, I think," Kate said, bending her head over the music again. She much preferred to concentrate on it rather than look at Master Rob's teasing blue eyes. She didn't know enough about him to be able to afford being interested in him. "The song is very beautiful, but the words are quite melancholy, I see."

"Aye, the princess of Carthage must bid farewell to her husband, who will be executed by their enemies in the morning," Rob said. "She sees the light from his prison window and sings this to him, hoping he will hear her."

"It is very moving," Kate said, and indeed it was. She could just envision the scene through the melody, the yearning and despair of the princess. "But is it truly the best choice for my lady?"

After all, Elizabeth had herself been an imprisoned princess far too often in her life, had seen people she loved ripped away from her.

Rob shrugged. "Sir William thought so when we performed a scene for him, as did my uncle until today. He has been most eager for us to learn it exactly right."

"Robert!" Master Cartman suddenly shouted.

Kate turned her head to see the man stomping toward them. His hair was on end, as if he had been tearing at it with his hands, and his eyes were wide and strangely lit.

"Cease flirting at once and see to the stage set," Master Cartman said. "Let the girl practice the song. There is much work to be done."

Rob gave Kate another smile, his brow arched. "Duty calls, I fear. But I hope we may talk more later, Mistress Haywood."

Kate bent back over her lute so she wouldn't watch him walk away. She found she did want to talk more to Master Rob, and not only because of his dashing smile and blue eyes. She wanted to hear more about court, about Lord Ambrose, about the houses Rob had visited and the people he'd talked to. The life outside Hatfield's walls.

She was also most curious to know why Sir William Cecil thought *this* play would please Elizabeth. And why now Master Cartman was in such hysterics over the playing of it. Surely there must be some hidden message within its words. She just had to decipher them.

CHAPTER 10

So there are actors at Hatfield?" Anthony said, a skeptical frown on his handsome face. "How did they come to be there?"

Kate smiled at him over the display of fine fabrics at Master Smythson's shop. Princess Elizabeth had sent her into the village to purchase more supplies needed for the play, and she'd met Anthony in the lane outside Master Hardy's offices.

"Sir William Cecil sent them, it seems," she said. "We met them on the journey back from Brocket Hall."

"And where did they come from before that? What was their purpose in seeking out the princess?" Anthony said, still frowning.

Kate laughed, though secretly she agreed with him. It *was* suspect. "You and your suspicious lawyer's mind. Perhaps Sir William thinks we need some diversion, which we most assuredly do, what with everything that has been happening of late."

"If that is all there is to it."

"I am sure that it is." But in truth Kate was not sure at all. The handsome Master Robert's uncle seemed most agitated, and Anthony was right— their appearance *was* most convenient. But she wasn't sure she could even articulate those doubts to herself, let alone to her friend, in a way that made sense at all. The days seemed upside down all around her of late.

"And the princess has you assisting them?"

"I am to play my lute to accompany their dances. And help a bit with the costumes."

"You? Sewing?" Anthony said with a teasing grin.

Kate laughed. "I am not entirely deficient in that womanly art, I would have you know. I am quite capable of mending a doublet or sewing on a length of trim. Speaking of which—do you like this gold ribbon?"

Before Anthony could answer, a piercing scream rang through the half-open door of the shop, shattering the tense calm of the village all over again. Kate instinctively ran out the door toward the noise, her heart pounding. But Anthony grabbed her hand and held her with him, his body slightly blocking hers as they skidded to a stop in the lane.

Kate stretched up on her tiptoes and peered past his shoulder, realizing they weren't the only ones who came dashing out to see what the noise was. Despite the periodic appearances of Queen Mary's soldiers of late, the village was usually a quiet enough place. People were wary and watchful always; after all, the burnings could spread to their neighborhood at any moment and care always had to be taken. But true uproars had been seldom.

Until now.

People peeked out of doorways and through windows, and crowded the walkways. Housewives wiped their hands on their aprons and tried to hold their curious children close. Everyone craned their necks this way and that, whispering together, trying to find that fearful scream, which was dissipating on the cold wind.

Kate knew she hadn't imagined it. The whole village had obviously heard it. She wrapped her hand around Anthony's arm and peered down the lane. *Don't let it be from Hatfield,* she silently pleaded. *Don't let it be my father. . . .*

Then it came again: a sharp scream, then another and another, all piled one on top of the other. A young girl came racing up the middle of the muddy street, waving her arms frantically in the air as she cried out.

Kate recognized her. She was the daughter of a maidservant to Mistress Regan, the old midwife who lived in a cottage near the church. The girl didn't come from the direction of the cottage, though, and her face was stark white, her eyes wide and dark with fright.

And there was a wide streak of rusty red blood on her apron.

She stopped in the middle of the lane and looked around frantically. In that one still moment, no one dared to step forward, as if stillness could stop whatever horror it was from happening.

Kate knew no amount of silence could stop danger from barreling over them. It would come anyway, and Elizabeth had shown her it had to be met head-on and defeated. She slid around Anthony, even as he tried to hold her back, and hurried to the girl's side.

"What has happened?" Kate said gently. "Is it Mistress Regan or one of her patients? Or perhaps your mother?"

The girl swung toward her. For a second her face was rigid with fear, but then it crumpled and she covered her eyes with her trembling hands. "It—it is horrible! Blasphemy. We shall all be damned for heretics."

Kate heard a ripple of shocked whispers move through the crowd at that most fearsome of words. "Blasphemy." Accusations had flown about too thick and fast since Braceton had arrived, and someone would have to pay.

"What has happened?" she said again. "Show me."

The maid whipped around and ran back up the street without a word, leaving Kate to follow. Anthony took her hand.

"I'm coming with you," he said simply, firmly.

Kate hated to admit it, but she was glad to have him beside her. There was no telling what they would find, and she knew she had to be brave and face it. She nodded, and they hurried after the girl's fleeing figure. A few people followed—Master Smythson and his wife, the blacksmith. The others still watched with their tense pale faces.

The girl led them to the church, past the same tilting headstones that Kate and Anthony had talked beside, and up the overgrown pathway. The carved door stood open.

Kate's steps faltered a bit as she stared at the shadows just beyond the gaping doorway. She could see nothing in that dimness, and somehow that heavy quiet was the worst. The girl stopped on the stone steps and shook her head.

"In there, mistress," she whispered.

Kate nodded and took a deep breath as she stepped through the door. The air smelled cool and faintly musty, touched with the tinge of old candle smoke and wood polish. As Elizabeth kept her own chaplains at Hatfield since the church closed, Kate hadn't been inside the village church in some time. The windows that were uncovered were dirty, letting in very little daylight, and the old columns and pews were mere hulking shadows. A candle burned on the altar table, which seemed a very long way away. Faint sobs echoed in the empty space.

"You should wait outside, Kate," Anthony said quietly. "Let me see what this is about."

Kate shook her head. "Her Grace will want to

know exactly what happened. It might have to do with her—her guests at Hatfield. I am quite all right, Anthony, I promise. I will not faint."

He frowned deeply, but finally he nodded. Surely they had been friends long enough that he knew he couldn't stop her. They walked quickly up the aisle toward the circle of light, their boots echoing on the old stone floors, over the faded etchings of the memorial stones.

It was the girl's mother, the maidservant called Meg, who knelt at the front of the altar, sobbing. Kate remembered that she sometimes cleaned in the church, and there were buckets and cloths spilled on the floor around her. Meg didn't look up when Kate and Anthony stopped beside her.

Or even when Kate let out a cry at the sight that greeted her. The candlelight fell over a body sprawled across the bare altar table. A very still, very stiff body. A dark stain had dripped down the table to the floor.

As if compelled, Kate moved slowly closer.

"Kate, nay!" Anthony called, his voice loud in the stony silence. He reached out to pull her back, but she had already seen what it was.

Ned, the mute kitchen boy, was the body on the altar. But not Ned as she always saw him, scurrying around Hatfield, watching everything with his large eyes and long limbs. His little face was white and stiff, blank. Like the stone he lay on—except for the hideous, gaping red gash across his throat.

"Oh, Ned," she whispered, her heart aching as she stared down at him. That poor young man. He had surely never hurt anyone in his short teenage life. Who would do such a hideous thing? What evil had come upon them?

She reached out to touch his cold hand, and then she saw it. The girl's anguished shout echoed in her head. *Blasphemy. Heresy.*

Ned was dressed in the chasuble, cope, and surplice of a priest. Elaborate, richly embroidered garments meant for a feast day, much too large for his small body, but most carefully arranged. His hands were crossed on his thin chest, and a gold crucifix and onyx-beaded rosary were between his blood-reddened fingers.

Kate's stomach heaved and she feared she would be sick, profaning the church even more. It was as if she could feel the sticky black miasma of evil wrapping tight around her, around them all. No one was safe. Not even a child.

"Oh, Ned, I am so sorry," she whispered.

"Come away now, Kate," Anthony said, and this time he wrapped his arm around her waist and guided her down the altar steps. The others moved forward, blocking her view of the body, and Anthony took her out of the church and into the fresh, chilly air.

"Here, sit down," he said, leading her to one of

the flat stone crypts. It was cold, but she sank down gratefully. Her legs were trembling so much she feared they would collapse beneath her and she would lie in the dirt and the dead leaves, sobbing helplessly. And there was no time to be helpless now.

"That poor, poor boy," she whispered, her throat tight. "Such a vile, wicked thing."

"These are wicked days, I fear," Anthony said quietly. He took a clean handkerchief from inside his plain dark russet doublet and pressed it into her shaking hand. "Master Hardy returned from London yesterday and brought news of more burnings at Smithfield. But this—I have never seen the likes of this. It is . . ."

"Hideous?" Kate murmured. She wiped at her eyes and nodded. Surely she would never forget the terrible sight. Whenever she slept, it would be there, waiting for her. Poor Ned, horribly murdered and his body thus profaned.

"I should have tried harder to keep you away," Anthony said. "I am not much of a friend."

Kate laughed hoarsely. "How, Anthony? Tied me to a tree? Locked me in Master Hardy's offices? Nay, you know I will not be stopped sometimes. If only . . ."

She heard a ragged sob, and looked over to see that Meg had left the church and huddled beneath a tree with her daughter. Eager to speak with the woman, Kate made her best effort to compose herself. She slid down from her stone seat and made her way across the churchyard to them.

"You were the one who found Ned, mistress?" Kate asked gently.

Meg glanced up, her thin face gray and streaked with tears. She seemed to recognize Kate as one of Elizabeth's ladies, for she struggled to her feet and tried to curtsy, but Kate took her arm and made her sit back down.

"Aye, 'twas me who found—that," she said. She put her arm around her sobbing daughter.

"Such a dreadful thing," Kate said. "Dreadful" was such a small word, but she couldn't think what could fully encompass the horror of Ned's desecrated body.

"The door was open when I got here to do my usual cleaning, but I thought nothing of it."

"Is the door often open?"

Meg shook her head. "It's meant to be kept bolted, of course, but ofttimes old Master Payne likes to come in and look about. He shouldn't, but—well, it seems to do no harm and keeps him quiet-like. After what happened to him and all."

"Master Payne?" Kate said sharply. She remembered well the old vicar shouting "fornicators" at her and Anthony here in this very churchyard. His wild eyes. The way he lurked around the village, seeing sin and damnation at every turn. "Was he there today?"

"Oh, nay, mistress," Meg cried, her eyes wide.

She glanced around guiltily. "No one was about at all, especially not the old vicar. I went to light a candle—it's so gloomy in there—and that was when I found the poor boy."

"So you saw nothing at all? You heard nothing out of the ordinary? No footsteps or doors slamming?"

The woman went very still for an instant, and Kate was sure she would say something else. Something more. But Meg just shook her head, refusing to look at Kate. "Nothing at all. 'Twas silent, like it always is."

"A demon did it, Mother. I know it!" her daughter cried. "Master Payne is right when he says we will pay for our sins. God is punishing all of us for going back to popish ways—"

"Hush now!" her mother shouted. "You must not say such things. Not here. Who knows who might be listening?"

The girl's face went red, but she shook her head. "It *was* a demon. I saw it, that black cloak—"

"Black cloak?" Kate said. Braceton too had mentioned a cloaked figure who vanished into the woods after firing on him. And there was the veiled woman who frightened Ned in the halls of Hatfield. Could they be one and the same? What were they seeking? Was Braceton the only common factor?

But Braceton's assailant used bows and arrows

to kill from a distance. Ned's throat was slashed by a blade before he was dressed in those vestments.

A blade wielded not by a demon, but by an all too human attacker.

Kate knew whoever had done these things had to be human, someone embroiled in the complex, sticky web of the politics around them. But the hysterical talk of demons still made her shiver.

"You saw someone in a black cloak? Fleeing from the church?" she said.

"We saw nothing at all," Meg said, grabbing her daughter's hand. "She is upset, and rightly so. She knows not what she says. If it *was* a demon, we didn't see it. We are God-fearing people, of a certes."

"But then—" Kate began, only to be interrupted by a shout. She looked over her shoulder to see a man racing up the pathway toward the church. Some of the villagers ran after him, reaching out to try to hold him back.

He was an older man, thin and bent, one shoulder twisted higher than the other, clad in rough gray garments. Yet he managed to evade the people who chased him in a tangle of shouts and confusion, and kept running toward the door.

"You shall not hold me back, varlets!" he cried. " 'Tis my own son in there, and I'll see him."

"Ned's father?" Kate whispered. She hadn't even known the boy had any family. He was always alone at Hatfield. Yet as she hurried closer, she could see the old man had the same eyes as the boy.

He tripped on the stone steps, giving someone the chance to grab his arm.

Master Smythson appeared in the doorway. Blood streaked his doublet and his face was as gray as the sky, but he blocked the old man's path.

"You must not come in here," he said, his voice gentle but implacable. "It's not a fit sight for you."

"Not a fit sight!" the old man shouted. "They say my boy is dead in there, but I know 'tis not true. If I see, I can tell you it's not Ned."

"I fear it is him," Master Smythson said. "We are sending word to Hatfield—"

"Hatfield!" the old man spat. "I never should have let him go work in that place. 'Tis cursed, and now it's killed him. He should never have even looked on princes!"

First demons, now princes. Kate's mind was racing.

Master Smythson shook his head. "Until we hear back from there, you should go home and wait. Please, believe me. . . ."

"Nay!" The old man yanked himself free and dashed into the church, pushing Master Smythson out of the way.

Kate longed to turn away from the cloud of

grief that lowered over them, but she could not. She could only stand there, until she heard the terrible howl of raw pain.

"I will find whoever did this—and kill him in a thousand ways worse than what he did here on this day!" Ned's father shouted. "We are all cursed."

The cloaked figure watched from a distance all the comings and goings to the church. The old building had surely not seen so much activity in a very long time. Every person in all the village seemed bent on catching a glimpse of the horror in their midst—and then bewailing the judgment fallen upon them all.

They did not even know yet the full extent of judgment.

The watcher saw Mistress Haywood talk to the charwoman and her daughter, a most solemn look on her face before the handsome lawyer's apprentice took her hand and led her away. It was too bad she had had to see the kitchen boy, but alas it could not be helped. Sometimes terrible things had to be endured to reach the greater good. One day even sweet Mistress Haywood would know that.

Or not. It hardly mattered.

The figure saw the boy's father fight his way into the church, and heard him vow bloody vengeance on whoever had done the foul deed.

Vengeance—aye, that was something the watcher knew well, indeed. Perhaps one day the old man *would* have his blood price. Rumor said he had been a mercenary in old King Hal's day, willing to rid the king of any annoyance for a price. He would know how to do it, even weakened as he was. Everyone had his day eventually. But that was another thing that mattered not.

The old man was carried out of the church by the burly blacksmith, followed by the grim-faced shopkeeper Master Smythson, who locked the doors with rusty keys he had found who knew where. They did not bring the boy out, but several of the villagers stood sentinel outside the doors. They whispered frantically among themselves. The scene needed only Master Payne to come along shrieking of hellfire.

Aye, it would not be long now. The figure waited patiently, having learned long ago the art of staying hidden and going unnoticed. The quarry was within sight of the traps so carefully laid for so long.

Before the hour was out, the rickety churchyard gate slammed open and Lord Braceton barreled up the pathway, his men close behind him with swords drawn. He was shouting and furious, invoking the queen's name and her royal heresy laws, swearing her wrath upon them all. Just as full of threats and violence as the day he arrived in the neighborhood.

The day his manservant met the fate meant for Braceton himself. An unfortunate mistake, that. But it had all worked out for the best in the end. Because now Braceton had time to see what was coming for him. See it—and fear it.

The boy had mercifully seen nothing—the mere flash of a silver blade in the dark and it was over. He had been a sad sacrifice. But life taught many lessons, one of the most important being that when the cause was just, no sacrifice was too great. God would be merciful to His own.

And now, when the watcher glimpsed the flash of raw, burning fear in Braceton's eyes as he demanded the doors be opened and the blasphemy be shown to him, it seemed the sacrifice was indeed worth it.

His man Wat. The kitchen boy. Braceton surely knew he was next. And the man was deservedly terrified. He had used his religion as justification for his acts; now he could see where his Catholic God had gotten him.

The figure turned away with a satisfied smile and hurried toward the stream to rinse away the blood, leaving a black cloak behind in the water to wash downstream, unseen.

CHAPTER 11

Ned's father lived just beyond the edge of the village, in a cluster of older cottages. Most of them were tidy, but his had a distinct air of neglect about it. Kate studied the house from beyond the garden gate, unsure how she should approach the man in his terrible, violently wrenching grief. It had been hours since Ned was found, but she didn't want to further distress his family. Yet she knew she had to try to find answers now, before whoever did this to Ned could get too far away.

Perhaps Ned's father, with his palpable volcanic fury, knew more than he thought he did. Or perhaps he was more involved than she wanted to think he was.

In such complicated days, tangled up in twisted loyalties and religious ideals, anyone could be swept away on the bloody tides, even men who kept to themselves like Ned's father. Perhaps she was wrong in her surety that Ned's death had something to do with Braceton. Perhaps it was to do with Ned's own family. After all, she knew so little about them, even though Ned had lived in the same house with her.

And yet some urgent instinct told her it *did* have to do with Braceton. Why else would poor Ned be dressed like a Catholic priest, unless it was to somehow get at the ardently Catholic queen's man?

Kate shielded her eyes from the fading sunlight and studied the cottage more closely. Unlike Master Payne's hut in the woods, it wasn't falling down in squalor, but it was unkempt. The shutters were loose, the garden overgrown and tangled, but once it had been tidy and even somewhat pretty. It also seemed to be empty.

She glanced back over her shoulder to see that no one watched her. It was as if the terrible crime had already spread like a poisoned well. She would have to hurry back to Hatfield soon, as Anthony already thought she had done, or he wouldn't have left her alone. But she wanted to find out all she could to tell Elizabeth. She didn't have much time.

She pushed open the gate, which swung easily on its broken hinges, and hurried up the weed-choked path. Taking a deep, steadying breath, she raised her hand and knocked on the door. There was only silence.

"Please! I must speak to you," she called, just in case the man was lurking behind the walls. Even as she said the words she knew it was a vain hope. The house was too still, and unlike in the woods, she had no prickling sense of any eyes watching her.

She walked around the cottage anyway, searching

for any signs that someone was there, for any clues. She found nothing but more weeds, more peeling whitewash.

As she hurried back to the garden gate, she saw a woman in the doorway of the nearest cottage. The woman leaned on her broom as she watched Kate with frowning suspicion on her reddened face.

"You won't find him there," the woman called. "His sister came and took him away already. Drunk he was, almost falling down from it. He probably was at the tavern before he stumbled here."

"His sister?" Kate answered. She could tell the woman wasn't inclined to be helpful, but perhaps she would be nonetheless. Kate carefully shut the gate behind her and made her way toward the housewife's doorway, trying to seem as non-threatening as possible. "Poor Ned's aunt, you mean?"

"Aye. She came to keep house for them once in a while, though you wouldn't notice anyone cleaned at all. Not since he came back from the wars and his wife died," the woman said with a sniff.

"He was in the wars?" Kate asked. The man had seemed in no fit shape to fight, but so often the war took men like that, making them not right in the head.

"Aye, once. I even heard he fought with that

high and mighty lord that's up at Hatfield now. Hard to believe."

"With Lord Braceton?" Kate asked, shocked. Ned's father somehow knew Braceton from long ago?

"Aye, so I heard. But you can't believe anything he says."

"And he is gone now? I need to talk to him."

"I told you. His sister came as soon as she heard what happened to the boy today and took her brother away. He was shouting and angry, but at least he went with her. So you won't find him there anyway."

A sister. Kate glanced back at the empty cottage, remembering Ned cowering in fear at the veiled figure who fled Hatfield. "Does this sister wear a veil, perchance?"

The woman scowled. "Nay, never."

That was one thought vanished then, that Ned's kinswoman could have been the veiled woman. Unless of course it was a disguise of some sort. Kate murmured her thanks as the woman turned back to her sweeping, and then went on her way back to Hatfield.

The lane was deserted, silent, giving her room to think about the terrible thing that had happened. She was so lost in her thoughts, she almost missed the tiny thing snared on a bush, until a ray of sunlight caught on it and made it shimmer against the grays and greens all around. Kate knelt down and carefully plucked it off to turn it between her fingers.

It was a feather, a finely cut, small fragment in peacock colors.

She knew enough of weapons from playing archery at court when she was a child to see it could only be one thing—the fletching from an arrow. Was it the same sort of arrow that had killed Braceton's servant not far from this very spot?

Kate tucked it carefully in her cloak and rushed on. It wasn't a veil or a black cloak, but surely it was some kind of small clue that would help her in her search. She had to hold on to it and let it tell her its secrets.

CHAPTER 12

Dressed in priestly vestments? And you saw this yourself, Kate?"

"I did, Your Grace," Kate said, as she stood before Elizabeth in the quiet of her chamber. The day was fading; outside the window, the light was tinged a pale rose-gold through the clouds, and soon night would be upon them. Braceton was still in the village surveying the gruesome scene, though he would return too soon. Kate was aching with weariness, but she knew that as soon as she closed her eyes, she would see poor Ned again. "It was—terrible."

"I'm sure it was. You should not have had to see such a thing. That poor boy." Elizabeth took Kate's arm and led her to the chair by the fire. She poured out a goblet of wine and pressed Kate's numb fingers around it. "Who would do such a horrible thing? And why?"

Kate shrugged. "I have been asking myself the same thing all afternoon. Surely it could not have been an attack on Ned himself. He has never hurt anyone at all. It seemed more like a—a message."

"Aye, it does. But a message to whom? To what purpose? I have seen many strange things in my life, but none quite like this." Elizabeth paced to the window and sat down on the cushioned seat. Her fingers tapped restlessly on the windowsill as she stared outside. "Did it look as if he had been killed there? Or was he moved from someplace else?"

Kate closed her eyes and forced herself to remember the details of the terrible scene in the church. "I know naught of murder, Your Grace, but I have seen pigs slaughtered in the farmyard before. I think he must have been killed there in the church, as there was such a quantity of blood on the altar and the floor. And it was beginning to dry, so it had not just happened. But—" She paused, frowning, as something struck her.

"But what?"

"But the vestments had very little blood on them at all. He was so carefully presented, as if he lay in state, like a true bishop. His hands were crossed with the crucifix and the rosary, and his eyes were closed."

"So he was killed, and then dressed and arranged."

"He must have been. I saw no signs of a struggle there either, Your Grace. I suppose he went to the church on his own for some reason, though I cannot see why he would go there at all."

"Nor can I." Elizabeth sighed and rubbed her hand over her eyes. "This whole matter has me puzzled exceedingly. Do you think the veiled woman you say Ned saw here had anything to do with it?"

Kate remembered the strange sighting here at Hatfield, the veiled figure she had chased and who vanished. The person in the cloak she heard about in the village. Surely they were one and the same, or at least connected? Mysterious figures such as that were a rarity in the neighborhood. She also remembered Ned cowering in fear, as if he knew something he could not communicate about the veiled woman. "I couldn't say, Your Grace. I haven't seen her again. It could very well be."

"But no one in the village saw anything?"

"They say not. There was much confusion, especially when Ned's father came running in, vowing vengeance. Meg and her daughter claim they saw naught before they discovered the body.

Surely if someone *had* seen anyone about the church, they would say."

"Perhaps. Or perhaps not, and who could truly blame them?" Elizabeth said quietly, still staring outside. "In these days it would be terribly dangerous to be associated with anything that smacks of deepest heresy. Best to keep one's head down."

Kate nodded. Who would wish to come to Braceton's attention, if they could help it? Poor Ned was dead; there was no help for him, and few would endanger themselves for a mute kitchen boy, except his own grief-stricken father. Yet Kate had to help Ned if she could.

"There was one odd thing, Your Grace," she said. "Master Payne was not around the church. I did not see him at all."

Elizabeth turned toward her. "The old vicar?"

"Aye, Your Grace. He is usually lurking about there, shouting about sin and hellfire to anyone who crosses his path. He hates the Catholics. This seems like the sort of thing that would have him in a great fit of passion."

"Master Payne does seem mad, but usually harmless. I have never heard of him actually harming anyone, though if he thinks someone is in danger of damnation, who knows what he will do? I wonder where he has gone."

"Perhaps he *did* see something, and has fled from fear. Meg's daughter did say it was a demon who did the foul crime." Kate shook her head. "Or maybe . . ."

"Maybe he did it himself."

"It could be anyone, Your Grace. It feels as if madness has come upon the whole world."

A shadow flickered over Elizabeth's eyes. "The world is always mad, my dear Kate. And sometimes it claims the most innocent among us as its worst victims."

Kate thought again of Ned, so white and still, and she feared the princess was right. The world was afire. Who would be the next consumed?

Elizabeth suddenly rose in a rustle of satin and paced to the other end of the chamber and back. "Finish your wine, Kate. 'Tis almost full dark, and you must get to the great hall soon. The play will begin directly after supper."

"The play, Your Grace?" Kate asked, surprised. "But—won't Lord Braceton stop it now? He never liked it."

"Lord Braceton has not yet returned from the village. When he does, he is sure to be full of more fury and choler than ever, but it will be too late to stop the play going forward." Elizabeth paused at the small looking glass on the wall and studied her reflection—the pale pointed face framed by a small frilled ruff, the red-gold hair drawn back under an embroidered cap. She had no expression at all. "I feel we could all use a little diversion, don't you, Kate?"

"Of course, Your Grace," Kate said uncertainly. She wasn't sure of any such thing. She wanted her own fireside, a piece of music to study, her father to talk to. Quiet, familiar things. Yet she knew Elizabeth rarely did anything without a purpose. If she wanted a play on this most inauspicious of nights, there was a reason.

"You have worked a bit with those actors, Kate," Elizabeth said. "Have you learned much about where they have been of late? What they were doing there?"

"Not very much. We mostly talked of music," Kate said. She thought of the handsome Master Rob, how open he seemed—and then how mysterious. "They were at Gorhambury, then went to Sir William. Probably Sir Nicholas sent them there. I know not where they were before that. London, mayhap."

"Yet Lord Ambrose is one of the queen's men. A most devout Catholic, they say. Why would he send his troupe to houses known to be of the new faith?"

"They say Lord Ambrose is abroad right now."

"Even curiouser, then." Elizabeth turned away from the looking glass and picked up a gown that was draped over the clothes chest. Kate saw it was a kirtle and bodice of tawny silk with ivory ribbons, and an air of darker gold damask sleeves. Beneath it was the fine red cloak Kate had worn before.

"Here, Kate," Elizabeth said. "Take this and wear it tonight. You have been working so hard, and deserve to look your prettiest."

Kate took the armful of fine fabric in surprise. Elizabeth had given gifts of clothing and food before, but these were very rich. It had been so long since she wore anything like that. "I—thank you, Your Grace," she stammered as Elizabeth fluffed one of the ribbons on the skirt. "But I will only be playing to the side of the stage. No one will see me."

Elizabeth's solemn expression cracked as she gave Kate a teasing smile. "What of Master Cartman's beautiful nephew? So golden—a veritable Apollo."

Kate had to laugh even as she felt her cheeks become embarrassingly warm. For had she not thought that very thing about the handsome, dashing Master Rob? The man had appeared in the neighborhood too conveniently, and could well have been involved in the violent murders. She would be foolish to entirely trust him. "He is only a player, Your Grace. I know they flirt and flatter, and mean not a word of it."

"Most wise, Kate, for I vow almost all men are the same. Peril to the woman who takes them seriously. But what of your other friend? The young lawyer?"

"Anthony Elias, Your Grace?" Kate said, surprised again that Elizabeth knew Anthony at all, though Master Hardy had done some legal work for Elizabeth from time to time.

"Aye. He seems of a more serious bent of mind, and just as handsome as Master Cartman, in his own way."

Handsome? Of course Anthony was handsome; Kate couldn't help but see that. But he was her friend, nothing more. Surely he only saw her as that? And she had no time for anything else, from either Anthony or Master Rob. "Anthony and I are merely friends, Your Grace. Do you yourself not say a woman's happiest state is the single one?"

Elizabeth shook her head, still smiling. "You *do* pay too much attention, Kate. I say many things for many reasons. The single state must surely be the most prudent, but it is sometimes a lonely one. You are so young still, and have so many choices before you. You must ponder them all well."

"I shall, Your Grace," Kate said, mystified as to what might have brought this on. Elizabeth was not usually one to pry into her servants' private lives, as long as they worked hard and were loyal to her. Kate herself knew she couldn't think of the future any more than Elizabeth could, not until her father was better and their lives more settled. "Most carefully."

Elizabeth nodded and turned away. "Then wear the gown tonight, if only to cheer me. And keep the cloak. The red suits you better than it does me."

Kate thought of how the cloak kept her so warm on the chilly days. "Thank you, Your Grace."

"And send Penelope to me. I must dress for the evening's festivities."

Kate played a song on her lute as she watched the servants carry in chairs and benches from the dining hall and line them up in front of the make-shift stage. The players were in the curtained-off area behind, and she could hear the sound of their voices as they ran snatches of lines, shouted and murmured, complained about costumes, but she could make little sense of the words.

She wondered if they were to perform the Princess of Carthage play, or if old Master Cartman had truly changed his mind to go with the older, more comic work. All Master Rob had done when she appeared in the great hall was send her to this seat with a distracted smile. He hadn't even seemed to notice her new gown, or the way Peg had styled her hair with ivory ribbons. When she asked what music she was to play, he answered, "Something that will hold their attention."

Which was not terribly helpful. Kate supposed she would just have to wait and see what happened when the curtain went up.

In the meantime, she softly played some of the

Spanish songs she'd taken to Brocket Hall and watched as the audience filed in after supper. Elizabeth came first, and she sat down in the front row with Sir Thomas and Lady Pope. Sir Thomas seemed gray-faced and distracted, constantly scanning the room as if he feared attackers would leap out of the woodwork. Kate could hardly blame him; she felt that way herself, wary and shivery.

Lady Pope sat with her hands folded and her lips pinched together, disapproving as always.

Penelope sat behind Elizabeth, staring down at the lap of her skirt as she pleated the fine damask fabric between her fingers and smoothed it out again. Kate's friend looked unusually introspective, as if she was as haunted by feelings of dread as Kate was herself. Kate tried to catch her eye, to give her a reassuring smile, but Penelope didn't look up. The rest of the servants filed into the back of the hall.

Once Elizabeth and the others were settled, the doors swung open again and Braceton came in. Kate was shocked by his appearance. She'd heard the echo of his shouting when he returned from the village, the terrible threats of the queen's holy wrath on anyone who had so profaned her church. Just what everyone had come to expect from him—threats and danger, destruction. The whole house seemed to hold its breath to see what would befall it next.

But then a taut silence lowered over the place, like the gray clouds outside and the cold wind that had swept up again. And Kate would hardly have known the man who sat down behind Penelope as Braceton at all. His burly, red-faced bluster was gone, leaving his face white and drawn behind his beard. He took in the stage with narrowed eyes, his fists braced on his knees, yet he said nothing. Merely watched, and waited.

Somehow that quiet attention was worse than anything else had been. Clearly the manner of poor Ned's death was meant as some sort of message to the queen's man. A taunt, perhaps—a grotesque warning centered around his Catholic religion. Perhaps the murderer was someone who had lost Protestant relatives to the queen's fires? Braceton would never let such a thing go unpunished, unanswered. But who would pay?

No demon, as the girl had wailed, but someone very human.

"Psst! Mistress Kate," someone whispered.

Kate tore herself out of her dark worries, and glanced over to see Rob Cartman peering at her from between the curtains. His golden hair gleamed in the torchlight.

"'Tis *The Princess of Carthage* tonight," he said. "You can start the prelude."

Kate nodded, and launched into the lively piece she had just finished learning. It was an interesting song, with an atmosphere of sunnier climes in its tune, a feeling of dancing nymphs and decadent banquets, of sea waves sliding across warm sand and birds swooping low over perpetually green trees.

Yet there was an air of sadness that lay over its lightness, a faint hint of darkness ahead that seemed to suit the night they now found themselves in.

She could feel the eyes of the audience on her as she played, Pope's wary, Braceton's piercing, Elizabeth's encouraging, but Kate let herself sink into the music and become lost. Sometimes music was the only escape, though surely it could never last for long.

As the last notes of the song faded away, the stage curtains swept open, and Master Cartman stepped forward. A gold-edged white toga was draped over his fine dark red doublet and black hose, and his graying hair was covered by a plumed helmet. A blunt-nosed stage sword hung at his side, rattling as he bowed low before the princess.

"My lady, and good gentles all," he said in a booming voice. He swept a grand gesture over the room, and Kate was amazed that he suddenly seemed not like the changeable, bad-tempered, nervous man who stormed around shouting unpredictably at the other actors. He seemed large, regal, almost otherworldly, and she knew she was back in the magic of playacting. It had been far too long, and despite everything she found herself drawn in. She could tell from the rapt looks on the audience's faces that they were, too.

Except for Braceton, who still scowled.

"Imagine yourselves not at Hatfield House, not in the midst of the cold and the rain," Master Cartman went on. "But be transported to a warmer shore, in a place and time far away. A time where emperors of great kingdoms wage wars on one another to win the fertile fields and the shore of the sea, where virginal maidens tend sacrificial flames in vast and rich temples, where conquered peoples are enslaved to the powerful. And where forbidden love blooms. . . ."

He bowed again, and left the stage as the curtains swept open. Kate leaned forward over her lute to examine the scene. The props she'd seen spilled out of trunks and cluttered around the hall now set a classical milieu. White columns set to either side of the stage framed a painted cloth of palm trees and green hills. A pasteboard chaise was set to one side, and one of the young apprentices lounged upon it. He too was transformed, by a long blond wig and a pleated white gown.

He pressed the back of his hand to his brow in despair and glanced at Kate. As she launched into the first chords, he began to sing.

I am Melsemene, princess of Carthage.

He sang in a sweet, pure voice, not yet cracked

by adulthood. His words told the tale of how the princess was her father's only child, the fount of all his ambitions, protected and cosseted, educated in all the finer arts and languages, the most beautiful and kind lady in all the land.

But then her father the king angered the gods, and in retaliation they demanded that Melsemene be married to Guyal, the cruel, ugly son of a neighboring king. Even though Melsemene wants only her life of study and contemplation, she is forced to agree to the marriage to save her father's life.

The song ended in a roll of thunder from metal sheets beaten backstage; then a new painted cloth dropped down, a scene of dark clouds and lurking creatures hidden among the trees. More actors crowded onstage, dressed in their costumes of armor and swords. War had come to Carthage, thanks to the princess's new prospective father-in-law, who wished to steal her kingdom and imprison her and make his own son king.

Kate didn't have to play again until the interval, and she was quickly caught up in the story. The princess and her father were locked away in a tower, but even there, love and hope could bloom. Melsemene glimpsed a handsome prince, played by Master Rob in fine velvets and furs, who was locked in the tower across from hers. They sent messages of poetry, sang to each other and, in one scene that had Kate almost in tears, met to embrace in person. The lovers planned a peaceful life away from the strife of wars and kings.

Melsemene was even willing to give up her rightful kingdom for love and a life of scholarship. It looked as if she would be set free and exiled, alive, united with her true love, and Kate held her breath as she watched their joy, forgetting it was Rob and the apprentice. But then the evil king took back his bargain, and condemned the lovers to death, along with Melsemene's father.

Kate frowned as she watched the princess fall to her knees to beg for their lives. This tale began to sound all too familiar. A young, scholarly princess dethroned, imprisoned, betrayed by false promises, used as a pawn in the power games of others. Murdered through no fault of her own.

It sounded very much like the story of Lady Jane Grey. Startled, Kate quickly glanced over the crowd, searching their faces to see if they made the same connection. Princess Elizabeth's face went even whiter, and her beringed hands clutched the arms of her chair.

"Enough of this!" Braceton suddenly shouted, as a hooded executioner raised his pasteboard blade above the princess's neck.

The actor playing the princess froze, stuttering to a confused halt in the middle of his final speech, and the executioner squinted past the torchlight. Rob, who stood at the side of the stage, held back by two "guards," closed his fist around the dagger at his waist. Kate saw it was no stage prop, but a real blade. Had he been expecting trouble all along?

Clutching her lute, she slowly rose to her feet and watched as Braceton stormed up the aisle. He reached out and pulled down the curtains, sending the actors waiting for their cues off in all directions. The apprentice leaped up from the block and fled, but Rob stood still and faced Braceton.

"There is still one scene left," he said. "The death of the prince—"

"I will hear no more of this nonsense!" Braceton roared. "First the church is befouled, and now you vagabonds spout your treasonous poison in this very house."

Master Cartman slowly emerged from behind the stage, his face-paint streaked by the sweat pouring down his forehead. He wrung his hands together, no longer the regal king. "Nay, my lord, we speak no treason, I vow! 'Tis merely a play, one Master Cecil thought would please the Lady Elizabeth . . ."

Master Cartman surely knew immediately he had said the wrong thing. Braceton leaped onto the stage, and with one powerful backhand sent Master Cartman tumbling to the floor. A woman in the audience screamed, and the young apprentice sobbed loudly.

"I should have known this was the work of

Cecil," Braceton said, tossing the torn curtains down atop the cowering Cartman. "I should have known you carried messages hidden in your pretty words."

"No messages, my lord. I swear it," Master Cartman cried.

"I see the meaning in your story, and I will not let it pass," Braceton said. "The queen's justice will always be done. No more of your lies! Begone from my sight now, you foul hedge-pigs."

"Lord Braceton," Elizabeth called. Kate turned to see the princess had come to the edge of the stage, Sir Thomas hurrying after her. Everyone else was huddled at the end of the hall, watching the scene with wide, fearful eyes, and Kate was glad her father was still tucked up in his chamber and not here to see this. "I fear the terrible events of this day have made you see treachery where there is none. 'Tis merely a play."

"You know very well, my lady, this is no mere play. You see the tale as well as I do," Braceton said. He turned away from the shambles of the stage to face Elizabeth, giving Rob time to help his uncle to his feet and lead him quickly offstage. "And such treason will not be allowed to stand. I will have justice if I must tear this house apart board by board to do it."

Dark pink streaked across Elizabeth's pale cheeks, and her dark eyes burned. "Then tear it apart! Send us all to the Tower, including these innocent players who only do the bidding of their masters in trying to amuse us. But you will find no treason."

Braceton stared down at her, huge and glowering, and Elizabeth looked tiny and frail next to him. But she did not turn away. Neither of them would ever back down in this clash of wills. "We shall see, my lady. I have been kind until now, gentle for the sake of your sister the good queen, who still has a care for you even though you have betrayed her again and again. But I will serve her despite that care. No more kindness."

He kicked out at a fallen column, shattering it. "And get these worms out of my sight, or their heads will be on pikes at your gate by morning."

CHAPTER 13

Kate found the players' cart in the sheep meadow beyond Hatfield's gates, near a large old oak tree, under which was a favorite picnic spot of Elizabeth's in the summer. Tonight the field was cold and damp, the moon obscured by the slide of purple-gray clouds. A few torches stuck in the earth illuminated the makeshift campsite, blankets on the ground, hastily packed chests still piled around. A woman sobbed quietly inside the cart.

They'd left in a hurry after Braceton stormed

out of the great hall, but it was impossible to travel on such a night.

Kate drew her shawl closer around her shoulders as she cautiously scanned the darkness for any movement. Was someone out there right now, with their arrows or their blades?

"Who is there?" a man called, his voice hoarse with caution. Rob Cartman stepped out of the shadows beside the cart and into an amber circle of torchlight, his sword drawn. Kate sensed a few other people by slight stirrings of movement under the blankets, but no one else showed themselves. It was as if they had all gone to earth, hiding.

Which was no bad thing. Not with Braceton tearing through Hatfield. "It's me. Kate Haywood. Her Grace sent me to see how you fared, and to give you this." She held out the purse of coins.

Rob slowly lowered the sword, which she saw was not a blunted stage prop, but a raw blade, like the dagger he had carried earlier. He raked a hand through his rumpled hair, and Kate could see the weariness etched on his face, the slump of his strong shoulders under his thin linen shirt.

"How did you get away?" he said.

"The same way you did—while Braceton was not looking," she answered. "He is too busy questioning the princess and the Popes to bother with me."

"Nor hopefully with us. We will be away at first light."

"Princess Elizabeth said to tell you she is heartily sorry for bringing you into her troubles."

Rob gave a harsh laugh. "I would say we brought it on ourselves. For did we not seek you out on the road to Hatfield?"

"Because Cecil sent you? And asked you to perform that play for the princess?" Kate said, exceedingly puzzled. Did Rob work for Cecil? Or for more sinister forces? "He is usually more subtle than that, I'm told."

"What do you mean?" Rob asked sharply.

Kate remembered what Elizabeth sought to know, what she'd whispered so quickly before she sent Kate out to find the actors. She remembered her own startled realization that the play was far more than it seemed. She needed to get to the bottom of it all before anyone else was hurt. "Is the play not about Jane Grey? The sweet young scholarly maiden, dethroned and imprisoned? The pawn to the power of others?"

"Hush!" Rob grabbed Kate's arm, and led her beyond the light, beyond the hearing of the others. "I know not what you speak of. It is merely a classical myth, as so many other plays are."

"It is not a myth I have ever heard," Kate argued. "And why would Lord Braceton react so? What had he to do with Jane Grey that would make someone want to send such a message?"

"I don't know!" Rob almost shouted. The woman in the cart sobbed louder, and he went on more quietly. "I don't know. You would have to talk to my uncle. He is the one who brought us the play and said we must learn it quickly."

"After you visited the Cecils?"

Rob shook his head. "Nay, it was before that. But I don't know when he got it, or who wrote it. It could be by any number of the writers we patronize, and they would pen anything asked for a few shillings. My uncle has seemed nervous about something these last few days, and changed his mind several times. I questioned him most ardently whether we should perform it, sensing that it could be too dangerous to bring up such dark memories. Yet in the end we deferred to Sir William."

Kate could make no sense of it all. "Can I speak to your uncle?"

"He has ridden ahead to see if we are still welcome at the next manor house. He told us to stay with the cart, as it's not safe to move it on these muddy roads till daylight."

"He has abandoned you here?" Kate cried. "So near to Braceton?"

"Our livelihoods are tied up in what's in the cart, Mistress Kate, these expensive properties and costumes. Without them we are truly nothing better than vagabonds."

It sounded plausible enough. But why would Master Cartman abandon his nephew and his possessions if he was not guilty of something? What was behind the strange play and his odd behavior? How were the play—about Jane Grey, who had been so passionately reformist in her religious ideas—and the Catholic priestly garb Ned wore connected? "Then you really know not what message was being sent in that play? If there was any message at all there."

"Truly, I do not know, Mistress Kate, or I would tell your princess. After what I have seen in London, she is truly our only hope now." Rob sighed wearily and leaned back against the tree. "There is one thing, perhaps."

"What is it? Surely even a fragment of knowledge would help."

"Lord Ambrose, our patron, was on the jury that condemned Lady Jane and her husband to death. But it is not a matter he is proud of, and he would never advertise it in a play to Princess Elizabeth. Not seeing that Lady Jane was her cousin."

"If such a play would have displeased your patron, your uncle should never have mentioned it to Sir William. Truly, I do not understand," Kate murmured, turning over everything she knew, all the jumbled-up, half-seen images. Who had paid the troupe to do the play? How did they know both the actors and Braceton, and poor

Ned? The answers were out there somewhere, surely nearby. She just had to find them.

"Nor do I," Rob said. "But it would seem, Mistress Kate, that we will pay for it all the same."

Edward Cartman stumbled over a knotty tree root in the darkness and fell to his knees, almost sobbing with fear. He had counterfeited terror and panic on the stage hundreds of times, but never before had he felt it as keenly as he did tonight. A cold wind blew around him, rustling the leaves over his head and seeping through his doublet.

It had been a great gamble to present the play, but the promised payoff was so large it seemed worth it. Edward had lost much of the season's receipts playing primero in the back parlor of the Rose and Crown, and with Lord Ambrose out of the country there was no chance of court engagements. The offer had seemed to come at a perfect moment, and at first seemed so easy.

Until he realized what was really going on beneath the harmless commission. Until Braceton knocked him to the floor, and he knew he had lost the gamble.

Edward pushed himself up from the dirt, the damp earth that smelled of rotten leaves and old smoke. His lungs felt as if they would burst. Surely he'd been running ever since they fled Hatfield. But it wouldn't be far enough.

He'd been a fool. He'd spent a lifetime clawing his way up from a boot-boy and apprentice to the leader of his own troupe. His brother, who had stayed sensibly on the family farm, had laughed at him. Until Edward came home wearing velvet and plumes, under the patronage of the wealthy Lord Ambrose. He'd shown them. And now he even had charge of his brother's treasured son.

But had they been right, in the end? Edward lost his head when he saw the great bag of coins on offer, just to perform one short play. And there was a chance the gamble could still pay off. He just had to ease his panic and think clearly.

He leaned against a tree, trying to catch his breath. Suddenly there was a soft rustle, a mere whisper of movement through the wind, and a figure slipped between the trees.

Just as on the night they met him to offer the coins and the play's script, the tall figure was muffled head to toe in a dark cloak. In the deep shadows of the hood could be glimpsed a black velvet visor in place of a face. The only color visible was the glint of the moon on the eyes that peered through the mask's slits. Edward couldn't tell if it was a man or a woman, or even human. Perhaps it was a demon, such as the one whispers said had killed the kitchen boy.

"So you performed the play, as I asked?" the figure demanded, voice muffled by the mask and the cloak.

"We did," Edward managed to say, even though he still couldn't seem to catch his breath. The whole scene had such a nightmarish air about it, like a witch's gathering at midnight. But it was terribly real.

The cloaked figure laughed. "And garnered a rare reaction, I'm sure."

"Braceton did not like it. Just as you said. Nor did Princess Elizabeth, I vow. Her face was white as milk."

"Good. You've fulfilled your bargain with me, then."

"Our dealings are at an end?" A faint spark of hope kindled in him.

The figure reached a gloved hand into the folds of the cloak. For one terrible moment, Edward felt panic crawling like a cold, living thing up his throat. He feared he would see a blade emerge. He almost collapsed to the ground as a purse came out instead. The figure tossed it at Edward, and it landed with a metallic clink at his feet.

"Yes. Begone from this place," the figure said, turning away. "And never speak to anyone of that play. It never existed."

Edward scooped up the bag. The weight of it in his hand, the clatter of the coins, swept away the panic. The risky gamble had paid off! It truly had! His great luck had not deserted him.

The relief made him bold. Without thinking, he called out, "If you ever do wish the play performed again, or any other nobles disconcerted, we know the lines well now. Surely others would be interested in it."

The cloak swept through the leaves as the figure spun around. "What *others* do you speak of?"

Horrified, Edward saw his mistake. "None at all! I only meant—"

"That play is for once and once only. But you go on to Leighton Abbey next, do you not? Or perhaps you wait for the return of Lord Ambrose."

"Nay," Edward protested. He took a step back, only to stumble over the root. "I only wished to see if we could serve you again."

The figure moved so quickly, almost like a ghost. It was upon him in a swirl of the cloak, and gloved hands shot out to grab him by the neck.

"I see I was mistaken to think I could be merciful," came a muffled whisper. "My enemies show no mercy. God's justice must be done. I cannot afford to be merciful either."

Suddenly the moonlight glinted on a blade, and it flashed down. Edward felt a sharp, horrible pain as the blade plunged into his chest and was pulled out again. The pain burned and then froze, and bitter blood bubbled up in his throat to choke him.

He tumbled to the ground, and the last thing he felt was the sweep of a cloak hem over his cold face.

CHAPTER 14

K ate was torn out of sleep by the sound of shouting and the crash of furniture tumbling to the floor. At first she was sure it was only a nightmare, of the dark and confusing sort that had disturbed her sleep too often of late. But then a cry rang out again, along with a deeper, rumbling threat, and she knew it was no dream.

She sat up straight in her bed, and for a moment she could hear nothing past the rush of blood in her ears. She pushed the bedclothes back, and as she swung her feet down to the cold floor, she heard her father cry, "Nay, I beg of you!"

Kate snatched up her shawl from the foot of the bed and quickly wrapped it over her chemise as she ran to the door. She pulled it open to find her rooms invaded by Braceton and his men.

After what happened in the courtyard, Kate had taken the precaution of carefully hiding her lute, but their sitting room was being overturned. Papers were scattered over the floor, plates swept from the sideboard, the chairs toppled over on their sides. A trunk Kate recognized as her father's, a small case he always kept locked and in his own chamber, stood open as Braceton sifted through the contents.

Her father knelt by the fireplace in only his nightshirt and cap, scrambling to try to gather up some of the papers. One of the men kicked them away, leaving a muddy bootprint over the musical notes.

"What are you doing?" Kate cried. She rushed over to grasp her father's arm, trying to lift him to his feet. He didn't even seem to see her, he was so intent on saving his work. "You have already been through all of our things!"

Braceton peered over at her, his eyes narrowed. "Ah, yes. The girl with the lute. You should have a better care with your father. It seems he was hiding this box from us beneath the floorboards. Surely that is a signal of some guilt."

"How ridiculous," Kate said. She managed to get her father to sit on one of the stools, and kept her hands on his shoulders to hold him with her. "That box is always out on his table. There is nothing in it that has to be hidden."

"Well, it was hidden." Braceton held up a pamphlet, his face turning brick red as he studied it. "What is this, then?"

Kate's father gave a strangled cry, and suddenly shot forward as if he would snatch it back. Kate grabbed a handful of his shirt, but it took every ounce of her strength to hold him.

"That is something very old; I don't even know why it's there," her father said.

"Then perhaps it is your daughter's," Braceton said with a terrible smile. "Is it yours, Mistress Lute-girl?"

He took a step closer, and held it up where Kate could see it. It was a cheaply made thing, with smudged ink and rough-cut pages, as if it had been produced and distributed in haste.

It did not belong to Kate, but she knew what it was. She'd seen them after Jane Grey was killed, passed furtively around the neighborhood. It was a compilation of Lady Jane's own letters and writings on the Protestant cause, along with a detailed description of her conversations with Queen Mary's priest in the Tower. It was accompanied by an account of her execution, as well as a prayer for her written by John Knox himself.

It was to all appearances a martyrology, for a martyr of the new religion. It was not known how all the documents had been unearthed, but it was rumored that the pamphlet was produced at Sir William Cecil's estate on a secret press.

And it was not at all a good thing to be found with. The death of young Lady Jane had blackened the queen's name even more than the Spanish marriage had, and surely Mary wanted her cousin forgotten. Her priests condemned such memorials to a girl who was to them an avowed and passionate heretic.

But what was her father doing with it?

Braceton smiled. "Do you know what this is? Perhaps you agree with your father that this deluded, treasonous girl was a saint?"

"Nay, she knew nothing," her father said. His

face had turned an ill greenish color and he slumped down on his stool.

"You worked in the household of Dowager Queen Catherine, did you not?" Braceton said. "Surely you knew Lady Jane in the queen's household. Perhaps you have fond memories of them both."

Kate had no answer to that. She *did* remember Lady Jane, though only vaguely. She'd only been a child then, and Lady Jane not much older. A small, pale, deeply serious and earnest girl who was always deep in a book. She conversed mostly with adults about very adult matters, such as religion. Her name hadn't been spoken at Hatfield in years, yet lately she seemed to haunt them all.

"Queen Catherine was a great lady," her father said stoutly.

"A lady who fostered heretic serpents in her household," Braceton scoffed. "If old King Henry hadn't died when he did, she would have been fetched to the Tower where she belonged. But you, Master Haywood, obviously long for those days to return. The possession of such writings is treason to the queen, so I am placing you under arrest. Since it's clear no one here at Hatfield can be trusted, you will be sent to the village gaol until you can be brought to London for questioning."

Arrested? Kate watched in stunned shock as two of Braceton's men grabbed her father by the arms and dragged him to his feet.

"Kate . . ." he cried, struggling feebly. "Kate, what is this?"

The sight of her father, her brilliant father, treated like the commonest criminal made a burning anger sweep over the chill.

"Nay, let him go!" she shouted. "He has done nothing at all. He only sits in here working on his music; he knows nothing of the world outside. How can he have committed treason? He can barely walk! He has gout."

Braceton reached out and grabbed her wrist, hard. "Then perhaps you assist him? I've seen you tiptoeing about, Mistress Haywood, thinking no one can see you. Maybe I should arrest you as well."

"Let her go," her father said, his voice suddenly calm. Kate twisted around to find him watching her. His eyes implored her to keep silent, to hold her temper. "She has done nothing. She's just a foolish girl. Take me to your gaol, and I'll tell you what you want. Whatever you want."

"Father, no," Kate insisted, deeply afraid. The gaol was a small, cold stone structure, damp and dismal. It usually held only ale-shot fools who caused fights at the tavern or petty thieves. One man had died of a lung-fever after being held in its drafty cells too long.

"My father is ill; he cannot be left there," Kate insisted, more afraid than she had ever been.

"Then he had best talk quickly," Braceton said

abruptly. He pushed Kate aside, and got between her and her father as they bundled him out the door.

Her father went quietly after Braceton's threat to Kate, but Kate could not keep silent.

"He does not even have shoes or a cloak," she cried, desperately trying to reach her father. "Is this the queen's justice now? To kill an ill, innocent old man with the ague?"

"The queen's justice?" Braceton shouted. "A slew of murders have been committed here, and you dare speak to me of justice, mistress? I will find out what treason lurks here—"

"What is the meaning of this?" Elizabeth suddenly said, her voice calm and cold, but easily floating over Braceton's fury.

Kate strained up on tiptoes to see into the corridor. Elizabeth had obviously just been roused out of bed, as they all had. She wore her fur-trimmed robe, and her hair was hastily braided. Penelope stood behind her, watching with wide, frightened eyes.

"This man has been found to possess heretical writings," Braceton said. "After *you* protected him. He is being taken to the gaol for further questioning. And I will tolerate no more inter- ference in this matter. Not after the queen's church was so befouled."

"My lady, please!" Kate beseeched, terrified for her father.

"I will write to my sister this instant and tell her of your atrocious behavior," Elizabeth said. She sounded just as angry and confident as ever, but Kate could see the flicker of uncertainty in her dark eyes. The terrible events of the last few days had taken their toll on everyone, and now matters were running over them all like a sudden winter blizzard.

"Do that, my lady," Braceton said with one of his cold smiles. "But I *will* question this man. And anyone else who might know of the plots that are afoot in this very house."

He and Elizabeth stared at each other in tense silence for a long moment, before Braceton gave a loud snort and pushed Kate's father farther along the corridor.

"He will not go without warm clothes," Elizabeth called out.

Braceton slowly nodded. "Very well. But his daughter will not gather them. Who knows what she would slip into the packing."

"Go, Penelope, and fetch some garments for Master Haywood," Elizabeth said, without taking her steady, cold stare from Braceton.

With a sob, Kate ran over to throw her arms around her father. The confusion and fear had faded from his eyes, but Kate could feel how frail he was in her arms.

"Don't be afraid, my dearest girl," he whispered as he pressed a kiss to her brow. "I was a fool to forget about that pamphlet, but we are innocent of any wrongdoing and the truth will always come out."

"But you will be ill in that place," Kate protested. "Your leg . . ."

"The princess will see to it I am comfortable. And she will take care of *you*. Stay very close to her."

Kate shook her head, still afraid. "I will find who has done this, Father, I promise," Kate said, though she wasn't sure how she could do that. What little knowledge she had gathered seemed so jumbled up and senseless. She only knew she could do it; she had to.

"Nay, Kate," he said, suddenly fierce. He took her face between his hands and looked down into her eyes. "You must take care of yourself now. Promise me that. I can bear anything if I know you are well."

That was how it ever was with them. One was well if the other was. "Father . . ."

"Promise me! We haven't much time."

Kate slowly nodded. "I will take care, Father."

Penelope came back with a bundle of clothes, as well as a cloak, a pair of stout boots, and a walking stick. She handed them to Kate's father, and suddenly reached out to kiss his cheek. He laughed in surprise.

"The princess will have you back here very soon, Master Haywood," Penelope said. "Before nightfall, I would say."

Without giving anyone the opportunity to say another word, Braceton hurried Matthew away. Elizabeth whirled around and followed them.

"Stay here, Kate," she called back. "I will see to this."

Penelope put her arms around Kate's shoulders, and Kate was glad her friend stood there to support her or she was sure she would fall. Tears of grief and rage choked her, yet she knew she had to stay strong for her father.

She had to stay strong for them all.

"I am sorry you could not see him."

Kate smiled at Penelope as they walked home from the village gaol. Penelope had stayed with her all morning as Braceton tore the house apart, including Kate's own rooms. She'd helped Kate gather a case of belongings to take to her father and walked with her all the way to the village in the cold wind, waiting with her as the gaoler went through the clothes and books and declared that Master Haywood could have no visitors. Penelope was quiet, but always there, and Kate was grateful for her company. She needed a friend with her now, to help her be strong.

Because she needed strength now more than ever before.

"At least they took the things to him," Kate said. "If he can stay warm, and distracted by the books, he should be well enough for a time. And they agreed his meals should be delivered from the Rose and Crown."

"Thanks to the coin you gave them."

Kate gave a rueful laugh. The money had been all she could scrape together so quickly, which was not much. "Needs must, I suppose. But he won't be there long."

"You agree that Princess Elizabeth can have him out soon?"

"I know she will do everything she can, but Lord Braceton is furious with her. He will thwart her at every turn." Kate remembered the way Braceton looked at Elizabeth, with the burning hatred of a general about to order his legions to charge an age-old enemy. "And I fear he is the one with the power at the moment. While Queen Mary lives . . ."

"Which could be for some long time yet. She has recovered from illnesses before."

Kate sighed. Waiting, not knowing, always being afraid, had been their lot for such a long time. It had been grinding, exhausting. Now it was desperate.

"There is only one thing to be done," she said.

"Break your father out of the gaol in the middle of the night?" Penelope said, a hopeful note in her voice.

Kate laughed, knowing that she had to restrain her more impulsive nature. "That could be rather exciting! Like something in a play. But I fear it would only cause us more trouble in the end."

"Then what will you do?"

Kate stopped next to a gray stone wall encrusted with moss, and leaned against it as she stared out over the empty windswept fields. She had been thinking about just such a question on the walk to the village, and it was a vexing one. She'd spent so long—her whole life, really—wrapped up in music and her own small world. The greater concerns had always been there, all around her in the people her father worked for and the places they lived. Politics, intrigue, danger, power and its loss—she knew of it, heard of it, was interested in it, but now it had come so close and become so real.

She knew she had to leave the cozy familiarity of her lute and her manuscripts to be a true part of it all. If she wanted to save all she held dear, her father and the princess, she had to.

The cold wind tugged at her hair, and she tucked the unruly brown strands into her cap. She wished for the fine fur-lined cloak given to her by Elizabeth, but a sense that Penelope, who was Elizabeth's close servant, would be hurt knowing of the rich present had kept her from wearing it while her friend accompanied her. "I am going to find out who is truly committing these crimes. Then Braceton will have to see it has nothing to do with us at Hatfield and release my father."

"Kate, nay!" Penelope cried. "It is too dangerous. Look what happened to Ned."

Kate closed her eyes as a spasm of pain rippled through her. "Aye. Poor Ned. I must do this for him, too. And I know to be cautious."

Penelope leaned on the wall beside her, and Kate could feel how stiffly her friend stood. Kate glanced over to find Penelope watching her with worried, shadowed eyes. "We could not bear it if we lost you as well. So much horror all around . . ."

"All the more reason to do what I can to stop it. No one else must be hurt."

"If you insist, I will help you however I can, of course," Penelope said earnestly. "We must keep the princess safe, no matter what. But how can we? Do you know something the rest of us don't, Kate?"

"I know very little, I fear," Kate said. She thought over the few things she had gleaned since Braceton came storming into Hatfield, bringing the darkness with him. What the cook at Brocket Hall told her about the estates. The play about Jane Grey, and Master Cartman's strange behavior surrounding it. The pamphlet in her father's possession. Ned clad in the vestments of a priest.

The only connection seemed to be religion, and Jane Grey, who had made religion the focus of her short life. But faith was always around them. It bound them together and tore them apart, as people had to grapple with faith to the monarch and the country versus faith in their immortal souls. It caused arrests and burnings. But what about it tied the terrible events at Hatfield together?

And what did it have to do with the attack on Braceton before he arrived? Did he covet someone's land? Whose?

"Very little indeed," Kate murmured.

"I doubt there is much to know," Penelope said sadly. "The world has gone mad and that is all there is to it. We should take care not to get drawn into that madness. It would surely drown us."

"But we are already involved! Ned is killed, my father in gaol, old Cora attacked by Braceton. Braceton's manservant murdered on our own doorstep." Kate pounded her fist on the wall. The rough stone hurt her hand, but that pain was as nothing compared to the fear in her heart. "Aye, we are involved, whether we will it or not. We must do our best to see it finished."

Penelope was quiet for a long moment. They stood there together, listening to the whine of the wind, the faint echo of noise from the village down the road. Life seemed to move on as usual there, but Kate sensed it was merely a facade. Like the kitchen maids at Hatfield kneading their bread, or the laundresses hanging out the wash, the princess reading, Penelope sewing. The things they did every day now seemed like playacting, a pretense to keep the wolf from the door.

But the wolf was already there.

"Your father is your only family, is he not?" Penelope said.

Kate nodded. "My mother died when I was born, and I have no aunts or uncles living, no cousins."

"I lost my mother long ago, too."

Kate looked at Penelope in surprise. They had been friends ever since they both came to Hatfield. They were close in age, and interested in plays and fashion. Kate could laugh with Penelope as she could no one else in the house. But they had never really shared such deep confidences.

"Did you?" Kate said. "I am truly sorry. I don't remember my mother at all, but I think of her often." And she missed her when she played her mother's lute.

"I do remember mine. She was so beautiful, so kind. Too kind, perhaps."

" 'Too kind'?"

Penelope gave a sad smile. "It was her soft heart that made her too good for this world, I think. After I lost her, Princess Elizabeth took me into her household as a kindness. But I miss my mother very much. Loyalty to family, to friends, is so important, is it not? The most important thing."

"It is," Kate agreed, hating the sadness in her friend's eyes. The ache of loneliness that never quite went away. "It is all we can really know there is in this world. All we can trust."

"When you were talking to the gaoler, I met Master Johnston, innkeeper at the Rose and Crown, in the lane," Penelope said. "He said that Ned's father has disappeared."

"Ned's father! But that is terrible." Kate recalled the last time she saw the man, frantic and wild with grief in the church, vowing vengeance. Then there was his empty house, the sister who had come and taken him away. "No one knows where he has gone at all?"

Penelope shook her head. "Master Johnston says he was quite ale-shot in the tavern before his sister arrived to fetch him, and was promising to find Ned's killer and flay him alive. Then his sister came, and no one has seen him since. The door to his room was open, but the bed was not slept in."

"How strange," Kate mused. Could the poor, grief-struck man be responsible for some of what had happened? Could he have been somehow involved, and was that why his son became the target of a murderer? The neighbor woman had said Ned's father was once a soldier and served with Lord Braceton, until drink took him over.

"Perhaps he really has gone to seek his revenge," Penelope said.

Before Kate could answer, she heard the rattle of wheels in the road. She turned to see Rob's cart slowly creaking toward them, Rob at the reins.

In stark contrast to how they had appeared on the way to Hatfield, all bells and drums and bright colors, today the players were silent, saddened. Most of them trudged along the lane, muffled against the cold, and Kate could hear a woman sobbing loudly inside the cart.

"Master Robert," Kate called out as they drew near. "Did your uncle return? Are you leaving for Leighton Abbey?"

Rob pulled up the horses and the cart lurched to a halt. He looked tired, his handsome face sharply drawn beneath his cap, and Kate could see the glint of blades hidden beneath his short cloak. It reminded her that he was not to be trusted.

"We are going to Leighton, aye," he said. "But my uncle has not returned. We couldn't wait for him any longer."

"*You* couldn't wait, you heartless varlet!" the woman in the cart cried.

Rob didn't glance back. "My uncle's leman disagrees, of course, but it wasn't safe for us to stay. Not with all that—well, all that was happening this morning. People have a tendency to blame players if they can."

"My father being arrested, you mean?" Kate said.

"I'm sorry for that, of a certes," Rob answered solemnly. "How does he fare now?"

"We were allowed to bring him some comforts from home, so he is well enough for the moment. But I must get him out very soon. He has done nothing wrong."

Rob nodded, and he looked as if he would say something more. But Penelope spoke first.

"I doubt you can say the same about your uncle, Master Cartman," Penelope said in a hard voice, one Kate had never heard from her before. "There is surely a reason people blame players when matters go awry."

Rob's jaw tightened as he stared down at Penelope.

"Penelope . . ." Kate said. Her head ached with all that had happened on that long day, and she didn't need quarrels to cloud her thinking. Besides, Penelope could certainly be correct.

"Wasn't his uncle the one who brought that dreadful play into the house?" Penelope said. "The one that angered Lord Braceton so much he took it out on your poor father. Perhaps he even brought in that pamphlet, and hid it in your father's things when he was afraid of being found out."

"What pamphlet?" Rob demanded.

Kate shook her head. She knew the pamphlet was her father's; he had just forgotten he possessed it, so wrapped up in his music was he. Yet it *was* strange it had appeared in such an obvious place just as Braceton looked for it. Right after the play about Jane Grey. Which, as Penelope had pointed out, was brought into the house by Rob's uncle, who was now gone.

"It was a work of Lady Jane Grey," Kate said. "A collection of her letters and such, printed soon after her death."

"I have seen such a thing," Rob admitted. "They were much circulated."

"Braceton arrested my father for having it amid his things. Yet I think it was all merely some ploy to flush out the real villain he seeks. The one who killed his manservant."

"My uncle could have had such a publication," Rob said. "But I doubt he would have hidden it in your father's room. Surely he would have buried it when he found out Lord Braceton was here."

"Then why has he vanished?" Penelope demanded. "Why did you perform that play?"

Rob shook his head, and Kate saw a fierce frown flicker over his face. "I vow I do not know, mistress! My uncle was never in the habit of confiding in me. But I intend to find out."

The woman in the cart wailed again, and Kate was suddenly very aware that they stood talking of dangerous matters in the middle of the road. She hurried closer to the cart and peered up at Rob over the brightly painted rim of the wheel. Penelope tried to stop her, but was not quick enough.

"You remember Ned, the kitchen boy who was killed in the church?" Kate said.

"Aye," Rob answered. " 'Tis hard to forget such a thing."

"His father has also vanished, as your uncle did," she said. "Did they know each other at all? Could it be connected somehow?"

"I don't see how it could be. My uncle surely did not know the man. Yet why should they both disappear on the same night?"

Kate shrugged helplessly. There was so much she did not understand. So much she was determined to discover. "You say you are on your way to Leighton Abbey now?"

"Aye. No matter what has happened to my uncle, we must eat. I will see to it we still have work. And perhaps there is something to discover there as well."

Kate nodded. The Eaton family, who lived at Leighton Abbey, was another Protestant family who had gained their estate in the Dissolution of the Monasteries. And Lady Eaton, as well as being related to William Cecil's late first wife, had once been a lady-in-waiting to Frances, Duchess of Suffolk—mother of Jane Grey. Surely there would be much to know at their home.

"If you will send me word, I will let you know if we hear anything of your uncle," Kate said.

"Kate, we must get home now," Penelope said insistently. She hurried over to tug at Kate's arm.

Kate nodded and stepped back as Rob set the cart in motion again. His mournful band trailed after him, and Kate watched them until they vanished down the road. She felt quite unaccountably sad as they disappeared from view. Their departure was so very different from their first appearance.

"Come, Kate," Penelope said, and they continued on toward Hatfield. "They brought nothing but trouble. And now they can run off, free, while we must stay and face Lord Braceton."

"They are hardly free," Kate said. "Their leader has vanished."

"And does that not seem like a sign of some guilt? Or perhaps some cowardice."

Kate feared her friend might be right. Rob had said his uncle acted strangely before they even came to Hatfield. And Master Cartman was the one who insisted on the play that infuriated Braceton so much. He had surely been up to something. But what? Why? Could the forbidden books she had seen in Master Payne's hut also be connected?

She was distracted by a sudden sound, like the cry of a wounded animal carried on the wind. She glanced back to see a man standing at the rise of a hill, beyond the wall that snaked along the side of the road. It took her a startled moment to recognize the man, outlined as he was by the glare of the gray sky. Then she saw it was Master Payne.

The vicar wore his usual dark, ragged old vestments, but his cap was gone and his long gray hair blew around him. He waved his hands in the air, then pointed at Kate and Penelope as they stared at him in astonishment.

"You are all damned!" he shouted. "Just as I warned. But you did not listen. If you disobey God's word, you will be punished. All the sinners will be struck down!"

"He should be in a play himself," Kate murmured, yet she couldn't help but shiver as she stared up at him. It was said the mad knew things, saw things, the sane could not. What had Master Payne seen?

"We should get home," Penelope said. "Master Payne should have been locked away long ago."

Kate nodded, and they quickened their steps until the man's warnings faded behind them and they went through Hatfield's gates at last. The dark redbrick house loomed before them, seemingly quiet behind its old walls, the gray sky reflected in the empty windows. Not even the gardeners were out yet, and when they went around to the kitchen doors no maids were hanging out the wash or throwing out slops. It seemed everyone was in hiding.

" 'Tis most strange," Penelope said. "Surely we must still eat. Why is no one out?"

A clattering sound came through the half-open door, and Cora's voice berated one of the maids.

Kate sighed in a measure of relief. "It seems we will eat, then. Something, anyway. We just have to stay out of Braceton's way while we can."

She turned to take the pattens from her boots, and her attention was caught by a flash of color that interrupted the expanse of gray-green lawn beyond the low herb garden wall. Slowly, she moved nearer to investigate. There had been too many unpleasant surprises that day.

And it seemed there would be yet more. It was a man lying amid the grass, his blue and green clothes bright in the dismal day. From that distance, Kate couldn't see who it was, but she remembered that Master Cartman wore bright garments.

"Kate, what is it?" Penelope said.

"Stay here, Penelope," she answered, and took a deep breath as she made her way out of the kitchen garden. She had to steel herself before she looked, especially after the way she had found Ned. She wasn't sure she could bear any more blood, even as she knew she must. This person might need help.

Holding her skirt hems above the damp grass, she crept closer. The figure lay so still she could see the person was beyond help.

When she was a few feet away, she found to her shock that it was *not* Master Cartman, or even Ned's missing father. It was Lord Braceton himself, stretched out on the grass, his open, glassy eyes staring up at the leaden sky and a trickle of blood from his gaping mouth matting his beard. He looked as if he had been there for some time, as the moisture from the grass dotted his doublet and he was growing stiff.

Two arrows had pierced his chest.

Penelope screamed, and Kate whirled around to find her friend had followed her. A scream escaped Penelope's mouth again, and her hand flew up to cover it. She stared down at Braceton, her face a terrible shade of green, and Kate feared she would be sick. That they would *both* be sick.

She grabbed Penelope's hand and they ran for the house.

CHAPTER 15

House arrest! God's blood, but now I am even more a prisoner in my own home."

Kate watched as Elizabeth pounded her fist on her table, rattling books and papers set out across the flat surface. Since Braceton's body had been discovered, more of Queen Mary's men had overrun Hatfield, swarming through the rooms and the gardens. The queen had roused herself from her sickbed to write to Elizabeth and declare her outrage that such a thing had been allowed to happen to her own agent in her sister's house.

Elizabeth was confined to her chambers until the murderer was caught.

Word had even come from the village that the lawyer Master Hardy, Anthony's employer, was intercepted on his journey from London. Master Smythson had closed his shop, and everyone stayed home, hiding behind closed shutters. A priest was being sent forthwith from court to purify the church and instruct Elizabeth on what she must do to save her soul. There would be no more prevarication.

And Kate's father was still in gaol. Captain Souza, one of King Philip's soldiers who now led the regiment of burly men in the queen's livery who filled the house, said he would remain there until he was told everything there was to know about the "treason rotting this cursed place." He also muttered many Spanish words Kate was sure they were better off not knowing.

Like Braceton, Souza railed about treason. But Souza was a spare, ascetic man of staunch Spanish Catholicism, a man of few words and much action. He would obviously be a difficult person to get around, and not someone Elizabeth could charm or befuddle. There were no journeys to Brocket Hall, no plays in the great hall.

And there were always guards at the princess's door.

Elizabeth sat down and tapped her fingers on the table, a hard, staccato rhythm. "I have long been a prisoner in truth, but now there is no pretense about it."

"I am sorry, Your Grace," Kate said.

Elizabeth shook her head. "You have nothing to be sorry for, Kate. You are the only one I can rely on now. Everyone else is so panicked they cannot see straight. Even Penelope, who has been such good company since she was sent to my service, weeps in her bed. She seems much more shaken to have found Lord Braceton's body than you are."

Kate swallowed hard, twisting her hands in her skirt as she thought of how Braceton looked when she stumbled over him. "I— In truth, Your Grace, I have been able to see little else in my mind since we stumbled across him lying there. But surely it's at moments like this that we must remain the calmest. Only by keeping control can we solve this crime and save ourselves."

Elizabeth's eyes narrowed. "Quite so, Kate. Where did you learn such a wise thought?"

"From you, Your Grace," Kate said with a small smile. She'd watched Elizabeth walk the dangerous tightrope of courtly politics with only her wits to hold her up for many months. And now, when they were so close to a safe haven, things looked darkest. It was no time to panic.

Elizabeth laughed. "Clever girl. Tell me again how Braceton looked when you found him."

Kate closed her eyes and reluctantly conjured

up the scene again. "He looked as if he was startled, I think. As if he died where he fell and did not expect danger. He probably wasn't moved to that spot."

"Sir Thomas did say Lord Braceton insisted he would go for a walk alone," Elizabeth said. "It was very early in the morning, and Sir Thomas tried to dissuade him, to make him take a guard, but Braceton said he was not going far. That he needed fresh air to clear the poison of this, er, snake pit."

"So there were no witnesses, even though he was not so far from the house."

"Most strange, indeed. The kitchen servants were all indoors, at their baking. But you say you saw Master Payne on your way home?"

"Aye, just at one of the hills beyond the woods. He was waving his arms and shouting at us. He looked even more ragged than usual."

"Could he have seen something?"

"Perhaps, Your Grace. If he could be found and questioned—and made to talk sense, which is probably beyond human effort."

Elizabeth slammed her fist down on the table again, sending a book crashing to the floor. "And I can find no one and nothing while I am locked up here!"

She pushed herself out of her chair and whirled around to stalk to the window. She stared down at the world outside, her palms braced on the glass as if she would push it out and soar free.

"I wonder sometimes if *they* felt like this, as if they would scream with fear and rage. Scream and scream, and never stop," Elizabeth said quietly, musing to herself.

" 'They,' Your Grace?" Kate asked, uncertain.

"My mother. And my young cousin, Lady Jane. They have been much in my thoughts lately, Kate."

"Lady Jane does seem to have appeared much in the house these last few days. The play, the pamphlet . . ."

"They say she made a brave end, with her faith to sustain her. She always did seem—not quite of this world." Elizabeth's finger tapped at the window, the band of her ruby-and-pearl ring clicking on the glass. "But in all her months of being trapped in the Tower, that terrible place, surely her mind could not always have been on a heavenly reward. She must have sometimes been afraid, longed for home, for her family. For the free, country breeze on her face."

Kate's heart lurched at the quiet sadness, and she hurried over to stand by Elizabeth at the window. Queen Mary's guard loitered in the courtyard below.

"This is not the Tower, Your Grace," she said. "And those men will soon be gone."

"Nay, this is not the Tower. It's meant to be my home, the home my father left me in his will, and once I felt safe here. But now it is a prison like any other. And I do think of them."

Kate didn't know what to say to that. Prisons, danger—they were always there, always fearful. And the dead were never entirely gone from them.

"They say the queen did not want to sign the warrant for our cousin's death," Elizabeth said. "That she had shown much mercy to the Greys after she ascended the throne, until Suffolk betrayed her and joined Wyatt's Rebellion. She wept for Lady Jane, but in the end her evil advisers persuaded her that it must be done for the safety of the realm. They say Lady Jane haunts her to this day. But would she weep to sign *my* death warrant?"

Suddenly Elizabeth turned around with a sweep of her silk skirts, and the cloud of old memories vanished from her eyes. "Kate, I need your help now."

"Of course," Kate answered. "I will serve you however I can—you know that."

"I do know that. You and your father are good and loyal servants, and I treasure that—but I fear what I ask may prove dangerous. I would not ask it if I hadn't seen how strong you can be."

Kate often feared she wasn't strong at all, that such terrible things as her father's arrest and finding dead bodies would send her weeping to her bed like Penelope. But she hadn't broken yet. She wouldn't until everyone she loved was safe.

"I will try, Your Grace."

Elizabeth nodded. She went to the table and poured out two goblets of wine. She handed one to Kate and said, "I cannot leave my rooms, but you can leave. You can slip in and out quietly, behind the backs of these guards."

"Oh, yes," Kate said. "I can use the secret passages if needs be."

"Then I need you to go to the village and talk to everyone you can. Find Master Payne, go after the actors to see why Master Cartman vanished, anything to find who might have killed Braceton. You are a sweet, personable girl; I have seen how people will talk to you."

Kate felt a tiny thrill of excitement to know she truly had the princess's trust. "I would be happy to do all that, Your Grace. I will go this afternoon."

Elizabeth nodded, and went to unlock a small covered chest that stood in the corner. She took out a purse heavy with coins and tossed it to Kate. "Use as much of this as you need. And, Kate . . ."

"Yes, Your Grace?"

"Be very, very careful," Elizabeth said solemnly. "I could not bear to lose anyone else."

CHAPTER 16

S o Master Hardy was detained in London?"
Kate asked Anthony as they picked up documents scattered across the floor of the lawyer's chambers. She had walked back to the village as soon as she could slip past the guards at Hatfield, only to find everything shuttered and silent. The queen's men had searched Master Hardy's rooms, but were now gone, leaving a mess behind them.

"Aye. He returned here for a short time, only to hurry off again, saying he had most urgent business," Anthony said as he examined a torn sheet of parchment and tossed it on the fire. The flames crackled with documents they'd burned, but was it too little too late? The rooms had already been searched, Master Hardy arrested. "It was most odd."

"He said nothing of what that business could be? You have no patrons in trouble that required his assistance?"

"Not a word. He has been doing much work for the princess and the Clintons of late, as well as the Eatons at Leighton Abbey, but Master Hardy is usually a most cautious man. His message to me after he was intercepted on the road was only to clean up the offices and be most careful with the papers."

Kate swept up scraps from under a writing table and added them to the fire. "It is surely impossible to be cautious now. Even people who live most quietly are thrown into trouble."

Anthony shook his head, his green eyes full of sympathy as he looked at her. "How does your father fare?"

"Well enough for the moment. I left him some clean clothes and more blankets before I came here, and he's hard at work on his lost Christmas music since the gaoler let him have paper and quills. If he has music, he doesn't care where he is. But I worry."

"Of course you do. We will have him out soon."

"Princess Elizabeth says so as well. But I know we have to find who is really behind these murders before the queen's men will free my father. Her Grace has asked for my help, yet it seems such a tangled knot." A knot she was most determined to unravel.

"What do you know so far? Here . . ." Anthony found some blank sheets of paper, a quill, and ink in the writing desk, and righted a fallen stool for her. "Write down everyone you suspect and why. Perhaps we can find some connection between them, or with Braceton."

Kate laughed. "Your lawyer's mind at work again, I see."

"We must be logical, even as events would

seem to have no logic at all. It's the only way we can begin to unravel your tangled knot."

" 'We'?"

"I'm here to help you however I can, Kate. I'm your friend, am I not?"

Kate glanced up at him as he leaned against the table next to her, his jaw tight and his eyes darkened as he looked down at the paper. Her friend—aye, he had long been that, and she was grateful for it. She'd had few enough friends in her life. But now she felt doubly happy to think she was not alone. That Anthony would stand with her, that in the midst of all the fear and confusion, she could hold on to him.

Yet she felt something else as she looked up into his eyes, something new and strange—yet another confusion. She thought of a line from one of her favorite songs, a plaintive tale of lost love and impossible hopes.

There was no time now to dwell on such things. No time *ever*, really. He had a future as a prosperous lawyer to look forward to, and he needed money and connections to do that. She was merely a musician singing for her supper. No matter how handsome and kind he was, how much she liked him, they could never be a match. Better to focus on what she *did* have some hope of solving—the mystery of Braceton's murder, not to mention the other tragedies that had fallen upon Hatfield recently.

She turned away from Anthony's steady gaze and dipped the quill into the inkwell. Her thoughts were racing.

"The main difficulty is that we know nothing of Lord Braceton's life at court," she said. "He made so many enemies here, in the short time he was among us, that I'm sure he must have dozens of them in London."

"Anyone who lives by the monarch and the court makes enemies," Anthony said. "But who is near enough physically to have done this thing? Let us just start with what we *do* know."

Kate nodded. "There is the vicar, Master Payne. I saw him just before we found Braceton's body, and he seemed wilder than ever, damning all the sinners. Braceton was a Catholic, a queen's man, surely associated with those who ousted Master Payne from his church and his comfortable vicarage. If he thought Braceton had something to do with leaving Ned in the church in such a vile way—"

"What if he killed Ned himself to leave a strong message for the papists?"

Kate glanced up to find him frowning down at her so far blank page. "Would he do such a thing? A churchman? I am sure they are connected, but I know not in what way yet."

"If his mind is disordered, who knows what he might do? Perhaps he thinks one sin would remedy a greater one, would punish the wicked

Catholics and show them what he sees as the evil of their ways. A necessary sacrifice for the greater good. And when that did not work, he killed Braceton himself."

Kate could see in his words a terrible kind of logic. So many people, Catholic and Protestant, had been willing to die terrible deaths for their beliefs. Would not some kill for them as well? Especially those like Master Payne, so obsessed with sin and sinners. She wrote "Master Payne" on the list, as well as her reasons for suspecting him.

But would the vicar have been cool and steady enough to fire those arrows so accurately? Kate tapped the quill on her chin as she considered that, and then added it to her list with a question mark.

"Who else could there be?" Anthony said.

"There is Ned's father, I suppose. He vowed revenge on whoever killed his son, and now he has vanished. Perhaps he thought Braceton was responsible for Ned's death and killed him before fleeing."

"Most plausible. But surely he did not kill his son, or shoot Braceton's servant with that arrow before they even arrived at Hatfield."

"He could have used the arrows to kill Braceton to throw people off his trail and make them think it was someone else, if he was involved in some plot."

"What do you know of the man before he came here?"

Kate shrugged. She had asked around the kitchens just such questions, but there weren't many answers. "Not much. Poor Ned couldn't speak, and I took little notice of the man, for I didn't know he was Ned's father. He worked in the stables at the Rose and Crown, I think. It was the innkeeper who asked Princess Elizabeth to take Ned into her household for kindness." She tried to remember what she had been told since Ned's murder. "I think he was in the army, perhaps with King Philip and Robert Dudley in France. And surely Elizabeth would take in anyone who knew Dudley."

"If he was a soldier, he would have the skills and nerve to do such a thing," Anthony said. "And the first bowman could have just been a highwayman, a random crime."

"Possibly," Kate said. "But it would be a strange coincidence indeed if Braceton was attacked with an arrow twice. It must be someone with some military expertise of some sort. And then there is Master Cartman, the actor. He has also disappeared."

"Ah, yes. The actors," Anthony said wryly. "They must always be considered."

"What have you against Master Cartman and his men, Anthony?" Kate said, unaccountably piqued that he would so dismiss the Cartmans. Rob especially.

"Did you not think it strange, the way they

appeared so fortuitously at Hatfield while Braceton was there?"

"Sir William Cecil sent them."

"And did Cecil have them perform that play you told me about? The one that made Lord Braceton so angry?"

Kate shook her head. "Master Robert said that his uncle claimed so, but Sir William has ever been a prudent and cautious man in the past."

"Aye. How else has he stayed out of Queen Mary's prisons?"

"He would not have brought Jane Grey to Braceton's attention, or the princess's, surely. But who would have sent that play? And for what purpose?"

"To make trouble, of course. Yet trouble for the princess, or for Braceton? What did Braceton have to do with Lady Jane?"

"I don't know. We must find out." Kate wrote Master Cartman's name on her list, along with a question mark. Master Cartman himself might have vanished, but perhaps Rob knew more than he had said thus far. "They have gone to Leighton Abbey, where they were engaged to perform before Master Cartman disappeared."

"Leighton Abbey. The members of the Eaton family are firm Protestants, and have lived most quietly since Mary took the throne. I wonder why they would want plays and merriment now."

"Their home was once one of the largest

religious houses in the area, I think," Kate said. "At Brocket, the cook told me many Catholics have been trying to seize Protestant estates before Queen Mary makes them forfeit to the church again. Perhaps the Eatons were one of the families so targeted. Maybe Braceton even had his own eye on the property. And Lady Eaton was great friends with the Duchess of Suffolk, Lady Jane's mother. Surely something would be known there about this scheme for grabbing estates before it's too late."

Anthony glanced down at her sharply. "You aren't thinking of going to Leighton yourself, Kate?"

"I might have to. The princess said I should find out whatever I can, and there isn't much to discover here."

"You will not go alone, then. I will go with you."

"Anthony, nay! You must stay here and watch over Master Hardy's offices." Kate suddenly realized she had taken over her friend's time to help with her own troubles, when he had plenty of trouble of his own.

"Master Hardy has been swept up in the events just as everyone else has. I can best help him by helping you." He quirked his brow at her. "And as your friend, I can't let you go running around the countryside by yourself. It isn't safe."

Kate knew better than to argue with him when

he sounded like this, so assured and determined. It was the lawyer's mind again, not to be swayed. And truth be told, she would be very glad not to be alone now. "Very well. Tomorrow we will go to Leighton Abbey. For right now, our list is very small." She read aloud what she'd written. "Master Payne. Ned's father, who as far as we know is still at his sister's house recovering from his grief. Someone who wants an estate that belongs to someone else, or an owner who wants to hold on to it. Master Cartman, or someone connected to him who gave him that play. Lord Ambrose, perhaps, or one of his enemies? He is a queen's man."

"Very possibly. He is said to be in France now, but he was one of the jurors who convicted Lady Jane and her husband."

"And surely Lord Ambrose knew Lord Braceton. Yet another question to answer." Kate added it to the bottom of her list. "I will think on this more tonight. Surely there must be somewhere else we need to go after Leighton."

After she sanded and blotted the list and tucked it away in her purse, she left Anthony to clean up the last of the papers from the office and right the furniture as best he could. They promised to meet outside the village the next morning to make their way to Leighton Abbey, and she hurried back to Hatfield before it could grow dark.

But at the kitchen door, she found a sight that

had become too familiar of late. Maids weeping, and guards everywhere.

"Oh, Mistress Haywood, thank heavens you have returned safely!" Cora cried, wringing her gnarled hands on her apron.

"I only walked into the village on a few errands," Kate said. "Why, what has happened?"

Cora gestured toward Peg, who sat on a bench by the door, crying into her sleeve. Her hair was in disarray, her skirt stained, and Kate feared that something bad had indeed happened. Again.

"Peg went into the woods to gather some mushrooms for the princess's dinner," Cora said, her face drawn and creased with worry. "And she found Master Cartman's body under a pile of leaves. The poor man was stabbed right through the heart."

CHAPTER 17

I don't think it is a good idea for you to look for this man alone, Kate," Anthony said with a scowl.

Kate laughed, even though this was all far from a lighthearted matter, what with Rob needing to be informed about his uncle's death. But she couldn't quite help it when she saw the black frown on Anthony's face. He had insisted on going with her to Leighton Abbey when he learned of her intentions to find Rob and tell him herself, and also take the opportunity to look for clues. To see Rob's reaction to the news.

"I am not alone, Anthony," she said as they turned a corner on the lane and found themselves just at the edge of Leighton's stone walls. "You are with me. I feel quite safe."

And she did feel safe, with him beside her. His presence seemed to comfort her. And she had to admit she would like to hear his reactions to whatever they found at Leighton.

"Only because I discovered what you intended and insisted on going with you," Anthony said, still scowling. "You should not be alone with that actor. I do not trust him, especially after this nasty business with his uncle. How can you be sure the nephew is not also involved?"

Kate shook her head. She could *not* be sure—of course she could not. But she wanted to be sure. "I don't think—"

"Who goes there? Show yourself!" someone suddenly shouted from beyond the wall, cutting off her words.

Kate peeked around the corner of the garden wall, but Anthony held on to her arm to keep her back. The sun was sinking below the chimneys of Leighton Abbey, and they had only just found where the actors were staying. The cart was lodged just beyond the formal gardens in a copse of trees, its paint brilliant red and yellow against the dark gray gloom. Trunks and cases were scattered around it, and a recently doused fire smoked, but it seemed most of the troupe was already in the house. Only Robert and a couple of others were still there.

"I demand that you show yourself!" Rob called out again. His fist closed around the hilt of the sword at his belt.

Kate tossed a reassuring smile at Anthony and slid away from his restraining hand to step around the wall. " 'Tis only me, Master Robert."

Rob's gaze narrowed and he drew his sword free. "Who are you? What do you want here, lad?"

Kate had forgotten she wore a disguise, a boy's hose and doublet she had borrowed from one of the Hatfield pages. She quickly snatched off her cap and let some of her brown hair fall free. "It's Kate, Rob. I'm sorry if I startled you."

"Kate! What are you doing here?" Rob quickly put away his sword and hurried toward her. "And dressed like that. Not that it doesn't become you very well."

"We had to travel fast, and it seemed we would attract less attention if I was a boy. And we didn't know if you would really be here. We had to be very careful."

" 'We'?"

Kate gestured toward Anthony, who moved to stand close behind her, watchful and protective as always. "My friend, Master Anthony Elias. He brought me here."

A crooked smile touched the corner of Rob's mouth. "Ah, yes. The lawyer's boy. Quite the lady's squire, I hear."

Anthony scowled. "'Tis more meet to find honest work in the law than roam the countryside like a vagabond. Kate insisted on coming here, and being her friend, I would assist her."

"And you took a most eager interest in her—insistence, I see."

Kate glanced between them. They watched each other with a taut, tense wariness that made her think of a bearbaiting. She didn't understand it at all. Surely they hardly knew each other? Yet they showed every sign of wanting to duel.

Kate gave an impatient sigh. There was no time now for such manly nonsense.

"Never mind that now," she said, stepping between them. She felt a bit silly, considering they were both so much taller than she was. "We have much to do and very little time."

Rob turned away from Anthony to smile down at her. "Why are you here, fair Kate? Dare I hope you missed me?"

"None of that now," she answered sternly. "I fear we bring you unwelcome news."

"Unwelcome news?"

"Aye." Kate took a deep breath and plunged ahead. "Rob, I am afraid there is no sweetened way to say this. It concerns—well—your uncle was found dead in the woods near Hatfield. He was murdered. I am so very sorry. I insisted on coming here to tell you myself."

Rob's teasing grin vanished and his eyes went dark. After a long moment he said, "I feared as much when he did not return."

"And Braceton too was killed. Which makes four deaths in only a few days."

"And you came all this way to tell me this? That was kind of you, Kate."

"She came because the Lady Elizabeth wants to be sure you had naught to do with these crimes, Master Cartman," Anthony interjected in a hard voice. "Your appearance at Hatfield, the play you performed—"

"Do you dare accuse me?" Rob said, his hand going again to his sword hilt.

"We wish only to find out all we can to discover the murderer," Kate said. She wished she could box both their ears. Time was wasting, and there was much she needed to discover. "Your uncle is dead, Rob, and my father and Anthony's employer have been arrested. The princess is confined to her rooms. We must find out what is happening, and quickly, before anyone else is hurt."

Rob fell back a step and rubbed his hand over his eyes. "You're quite right, Kate. Yet I fear I'm baffled."

"As are we all," Kate confessed. "Was your

uncle in some sort of trouble, then? In debt to someone who could force him to show that play?"

"I know nothing about the play, except what I've already told you," Rob said. "My uncle brought the manuscript back from one of his journeys to London and seemed most insistent we learn it quickly. But once we were here, he seemed to change his mind. He was restless, angry. He had always been quick-tempered, but was more so than ever."

"Yet he did have you perform it in the end."

"And you saw what happened."

Kate nodded. "It infuriated Lord Braceton. And seemed to frighten him as well. Most strange. Had he anything to do with Jane Grey?"

Rob shrugged. "He knew our patron, Lord Ambrose, I think, but Ambrose has been in France for some time now."

"And Lord Ambrose was on the jury that convicted Lady Jane," Anthony said.

"We had naught to do with any of that," Rob insisted. "We are merely vagabond players, as you so aptly point out, Master Elias. We can't afford to be mixed up in court plots."

"Yet it seemed your uncle was, in some way," Kate said. She carefully studied Rob's face. He did seem baffled and saddened by his uncle's death, but he *was* an actor. And he had been in too many places at too convenient a time.

Rob's face suddenly darkened, as if he sensed her suspicious thoughts. "I had naught to do with any of this. I did my best for my uncle because he took me in when my parents died. But I could not be a traitor." He reached inside his loosened doublet and took out a ripped and smeared note, holding it out to her. "I was meeting a lady when my uncle was killed, a lady whose company I have enjoyed before. She sent me this, and others, to tell me when it was safe to meet her. If needs be, she will vouch for me to your princess, but I would rather not involve her in any of this."

Kate felt a most unwelcome stab of what seemed horribly like jealousy as Rob told her about his mistress. But she made herself glance at the note, which was written in a pretty hand that surely meant the lady had some education.

"It does seem as if he was at an assignation," she murmured. Rob tucked the note away with a curt nod, and Anthony's frown eased the merest amount.

Kate turned to study the house, outlined by the setting sun. It was typical of a grand house built from monastic structures, its gray stone austere and chilly. The church was gone, but the living quarters were built over the old cloisters, which still stared out with blank arched windows. Two new octagonal towers stood at either end, no doubt built for banqueting and festivities. Not that people like the Eatons had found much cause for merriment since Mary became queen. She must get in there somehow.

"The Eatons are of a different mind than men like Braceton and Ambrose, I hear," she said. "They are associated with the Cecils and the Greys. How did your uncle come to be engaged here?"

"We've performed for the Eatons before," Rob answered. "At their house in London, before they left to live quietly in the country. My uncle never subscribed to any faction or ideology, Kate. He only knew the language of money, and would perform for any who would pay. Lady Eaton, as well as being rather sickly, is of a romantical sort of mind and enjoyed my uncle's performances."

"Lady Eaton—who was once lady-in-waiting to the Duchess of Suffolk," Kate mused. "I assume he had no plans to perform his *Princess of Carthage* here."

"Not that I know of. We were set to do *The Shepherd and His Lass*, a pastoral romance of the sort her ladyship prefers."

Kate turned back to Rob with a cajoling smile. He could be of use now, and she needed him, no matter what her old suspicions were. Or her new jealousies. "And is there a part among the shepherds for a poor musician, perchance?"

"This is some of the finest clover ale I have ever had, mistress. Truly the flavor is most—unique."

Kate sat quietly by the kitchen fire, listening to

Rob as he charmed and flattered the Eatons' cook. And flattery it assuredly was, she thought as she took a sip of the bitter concoction in her mug. But—as she had told Rob and Anthony—the servants were the place to go for information in any household, so they were waiting in the kitchens for the time to begin the play. As Kate was meant to be a boy, she tried to stay silent and unobtrusive, observing everything.

But that meant Rob had to lead the conversation, and watching him tease and laugh with the maids, making them all blush, was quite annoying. There was no time now for such silliness.

That was the only reason for her irritation. Surely.

Kate stared down at the cloudy liquid in her mug and listened as the cook, a portly elderly lady who should have known better than to be taken in by such flattery, giggled. Kate hoped Anthony, who, posing as a well-to-do traveler, had been taken in as a guest abovestairs, was having a more sensible conversation.

"Aye, 'tis my own recipe," the cook said. "A secret blend of herbs. I'm glad you like it, young man. You must taste many a blend of ales on your travels."

"We do visit a great many fine houses, mistress, in our line of work," Rob answered. He leaned back in his chair and stretched his long legs in their particolored hose out before him, as lazily as if he had hours to kill. The maids stirring the pots over the fire looked at him from under their lashes and fell into whispering together. "But few as fine as this one. You must be a very organized housekeeper, mistress, to keep it all running so smoothly."

The cook's cheeks turned bright pink. "I work hard—that's true enough. We've been shockingly short-staffed these last few years, and it's not easy to make do. But I've been here since I was a scullery maid, and won't leave now."

"These last few years?" Rob asked.

The cook poured more ale into his cup. Luckily, she seemed to have forgotten Kate was there and left her mug alone. "Aye. Lord Eaton was a privy councilor in young King Edward's day, as his father was before him for King Henry. Well-favored the family was then. But they left the court when the queen was crowned. Fortunes have been meager since then."

"Was it King Henry who gifted the Eatons with this estate?"

"So it was, for their good service. Their estate before was much smaller, but this was part of the old monks' holdings."

A former monastic demesne, just as Kate had thought. One Braceton and his men wanted? Just like Gorhambury?

"Times must have been merry back then," Kate said, keeping her voice low and rough, her cap tugged down over her brow.

The cook glanced at her, as if in surprise she was there. "Oh, aye. There were hunting parties and dancing all the time; we even had a cook from London who made only sugar subtleties, and four boys to turn the spits. It was especially fine when Lady Eaton served the Duchess of Suffolk. Grand people were here often. We prepared suppers of thirty removes at least, and I had a large staff of maids. Good, hardworking girls." She looked at the giggling maids, who were letting the contents of their pots burn while they whispered, and sighed. "We haven't seen a play in a year at least. Hopefully it will cheer my lord and lady to see you."

"There hasn't been company here of late?" Rob asked.

The cook suddenly frowned. "We had company of a sort only a few weeks ago. But he wasn't cheering in the least. Lady Eaton was ill with worry after he left. She's just now out of her sickbed."

"Not family visitors, then?"

"Nay. 'Twas a man sent from Queen Mary to question my lord and lady about their religious practices. A very rude and loud sort. He tore things up something fierce."

"And his servant was a great lout," one of the maids said. "Always down here pinching our bottoms."

The cook poured out a mug of ale and gulped it

down. "Such people came here before, of course, when the queen came to the throne, and then after that Wyatt business. They questioned Lady Eaton over and over about the Suffolks, and it made her so ill. The last one left in a great hurry, much to the relief of us all. We thought it was over until this new one arrived. He was much worse than any of the others."

"Was this man called Lord Braceton, by any chance?" Rob asked.

"How do you know?" the cook said, surprised. "Have you encountered him yourself?"

"Sadly, I have," Rob said. "Before we came here, we performed at Hatfield House."

"For the Lady Elizabeth?" The cook gasped. "May God bless her."

"Aye, for the Lady Elizabeth. Much like your master, she was in need of some merriment. Lord Braceton and his men were likewise examining her household. But he is dead now."

"Dead!" one of the maids squealed.

"Foully murdered," Rob said, and told them something of what happened to Braceton and his bottom-pinching manservant. "We heard tell he also visited the Bacons at Gorhambury."

"God protect us," the cook whispered. "What's to become of us all? Surely the queen will send even more men after us now."

"Did Lord Braceton find anything here at all?" Kate asked, still keeping her voice low.

The cook shook her head, obviously distracted. "I shouldn't think so, or he would have hauled my lord off to the Tower. But he tore things up something terrible, and one of the maids said she saw him hide a letter somewhere before he left, though I won't have anyone doing anything so stupid as search for it. We did think perhaps he was looking for that strange man who came here to sermonize once or twice, that Master Payne. Full of fire and brimstone, that one was."

Kate sat up straight in surprise. Master Payne had been at Leighton? To what purpose? And Braceton had left a letter here somewhere?

Before she could ask anything more, a footman appeared on the stairs and called down, "The hall is prepared now, Master Cartman, and my lord and lady are finishing their supper."

"Then I must go and make sure all is ready for the play," Rob said. He put aside his mug and stood up, gesturing for Kate to follow. "Shall you all come watch the play?"

As they made their way to the great hall, Kate examined the house around them. Traces of the old ecclesiastical structure remained in the pointed arches and cold stone walls, but the Eatons had added grand secular touches as well, in new mullioned window glass, fine tapestries, and cushioned chairs. The new furnishings did little to banish the worn, disused air of the place, though.

The house had a strange hush about it, as if it

stood still and waited for something. Patches of the paneled and plastered walls were bare and there was little furniture or plate. These days were indeed difficult for families like the Eatons, with fortunes low. Surely it was all they could do to cling to their estates. If a man like Lord Braceton went after them . . .

What lengths would they go to in order to protect themselves?

She followed Rob as he slipped into a small chamber just off the great hall, where the other actors were putting the last touches to their costumes and running through their lines. They gave Kate curious glances, but they said nothing to her. They seemed too wrapped up in their preparations.

Rob led her to a stool in a quiet corner and handed her a sheet printed with a ballad. "If you sing this at the beginning, while the shepherd is asleep and dreaming of his love, you can stand to the side of the stage and examine the audience with no one to notice you."

Kate nodded and quickly scanned the song. It seemed easy enough to follow, a sweet, simple pastoral with a repetitive lyric pattern. As she studied the words, she noticed that Rob seemed most distracted. He paced in front of her, running his fingers through the blond strands of his hair, and he frequently stopped to study the other actors.

"Shall you tell them about your uncle?" she asked quietly.

Rob shook his head, still watching his friends. "Not tonight. I need their concentration for the play—it would be a disaster if they were weeping and confused. With my uncle gone, I must lead them now. I will tell them tomorrow, after we leave this place."

"Will they have to look for new places in other troupes?"

"Not if I can help it. I am my uncle's heir. I'll have to negotiate with Lord Ambrose, or find another noble patron, to keep everyone together. My uncle had his faults, but thanks to him, we had begun to build a reputation for our plays. Writers want to sell their work to us, and noble families begin to engage us for their celebrations. We shouldn't squander it."

Kate saw a shadow of something like fear and doubt flicker in his eyes before he covered it with a quick flash of a smile. She was reminded again of the terrible toll these events had taken on so many people. And of how much else could happen if they didn't find the villain soon.

"Was your uncle your only family?" she asked softly.

Rob nodded. "My parents died when I was a boy, and my uncle took me in. His brother, my father, was a farmer, and I'd never left our home before that. Thanks to my uncle, I've seen cities and great estates, met many people."

"Found that you have a talent for the stage?"

"And that. I love the theater. As much as I grieved my good parents, I would have been a terrible farmer. My uncle, despite his gambling and some of his bad habits, gave me this life." Rob shook his head, a spasm of grief passing over his face before he quickly smiled again. "I can't believe he is gone, so quickly and so terribly. What shall I do now?"

Kate remembered Penelope telling the tale of how she lost her mother and was cast into the world alone. She thought of her own lost mother, of Queen Anne Boleyn, and of her own dear father, locked up so unjustly. So many losses. Her heart ached for Rob now, despite her previous suspicions of his motives.

"Who do you think the other man was?" she said.

"What other man?" Rob said, his attention turning from the actors back to her.

"The cook said men had come from the queen before to examine Leighton Abbey, including one who left in a great hurry before Braceton arrived to tear the place apart. Who could it have been?"

Rob shrugged. "Any one of dozens of the queen's men, I suppose. She's been sending them out ever since she took the throne, especially to places like this. Examining people's religious practices, their loyalties."

Kate nodded. He was right, of course. It could be anyone. Many families like the Eatons had fled abroad, and those who stayed had to be very careful. They could be searched at any time. Yet something about that worried at her. If he was a queen's man, why would he have left so quickly, without finding what he came for?

Word arrived that the audience was ready for the play. Kate followed the actors out of the antechamber and onto the stage. As at Hatfield, it was a makeshift space of a dais hung with draperies. Some pasteboard trees and painted boulders created the shepherd's sylvan landscape. Beyond the curtains could be heard the muffled murmurings and shufflings of the audience.

Kate stood in the shadows behind one of the trees and watched as Rob, playing the shepherd, took his place lounging against the boulder. The young apprentice, in a long blond wig and pale pink skirts, waited to make his entrance.

At Rob's gesture, the servants swept open the draperies and Kate launched into her song.

As she sang, she studied the people gathered on benches and chairs below the dais. Lord and Lady Eaton sat at the front. He was stout and sturdy in his dark red doublet sewn with rows of gold buttons, his graying hair and beard fashionably trimmed. He didn't seem much interested in the play, tapping his booted foot and glancing around distractedly, but it was clear Lady Eaton was entranced. Unlike her husband, she was small and delicate, pale as snow, in a saffron-colored gown that had once been the height of fashion. She studied the stage with shining eyes.

Kate wondered how such a frail lady had once served the Duchess of Suffolk, who was reputed to be very fond of the hunt and dancing. But maybe it was exile that had made Lady Eaton delicate.

Next to her sat Anthony, who appeared to be doing an excellent job pretending to be a gentleman traveler in need of lodging for the night. His good looks and fine manners made it a role he could easily play, and Lady Eaton turned to smile at him. Hopefully he also had gathered some useful information, yet somehow Kate wished he hadn't used his chivalrous ways to get it.

Behind them sat the Leighton Abbey household, in rows by their rank. It wasn't a large staff, and Kate remembered the cook said many had left, but there were still several young maidservants and footmen whose wages would not be as high as veteran staff. Kate carefully examined each one.

Suddenly a movement in the shifting darkness at the back of the room caught her attention. She scanned the paneled and carved walls, and for a moment could see nothing. Had she imagined it?

But no, the shadows moved again, and in the gloom she saw a woman standing near the doorway. She wore a plain black gown to blend in, and a veil covered her face completely.

An image flashed through Kate's mind, of the veiled woman fleeing through the corridors at Hatfield. Of Ned cowering in fear at the sight of her. The woman looked the same: not very tall, of slim build, the opaque veil concealing all her features. Surely there wasn't more than one dramatically veiled woman roaming about Hertfordshire?

Kate quickly finished the song, rushing so much through the final bars that the apprentice seemed most confused about making his entrance. Rob sat up and gave her a concerned look, but Kate knew there was no time to waste. She knew a musician was not needed for the first few acts, so as the play began, she crept off the side of the stage and made her way around the edge of the long, narrow hall, careful not to be noticed.

But despite her haste, the woman had vanished. There was no one standing at the back of the room at all. The door was open a crack.

Kate slipped through the door and closed it behind her. She found herself in a long, narrow, empty corridor. A scent of violets hung in the air, and as she stood very still and listened, she heard the brush of light footsteps on the floor.

She ran toward the sound, following it around a corner and up a narrow flight of stairs. The farther up she went, the more she left behind the lights of the house and the quieter the corridor became. She had no time for fear, though, no thought to turn back. She had to find the woman, talk to her, make her see she meant no harm. The woman surely held some important clue to what was happening.

Kate followed the sound of the steps around a sharp turn in the steps and found herself at the foot of an even narrower, twisting set of stairs. They seemed to lead up into a turret of some sort. She glimpsed a flash of swaying skirts above, and peered up to see the woman dashing up the narrow steps. Despite the tiny, sharply twisting staircase and the faint light, the woman ran with a sure step.

"Wait, please!" Kate called. "I mean you no harm. I only want to talk, I beg you."

Her only answer was the sound of a door swinging open. Kate ran up the stairs, glad of her boy's breeches and sturdy boots, which allowed her to move freely. To either side of her were cold stone walls, old arrow slits letting in the moonlight. A faint amber candle flame burned somewhere in the gloom above her.

At the top was a circular sort of foyer, with stoutly iron-bound closed doors all around. One door was half-open, and that was where the light emanated from. Kate dashed toward it to push it all the way open.

She glimpsed a narrow bed, a clothes chest, a small table that held the candle. But no veiled woman.

Suddenly she felt a hard blow land between her shoulders and shove her forward. She stumbled and fell painfully on her hands, the jolt going all up her arms and making her cry out.

Before she could push herself up, she heard the door slam behind her and a bolt fall into place. The candle sputtered, and a surge of cold panic rushed through her. She jumped to her feet, ignoring the pain in her hands, and ran to twist at the door latch.

Just as she feared. She was locked in.

"So foolish," she muttered. She pounded her fists on the door, even though she knew very well everyone was much too far away to hear. She should never have run after the woman like that. She needed to be back to the play before the next song was to happen, before anyone could miss her. But her fear that the woman would disappear once again had clouded her judgment.

Trying to breathe deeply and stay calm, Kate leaned back against the door to examine the room. It was such a small space, with rounded walls and meager furnishings, but tapestries hung over the cold stone and embroidered blankets were piled on the narrow bed. It was a comfortable hidden nest, high up here in this tower.

Who was it who took refuge here?

Kate hurried over to open the clothes chest at the foot of the bed. As long as she was trapped, she might as well look for clues.

More dark-colored clothes and clean smocks decorated with blackwork embroidery were neatly folded in the chest, amid violet sachets. They were good quality, wools and velvets, cut for a slim figure, but they weren't marked with any initials. There were caps and veils, shawls, but no books or papers. No paintings or letters. The veiled woman remained a mystery.

Kate sat back on her heels and studied the tapestries. The Marriage at Cana, not of the very best quality, but fine enough. She remembered such scenes in the rooms of Queen Catherine Parr. On the table was one book, a Bible in English, illegal since Mary became queen. Yet that was not really a clue to the woman's identity. The Eatons were known to be a family of the new religion. Perhaps they harbored the woman as a fugitive for her faith.

Kate went to open the book, checking for any inscriptions or notes. On the back page was written, in careful letters, *I remember. From your faithful daughter.* There were no names or dates.

As she set aside the volume, she felt a small rush of cool air touch her ankles, a fresh breeze in the small, stuffy room. She followed it to see that one of the tapestries stirred slightly at the floorboards. She pulled the stiff, heavy cloth back to find a narrow doorway cut into the stone.

Dizzy with relief, she tugged it open. The latch was stiff, as if it wasn't much used, but she set her booted feet and pulled hard until it squealed on its hinges and she could slip outside.

She found herself on a narrow walkway, held back from the night beyond by a low, crenellated stone wall. She peered past it to see a court-yard far below, deserted and dark. Past that she glimpsed the gardens of Leighton Abbey, the low, quiet roofs of the old monastic outbuildings. There was no sight of the veiled woman.

Kate followed the walkway around the wall, hoping to find another doorway or perhaps a window large enough to climb through. At last she discovered a stone stairway that wound its way down the outside of the tower. Breathless with relief to be free, she ran down it and hurried through a half-open door at the tower's base. Now she just had to find Rob and Anthony, and tell them about the veiled woman.

She was in a corridor, probably near the kitchens, she thought, as she examined the roughly plastered walls and flagstone floor. Buckets and muddy boots lined the baseboards. She couldn't hear any voices or catch a glimpse of anyone, but she dashed into the house.

She turned a corner, and found herself in a pantry of some sort—a small room lined with tall shelves laden with pottery pitchers and thick glass bottles, baskets of fruit—kept cool to preserve the food.

At the other end was another door, half-open to reveal a bar of light. As she crept carefully closer, she heard a man's deep voice, answered by another man, higher and younger.

". . . when these benighted actors leave. I never should have let them in the house."

"Why did you? Things have been going well of late. Quiet, since the queen's last emissary departed."

"Lady Eaton wanted to see the play. She misses the court life, I fear, being in the thick of things. But we need the quiet if we are to make what we so devoutly wish come to pass. Yet I fear this quiet will not last."

Kate carefully peeked around the door and saw it was Lord Eaton talking, along with a slim, dark young man she didn't recognize. Their faces looked most solemn. They were walking toward her little pantry, and she feared they would find her there. She knew she should show herself, claim she was lost, but something held her back. She wanted to know what the event they "devoutly wished for" was.

The Eatons harbored the veiled woman. What if they were not to be trusted? What if they threatened Elizabeth's well-being?

As their footsteps came closer, Kate ducked behind one of the shelves and crouched down as low as she could, praying she would not be seen. She held her breath as the door slowly opened.

CHAPTER 18

A ye, the actors seem harmless enough, I think," Kate heard Lord Eaton say as the men stepped into the room. Bottles on the shelf rattled, as if he searched for something. "My lady wife has been down in spirits ever since she was sent away from Bradgate Manor. She and Frances Grey were great friends, and she was much fond of the girls, especially Lady Katherine. She misses the liveliness of that life. Mayhap a play can remind her of those days."

"And actors do travel to many households. They might have news we do not."

The rattling abruptly ceased, and Lord Eaton sighed heavily. "They did bring word that Lord Braceton is dead. Murdered."

"Murdered!" the younger man cried. "But— surely blame will be somehow attached to us. Everyone knows the man was here."

"We must pray not. He went to Gorhambury after Leighton, and it's well-known the Bacons are more suspected than we are by the queen. We live quietly here and have for some time, ever since . . ." Lord Eaton's voice trailed off, and then he went on more quietly. "We have to, after the last visitor from the queen. No evidence was found against us then either."

"Because he left in such a hurry. What is to be done now?"

"What *can* we do? It's too late to flee, as others have done. With luck, Braceton can't be connected to us."

"Better that Hatfield should be blamed?"

Lord Eaton was silent for a long moment. When he spoke, he sounded deeply weary. "The Lady Elizabeth will surely not be blamed either. She cannot be; she's our best hope, since sadly the Greys are a spent force."

"Everyone knows the queen's hatred of her sister."

"And everyone also knows Queen Mary is ill. The Lady Elizabeth is clever. She has removed herself from tighter corners before. The Tom Seymour business, Wyatt, Dudley. Surely the death of a bullying functionary can be as nothing to her."

"Do you truly think that's all Braceton was?"

"Nay. He had the power to cause us trouble enough. But he is dead now. Hopefully anything he knew died with him."

Kate's legs were cramping where they were tucked up beneath her, and she bit her lip to hold back a groan as she tried to stay still. What had Braceton come to know here at Leighton?

There was the sound of a door slamming down the corridor, and running footsteps. Someone called out, answered by a shout of laughter.

"What was that?" the younger man said nervously.

"Naught but the servants, I'm sure," Lord Eaton answered. "They are overly excited to have those actors in the house, just as their mistress is."

"Was it truly a good idea to let them in? They could be spies."

"Spies for whom? We have nothing to find any longer, not by either side. And I told you, Lady Eaton needed the amusement."

"What about your—guest in the old bell tower? What if they came across *her?*"

The veiled lady? Kate leaned closer to the shelf, holding her breath as she waited to learn more about the mysterious woman. Who was she to be here at Leighton? To be creeping about Hatfield?

Lord Eaton paused again, and the bottles rattled as he seemed to sort through them. "How could they see her? She keeps to herself and never speaks to anyone. I'm not sure she *can* speak. And if someone saw her—well, everyone has a strange relative or two lurking about."

"You should have turned her out long ago. You can't afford reminders of past alliances. Not if you want to keep this estate. You know why Braceton and his ilk were scouring the country-side now of all times."

Ah—so it *was* true some courtiers like Braceton were taking advantage of the queen's piety to enrich themselves. And surely Leighton Abbey would be a prime target. The house was filled with possible culprits. And she remembered the cook's words about a letter of some sort Braceton left behind. Where could such a thing be? How could she find it, especially since she needed to be involved in the play and affect a servant's humble demeanor?

Kate's leg accidentally slipped, knocking lightly against the shelf. Her heart pounded and she held her breath. The men didn't seem to hear her, though. Lord Eaton took down some bottles and they turned toward the door.

"Lady Eaton would never send her away," he said. "Not after what they saw together. We must wait and bide our time. It has saved us thus far."

"For how long?" the younger man said impatiently, fiercely. "It has been years! It could be years more. We won't be so lucky forever. Braceton came so close—"

"Hush!" Lord Eaton hissed. Their voices grew fainter as they moved away, and Kate strained to hear them. "'Twas just such hotheaded nonsense that got men like Suffolk killed. He knew not when to leave well enough alone."

The door shut behind them, and for a moment Kate feared she would be locked in again, with no escape route this time. But she didn't hear the click of a lock or the thunk of a bolt, and once she was sure no one else was coming, she unfolded her legs and held on to the shelf to pull herself to her feet. Pins and needles shot through her skin, and she gasped.

I could be cozy at home with my music, she thought. What was she doing sneaking through strange houses, listening to half-understood conversations, and chasing veiled women up towers?

Yet deep inside, she felt a thrill to be doing something, anything, to help Princess Elizabeth, who had done so much for Kate and her father. True, she did not have the answers yet, but she was sure she was very close. So close she could nearly reach out and touch them.

She needed to find the veiled woman. And that letter.

Once the pain in her legs subsided, Kate tiptoed to the door and carefully pulled it open. She peeked out and found the corridor empty. She let out an impatient sigh as she felt a pang of disappointment. What had she expected? That the woman would be lurking about, waiting, when she'd already gone to such lengths to hide herself? It would be no easy task to find her at all.

Yet she had been at Hatfield. Not a terribly far journey, but surely not an easy one for a woman all muffled in black. Someone must have noticed her. And why was she at Hatfield, if she lived here at Leighton? Who was she there to see?

Kate made her way back toward the great hall. It was silent but for the buzz of low conversation, so it seemed there was an interval in the play and she was not quite as late as she feared. She needed to find Anthony and see if he had discovered anything from Lady Eaton, who seemed so happy with his company. And she had to beg his help in looking for that letter. He was disguised as an aristocrat and she as a servant; he would have much more freedom to wander the house.

She glimpsed Anthony near the doorway, talking to Lady Eaton, who was obviously trying to flirt with him. Kate carefully gestured to him, waiting just outside the doorway until he noticed her. He made his excuses to the disappointed-looking lady.

"What is it?" he asked quickly in a low voice.

She hurriedly told him about the mysterious letter, obtaining his agreement to search for it, and just in time, for as she stepped back into the small antechamber, someone grabbed her arm.

Kate gasped, cursing herself for her distraction. She whirled around to find Rob standing there, half-clad in his shepherd's costume and half in his own clothes. "Where on earth have you been, Kate?" he demanded. "We are in the midst of a play! The interval will not be long, and you need to know the song for the second part. . . ."

CHAPTER 19

W on't you join me for a goblet of wine, Sir
Anthony?" Lady Eaton said in her low,
breathy murmur as she took Anthony's arm and
led him from the hall during the interlude of the
play. Behind the makeshift curtains, the clatter
of changing scenery could be heard, and the
audience was talking together in a low rise and
fall of voices.

Lord Eaton had disappeared during the first act
and had not yet returned, but Lady Eaton was
most hospitable, Anthony thought as he studied
her flirtatious smile. *Find the letter for me, please,*
he remembered Kate whispering, her eyes wide
and beseeching as she touched his hand.

Anthony couldn't deny her any help he could
give. He feared it would be very difficult for him
to deny her anything at all; it had been thus ever
since he met her.

He had to admit that under normal circum-
stances, talking with Lady Eaton would be no
great hardship. She was still a pretty woman,
despite the trials her family had been through of
late, albeit too pale and too thin under her dark
brown velvet and brocade gown. A sort of quiet
sadness lurked around her faded blue eyes, and
he was a man who couldn't bear female sorrow.

God's toe, but he would do anything to help Kate, his sweet friend. But Kate had rushed off to hurl herself into even more danger with that damnable actor, and all Anthony could do was find the information that might stop her.

"My husband has a very fine Rhenish wine he recently received," Lady Eaton said. Her pale cheeks were flushed pink from the pleasure of seeing a play, and her fingers curled tightly, eagerly around his arm as she led him into a small library off the hall. "I am sure you would enjoy trying some."

Anthony carefully studied the chamber as Lady Eaton shut the door behind them and hurried over to unlock a cabinet against the tapestry-hung wall. Draperies were drawn tight over the small windows, keeping the room warm and stuffy despite the lack of a fire in the grate. There was little furniture beyond the cabinet, a writing table, and a couple of stools, and there were very few books on the shelves.

Had most of the shelves held forbidden books that were hidden away? The Eatons were, after all, a Protestant family, friends of the Greys. Anthony was sure that was one of the keys to getting into Lady Eaton's confidences.

"I would indeed most appreciate a goblet of your husband's new wine," he answered. "It has been some time since we've seen any wines from the German states, I fear."

"Many of our dear friends have been forced to make their homes there, sadly," Lady Eaton said. She took a pottery bottle from the cabinet and poured out a generous measure of the pale golden wine into two goblets. "We send them news of home and aid when we can, and they send us small gifts in return."

Anthony took the goblet she handed him and held it up in a salute. "To absent friends, then, Lady Eaton. May they return home very soon."

Lady Eaton gave him a tentative smile over the rim of her goblet. "I wonder, Sir Anthony, if perhaps we share some of the same friends? Your estate is near Hatfield House, I believe you said."

Anthony remembered the tale he and Kate had concocted to tell the Eatons. He was a Protestant knight, somewhat dispossessed under Queen Mary's reign, but still of good breeding, who had met with the actors on his way to London and decided to pay his respects at Leighton Abbey.

"Indeed it is," he answered. He took a sip of the wine. It was very good, sweet and strong, and he knew he would have to go slowly with it if he wanted to keep a steady head at this vital moment.

But Lady Eaton seemed to have no such concerns. She drained her goblet and refilled it. Most impressive for such a petite lady. "And are you mayhap acquainted with the Lady Elizabeth?"

"Only distantly," Anthony said, trying to seem cautious and reluctant. "She is carefully guarded. But I have been able to pay my respects to her and assure her of my best wishes and aid."

A brilliant smile broke across Lady Eaton's face, showing how very pretty she must once have been, when she was a young lady-in-waiting to the Duchess of Suffolk, Frances Grey. "I do pray for her daily. With the Grey family brought so low, she is our only hope."

Anthony leaned closer to her and said in a confiding voice, "So do we all. I think she will need our prayers now more than ever. I heard tell Hatfield has been descended upon once again by an agent of Queen Mary."

Lady Eaton's eyes hardened and she took another deep drink of the wine. "Lord Braceton, I would wager. The man is like the veriest plague."

"You know of him?"

"Know of him?" She laughed bitterly. "We had the hideous honor of a visit from him ourselves. It seemed he has been making a tour of the houses of known reformists, tearing up what little we have left. We feared he would be bound for Hatfield after he left here."

"But obviously you and your husband had naught for him to find, or you would not be here in your house now," Anthony said. "You must have been too clever for him."

Lady Eaton laughed again, this time an easier,

almost girlish giggle. "I am most flattered, Sir Anthony, that you would think me clever. I confess I have very little education, but I learned a bit about courtly life when I served the Duchess of Suffolk. Now that family was one of truly clever ladies. Lady Jane was so . . ."

Her voice trailed off sadly, her smile vanishing, and Anthony knew he had to bring her back hastily to the present moment, to the subject of Braceton. "So you hid your—valuables when Lord Braceton arrived?"

Lady Eaton shook her head, as if ridding herself of memories, and took another drink. "We had been visited before by the queen's minions, of course. By a man named Lord Ambrose. You have heard of him, I'm sure."

Anthony was surprised. He *had* heard of Ambrose, most recently. Ambrose sponsored the troupe of actors who even now were in the hall of Leighton Abbey itself.

His hand tightened on the goblet. He had known all along he could not trust that damnable Rob Cartman. And not because of the way he looked at Kate.

Not just because of that, anyway.

"Lord Ambrose has been sent by the queen to France, I think," he said.

"Aye, so he has. But after he left, his good friend Lord Braceton descended on us." She set one of her hands on Anthony's sleeve and smiled

262

up at him. "But I knew what he had come for, and I made sure he did not find it."

Ah—*now* he was getting somewhere. Anthony let his head dip close to hers and smiled at her in return. She smelled of wine and violet powder, nothing like Kate's fresh, crisp lavender. "What did he come to find, Lady Eaton? Something that could hurt the Princess Elizabeth?"

Lady Eaton studied him closely. "You are the princess's true friend, I think."

"I am, Lady Eaton. I vow it on my soul."

Tears suddenly welled in her eyes. "I confess I have been keeping a secret that has been heavy on my heart, and I have not been sure what to do with it."

"You can safely confide in me, if you so choose," he said. He led her to one of the stools and helped her to sit before he knelt beside her. She laid her hand on his arm again, and her fingers trembled. "I would be most happy to help you however I can."

"You are most kind, Sir Anthony. Truly a gallant gentleman, and I had feared there were none left in the world," she said with a sniffle. "It all happened when Lord Ambrose was here, you see. And then there was the fire. . . ."

CHAPTER 20

Out of breath, Kate had slid back into her place on the stage, just as the next act of the play began. As she picked up her lute, she secretly studied the gathered audience. Lord Eaton had returned to sit next to his wife, but he seemed restless, fidgeting in his chair, tapping his fingers on the carved armrest. The man she had seen him talking with stood at the back of the room, studying everything carefully. Kate knew she would have to be extra cautious and not draw attention to herself.

Lady Eaton had been gone for many long moments once Kate sat back down, but she returned with a small, secret smile on her pale face. And Anthony's seat next to her was still empty. It was very difficult to sit still, to concentrate on the music, when all she wanted to do was find out if Anthony was any closer to finding the letter.

Rob made his exit for the scene, and from behind the curtain just beyond where Kate sat, she heard his fierce whisper.

"Did you find anything?" he said.

Kate answered through her determined smile. "Perhaps so. This seems a very strange sort of house."

"What house is not, in these days? Do you think the Eatons had something to do with my uncle's death?"

"I could not say yet." Much depended on what might be in that mysterious letter. Kate saw Lord Eaton's watchful man glance toward her, his eyes narrowed. "Go away now. You are distracting me and I can't draw notice."

Rob muttered a curse under his breath, and she heard the rustle of footsteps as he moved away from the curtain. She finished her song and let the actors' lines take over. The watchful man's attention swung back to them, and she could take a breath again. Yet she couldn't help notice that Lady Eaton was growing restless as well, glancing at Anthony's chair more often as if she wondered where her handsome guest had gone.

Surely he should have returned by now, Kate thought. Her chest felt tight as she considered where exactly he might be, what he had managed to find. Had he been caught by one of the Eatons' servants? Attacked by the veiled woman? By God's blood, but she could not bear it if she had led her friend into danger.

The moments slid past painfully slowly, that tight feeling of dread growing closer around her like a vise, until at last Anthony slipped back into the hall. Kate's fingers faltered on the lute strings, but she quickly righted her song.

As Anthony returned to his seat, she saw that

his cap was gone, his hair slightly ruffled. But Lady Eaton beamed at him.

And he lightly touched the sleeve of his doublet, where she could see a tiny bulge that should not be there. He gave Kate a quick nod. However he had done it, it seemed he had found the letter. . . .

To Lord Ambrose, My dear friend,

My motive in writing you today, so quickly and in secrecy, sending this only by the most trusted of messengers, is to warn you of the danger we are in concerning the great matter of Lady Jane Grey. We have long been bound to silence over this, along with so many others, but I fear the silence may soon break and our role in what occurred become fully known.

Take pains, my friend, to conceal all the reasons behind these doings. For if the good queen should not reign longer, and the Spanish depart, we will be at the mercy of the Greys once again. Hold fast to our purpose, which is the purpose of God and the queen, after all, and in our own best interests.

—Braceton

"Braceton was on the jury that convicted Lady Jane, along with Lord Ambrose?" Kate asked in astonishment as Anthony helped her climb over a low wall on their way home in the early-morning light. She suddenly felt rather foolish. Surely she should have realized such a thing, should have known to look into the connection. She should not have needed Anthony to charm Lady Eaton to find out the information for her. "I should have known."

"How could you have known, Kate?" Anthony said.

They paused at the top of a hill to catch their breath, looking at the redbrick chimneys of Hatfield in the distance as they talked. From afar the house looked quiet, peaceful, with only the curls of silvery smoke rising into the sky to show anyone was there at all.

"It's not widely known who served on the queen's jury for that case," he went on. "Not many would want their names associated with such a business."

"Braceton didn't seem the sort to back away from admitting what he'd done, or even from being proud of it," Kate said. "He was very vocal in his hatred of 'heretics,' and Lady Jane was one of the chief proponents of the new religion. Is that where he and Lord Ambrose met?"

"Nay, it seems they were allies from court, from what Lady Eaton said. She is much attached to the Grey family, and after a few goblets of sweet German wine she was most happy to confide in me. She hates everyone who had a hand in Lady Jane's death, of course, but especially Ambrose and Braceton, since they searched Leighton."

"If Ambrose searched Leighton once and found nothing, why would Braceton go back there? When there are so many other houses of Protestants to raid?" Kate asked. Then she remembered what she had overheard Lord Eaton saying, that their first "visitor" had left in a great hurry. "Did Ambrose leave something unfinished?"

Anthony gave her a smile, a wide, dazzling grin that made him even more handsome than did his usual serious mien. It also made him look infuriatingly satisfied, as if he had a secret Kate didn't know. "Indeed he did. And Lady Eaton very kindly let me examine Lord Ambrose's chamber and talk to a chambermaid who cleaned after he left. 'Powerfully untidy,' she declared him to be, and was still most put out that he left behind such a mess. I must say, the ladies of Leighton Abbey were most kind and accommodating."

"Because you flirted with them and they liked your pretty green eyes!" Kate cried. "Don't tease me, Anthony. What did you discover?"

"A great deal, as it turns out. You were quite right, Kate, when you said the servants of a household knew everything that happens there. They're also very happy to share their knowl-edge."

"Of course they are. Because usually no one

listens to them, much to the detriment of those who think the servants beneath them."

"And it seems Lord Ambrose was a great one for standing on his rank. He tore apart the Leighton kitchens and tried to abuse one of the young maids. But one day he received a letter that had him much agitated. He locked himself in his chamber and would not come out. Until the fire."

"Fire?"

"Aye. It seems one night some sparks from a hearth caught a rug afire. The flames were contained in that one chamber, but not before most of the household was sent outside into the night for safety. Lady Eaton remembers it well because she caught the ague in the damp air."

"Is that the only reason she remembered it?"

"Nay. Also because of the theft. A small chest was taken from Lord Ambrose's chamber, but there was no one to blame, for everyone was out in the garden—in full sight of Ambrose himself."

Kate was fascinated by Anthony's tale—and by how much information a handsome young man could glean from lonely ladies in an isolated house. Obviously she had been wrong to not seek his help in the matter long before.

"Could he have simply misplaced it?" she said. "Nay, that does not seem like something a courtier like Lord Ambrose would do. Who took it?"

"The maid said everyone thought it was the ghost."

"Ghost?"

"It seems that Leighton Abbey, like any old house, is much haunted. By long-dead monks, thwarted lovers . . ."

"A veiled lady in black?"

"Of course. There must always be a veiled lady. Bess, the maid, declares she has seen the ghost herself. And everyone is sure that is who took the chest. Though how a ghost could carry a heavy box in its spectral hands, I could not say."

"They are scarcely spectral," Kate murmured. Even now she could feel the strength of the push that sent her stumbling in the tower room.

"What do you mean? Have you seen the spirit yourself?"

"I have seen her." Kate quickly told him about her two encounters with the veiled woman, at Leighton and at Hatfield.

Anthony frowned. "You should not have gone dashing into danger like that, Kate."

"I know. I am too impulsive sometimes. But I couldn't let her escape again. I need to find out who she is. And what she did with Lord Ambrose's box."

"Well, there I can help you. The box may have been carried off by a ghost, but it appeared quite safe and sound. In the chamber of the unfortunate maid Lord Ambrose tried to rape, who is friends with my new friend Bess."

Well! He might have said that in the beginning. "What was in the box, then?" Kate demanded. "Did they give it back to Lord Ambrose?"

"Of course not. If the Leighton ghost saw fit to steal the thing from him and give it to the maid, they knew there had to be a reason. They gave it to Lady Eaton."

"Who last night showed it to you," Kate finished for him. "Anthony, you truly worked miracles in only a few short hours."

Anthony grinned. "It seems Lady Eaton, despite being lady-in-waiting to one of the most educated families in England, cannot herself read beyond a few letters. She recognized the name of Lady Jane Grey in the letter that had caused Lord Ambrose such agitation, but naught else. Ambrose was predictably furious about the loss of his possessions, and out of fear, Lady Eaton hid the box and told no one about it."

"Not even Lord Eaton?"

"She said he has such a temper, she was afraid he would use the letter to create even more trouble with Ambrose and thus with the queen. It made her all the more ill, the fear of keeping the letter and also of getting rid of it. Several times she tried to burn it and then could not."

"Then what happened?"

"Ambrose was called back to court in a great hurry, before he could find the box, and then as we know he was sent on to France. Things were quiet at Leighton, until Braceton arrived and the searches began all over again."

"And Braceton needed to retrieve his letter."

"I would wager a guess that he came to Leighton only to try to retrieve it, even using the threat of seizing the whole estate to get it. But a ghost doesn't respond to threats."

"And neither does Lady Eaton, it seems."

"Not when the poor lady is paralyzed with terror. She kept the papers well-hidden, intending to give them to her husband after Braceton left."

Kate sat down on the low wall and quickly read over the words of the letter again. The ink was thick and blotted on the cheap paper, as Anthony had obviously written in a great hurry, but the story that unfurled before her was definitely a fascinating one.

As Kate reviewed the letter a third time, she glimpsed the workings behind what had happened to poor Lady Jane, thanks to men like Braceton. As Kate herself remembered from those dark winter days after Jane's father, the Duke of Suffolk, was arrested for his part in Wyatt's Rebellion, word had been given that Suffolk had lied about Queen Mary's impending Spanish marriage for his own ends. He spread falsehoods about King Philip's intentions toward England in order to set his daughter back on the throne.

At the time, it was widely believed that Mary, who pardoned Suffolk after his first rebellion and declared she meant to show mercy to Jane as well, could no longer protect her young cousin, no matter what her soft heart wanted. A second rising in Jane's name made the queen's advisers force Mary to sign the warrant for her own protection and that of the realm.

But this letter showed that was a lie, and the Crown knew it to be a lie all along. The way had to be smoothed for the Spanish alliance and the return of the Catholic Church to England, and Mary had to be rid of Jane. With her cousin out of the way, her troublesome sister, Elizabeth, could be next. With the help of men like Braceton and Ambrose. And word of this great concealment could ruin reputations of many high personages both in England and abroad.

Kate slowly refolded the letter and took a deep breath. "Jane Grey," she murmured. "All roads on this strange journey lead back to her, don't they? Jane Grey and Protestant estates. But how would that get poor Ned killed? Or Master Cartman?"

"Ned is a mystery indeed," Anthony said. "But Master Cartman and his troupe are associated with Lord Ambrose. Surely they cannot be entirely innocent in this matter, even if your Master Robert did have a liaison at the right time."

Kate tore the letter into tiny shreds and let them blow away on the wind. She couldn't risk smuggling it into Hatfield, and she knew the words very well now. "I should get back to Hatfield and tell the princess what has happened. You have been such a good friend, Anthony. I can't thank you enough."

Anthony suddenly reached out and took her hand in his. He raised her fingers to his lips, warming her chilly skin with a kiss.

"We work well together, do we not, Kate?" he said, looking into her eyes without a hint of a smile. "I only wish you would let me help you more."

Confused, Kate slid her hand free and looked away. A wagon was rumbling out past the gates of Hatfield, laden with beer barrels to be refilled in the village. It seemed Souza had at least somewhat lifted his strict quarantine, and she should take advantage of this moment to sneak back into the house.

"I—I must go, Anthony," she said quickly. "I will write to you of what the princess says of all we have discovered."

"Take care, Kate," he said. "Don't let your impulsive nature lead you into danger again, especially if I am not there to help you."

Kate gave a rueful laugh as she turned away. "I fear I can hardly stop it, Anthony. But I promise I will be careful. I'm the only one who can help my father."

She ran toward the house and slipped through the gates while they still stood open. No one was around but the porter; guards were no longer thick at the front doors, but she feared it was not a sign they were yet out of danger. Everything was *too* quiet.

And she had no time to sort out the confused feelings swirling through her.

As she drew closer to the house, Penelope appeared on the doorstep and waved her hurriedly inside. "Kate, there you are! Wherever have you been? Her Grace told me to look out for you. She said she sent you out on an errand, but not dressed like that." Penelope took the white wool shawl from around her own shoulders and wrapped it around Kate, covering her boy's doublet. Penelope led her quickly into the house.

Kate, suddenly very weary, leaned gratefully against her friend as they made their way up the back stairs. It had been such a long, strange night, and she'd had little sleep for days. "Princess Elizabeth did indeed send me out on an errand."

"I hope she didn't have you mucking out the stables!"

Kate had to laugh. "No, indeed. I almost wish she had. It would have been easier."

"What *were* you doing, then?"

One of the guards hurried past them, his heavy boots thudding on the floor, scattering the rushes. He gave them a disdainful glance, and Kate was reminded their home had been invaded. They weren't safe anywhere.

"We can't talk here," she said. "Is the princess still confined to her chamber?"

"I fear so," Penelope answered. "She was allowed to walk in the gardens for a few minutes this morning, after she shouted about the lack of exercise, but now she is closeted with that horrid Senor Souza. He is certainly a quieter man than Lord Braceton, but I think more difficult to deal with."

"I wouldn't be so sure of that," Kate murmured, thinking of the hidden letter at Leighton Abbey. True, Braceton had been all noise and bluster and threats on the surface, but he had coldly conspired to do away with a young, innocent woman and turn the blame from Queen Mary and her court. He had torn apart three houses—Leighton, Gorhambury, and Hatfield—to hide his blame.

"What do you mean?" Penelope said. She pushed open the door to Kate's own sitting room and led her to the chair by the hearth.

Kate sat back against the cushions, struck all over again by the terrible quiet of that familiar room. Without her father there, with his usual clutter of papers and books and the sounds of his music, the space felt cold and hollow. So many families had been torn apart.

She drew Penelope's shawl closer around her shoulders and watched as her friend coaxed a fire to kindle. Once the flames were crackling,

Penelope went to the sideboard and poured out two goblets of wine and found some bread and cheese wrapped in a cloth.

Kate eagerly devoured the small repast. It seemed like such a very long time since that meal in the Leighton Abbey kitchen. Once she felt a bit stronger, she sat back and smiled at Penelope.

"Thank you so much, Penelope," she said. "I needed that."

"You looked pale as milk when I saw you at the door," Penelope answered. She took a sip of her own wine. "We must all stay as close together as we can and help each other through these times. I fear we have no one else."

There was a hard note to Penelope's voice Kate seldom heard from her. Penelope's violet-blue eyes were blank and flat as she stared into the fire.

"Do you never think about marrying again?" Kate asked. "I know little of your husband, but perhaps he did ease your loneliness a bit after you lost your mother."

Penelope laughed. "Dear Kate. Nay, I don't think to marry again. I don't speak of my husband because there is little to say. I married him too young out of desperation, before I knew him or myself very well. It was a mistake. But luckily he died before much harm could be done."

Kate didn't know what to say to that, just as she was left speechless when Elizabeth warned against the perils of marriage. She had so little experience with such matters, she felt foolish.

"Perhaps you think of getting married yourself, Kate," Penelope said, refilling their goblets. "What of your friend from the village? The lawyer?"

Kate thought of Anthony, of his green eyes, the way his hand felt on hers, and she felt even more foolish. Despite his help at Leighton, there were still insurmountable barriers to their ever making a match. "We are only friends. He needs someone to help him in his future career, someone happy to keep a fine house and raise children without being distracted by the music in her head all the time." Someone with a good dowry.

"Just as you will. It is very true that sometimes we have other, more important matters to attend to than romance." Penelope flashed a smile. "But it doesn't mean we can't have fun sometimes. Even Princess Elizabeth thinks once in a while of matters of the heart."

Kate laughed. "Does she indeed? And who here, pray tell, would any of us have to think on? The stable boys?"

"You know who I mean," Penelope said with a wink. Of course Kate knew who she meant—Robert Dudley, whom Elizabeth had known for years. They were in the Tower together after Wyatt's Rebellion. But his name could not be mentioned these days. "The way he used to look at Elizabeth when they met at court—it's rather like the way your handsome lawyer looks at you."

Kate could feel her cheeks turn warm, and it wasn't from the fire. She looked away and shrugged.

"As you will, then," Penelope repeated. "As I said, these are no days for romance. Or surely you would be gone from here all night on an assignation, and not on some royal errand."

"I would rather have been on a romantic assignation," Kate said. She shifted in her chair, her body still sore from all the running and falling and chasing. "I wish this was all over and done, and all of us safe."

"Oh, Kate, my dear. I fear we will never be safe. Not living so near royalty as we do. Surely you've learned that, wherever you were last night."

Kate studied her friend. Penelope was a smart woman, one who had been at court as long as Kate or even longer. She had experience of people Kate did not. Perhaps Penelope could be of assistance, could help Kate sort everything out in her mind.

"I was sent to Leighton Abbey," she said. She gave Penelope a quick summary of the events of the night, of the journey to Leighton Abbey, the play, the letter, the veiled woman. Penelope listened in quiet thoughtfulness, turning the goblet around in her hand.

"It all sounds like a dramatic sonnet, I know,"

Kate said. "I wouldn't have believed it all if I wasn't there."

"So Lord Braceton was even worse than we thought," Penelope said. "He deserved his fate for trying to steal people's estates, when all the time he was conspiring to have innocents unjustly murdered."

"But the people who are caught up in this matter do not deserve it! My father, the princess, Anthony's employer, poor Ned—"

"Quite right," Penelope said. "One injustice should not lead to another. You say the letter is still at Leighton? I think—"

The door suddenly flew open, making Kate sit up straight, startled. The wine sloshed in her goblet. A frown flickered over Penelope's face as she turned to see who had burst in on them.

It was Peg, breathing heavily from running, her plump cheeks red and her hair falling from under her askew cap.

"What is it, Peg?" Kate said, nervous. "Is someone ill? Has word come about my father?"

Peg shook her head. "Nay, 'tis the princess. She has a visitor."

"God's teeth, but not another one," Kate cried. "An officer of the queen? Are we all to be arrested?"

"Come see for yourself." Peg spun around and ran off again, leaving Kate and Penelope to follow.

They made their way upstairs to one of the windows overlooking the courtyard. Peg pushed it open, and they leaned out to peer down at the arrivals.

It was a woman on a fine white mare, accompanied only by two grooms who wore no livery. Her garb was plain but very fine, a black velvet doublet and riding skirt of black wool trimmed with gold braid. Her face was hidden by a black plumed hat, but as one of the grooms helped her from the saddle she glanced up, and the light gleamed on golden curls.

Kate heard Penelope gasp, a sound that matched her own surprise. They looked at each other and cried, at the same time, "Jane Dormer!"

Kate glanced back to see the lady take a small case from her saddlebag and turn toward the house. It was indeed Jane Dormer, Queen Mary's favorite lady-in-waiting and the fiancée of the Count de Feria. What was she doing at Hatfield?

Kate had the sinking feeling it could be nothing good.

CHAPTER 21

"How are you feeling today, Father?" Kate tucked a blanket around her father's shoulders and pulled her own cloak closer around her. It was the fine red cloak Elizabeth had given her, but even it couldn't keep out the damp chill of the small cell.

"I am quite well, Kate dearest. You needn't worry," he answered, patting her hand. "I daresay it's quieter here than at Hatfield, and I can concentrate on my work. And the gaoler is not such a bad man. Of an evening we play a bit of primero, and he tells me about his son, who is taking an interest in singing."

He gestured to the small table, spread with his music, inkpots, and quills. And to the cot piled with blankets and bolsters Kate had brought from Hatfield. A brazier glowed at his feet, but it didn't warm much of the space.

Kate studied her father carefully. He looked thinner, his skin grayish under his silvery beard, and his eyes were bloodshot. When she changed the bandage on his gouty foot, it looked even more swollen. He stared up at her, and as he tried to smile it faded into a sharp cough.

"We must get you out of here very soon," she insisted. She poured him a goblet of the wine

Elizabeth had sent for him and stirred in a measure of Cora's special cough syrup concoction.

"I daresay I am better off here for the time being," he said again. "Is Her Grace still confined to her chamber?"

"She is allowed to take a bit of exercise, but she is much restricted. Queen Mary sent one of her husband's Spanish officers to look into Braceton's death."

"But you are allowed to leave?"

Kate shrugged. She wouldn't tell him of how she had crept out of the house when no one was looking, or about her adventures at Leighton Abbey. He had enough to worry about. And as Jane Dormer was still with the princess, not even Elizabeth knew Kate had gone. Penelope had gone off into the secret passageways to see what she could overhear.

"I am quite insignificant, Father," she said. "No one bothers with me." And that was a good thing. It meant she could go places most young ladies could not.

"Ah, my dear. If they only knew your true depths." He sipped at the wine. Outside the stout door, there was a sudden clamor, a shout, and a great banging noise.

"I must be getting a new neighbor," Matthew said. "The alleged blasphemer was sent off to London yesterday."

To London—to be burned? And her father's

supposed crime was to be in possession of heretical writings, another burning offense. Yet he had not yet been sent away. She still had time, a little time, to piece it all together. And the queen's lady's appearance at Hatfield could be a good sign—or a very bad one. It could mean the queen was more ill than ever and had sent her favorite lady to give word to Elizabeth, the queen's heir. Or it could mean the queen had just sent more spies into her sister's house.

The man outside screamed incoherent words before the cell door was slammed on him. The gaoler's heavy footsteps faded away, and everything was quiet again.

"How does your work progress, Father?" Kate asked, determined to be cheerful for him in the time they had left today.

When she left the village, the afternoon was growing late and she knew she had to hurry to get back to Hatfield before dark. She glanced toward Master Hardy's law offices. A candle burned in one of the upstairs windows, a tiny, solitary glow in the gathering gloom, and for a moment she wanted to go back and knock on the door. To talk to Anthony, go over her ideas of the murders, share her fears.

But she remembered how confused she was when they had parted at the gates of Hatfield, and she didn't need to cloud her thoughts now. She turned away and quickened her steps toward home.

The wind grew brisker and colder as she made her way down the lane. She wrapped her cloak tighter around her and pulled up the fur-edged hood, glad of the dagger she had tucked into the purse tied at her waist. The darkness past the trees seemed even heavier than usual, filled with the potential for watching eyes. Waiting eyes.

Kate walked even faster, and thought of the murders that had already happened rather than what might be lurking in the twilight. It still seemed so elusive, the connection between all the victims. Ned, Braceton and Braceton's servant, Master Cartman—how were they linked beyond Hatfield? It all kept coming back to Jane Grey.

Yet half the nobility of England had once been allied with the Greys. They had been at the very center of the elite of the new religion. And the other half had held them as enemies. She would have to trace all those connections. Try to remember all she could about her young life at court, which was not much. She had been such a child then, only vaguely aware of alliances and plots and families.

Kate turned a bend in the road, and glimpsed a rider ahead of her. Thus far she had been the only traveler abroad, as the day was chilly and everyone kept in hiding while the queen's men searched the neighborhood. She was startled to see someone else, and for an instant thought about hiding in the trees until they passed by.

But then she noted the horse, a sturdy brown cob that seemed familiar. She had last seen it drawing a brightly painted cart. And the rider had bright blond hair under a plain knitted cap.

"Rob," she called, and hurried to catch up with him. "What are you doing here?"

He turned in the saddle and watched her as she came toward him. Beneath his cap, his handsome face was drawn into stark, sharp lines, and dark circles were etched under his eyes. But he gave her a quick smile, and didn't seem surprised to encounter her there.

"I came to see what I could find out about my uncle," he said. He swung down from his horse and wrapped the reins around his gloved hand. They continued slowly on together down the road.

The wind had become even more biting, and Kate was glad of the fine cloak's warm hood, shielding her face and keeping the breeze from tearing at her hair. She was also glad not to be alone now, though she worried about the way Rob looked. The angry light in his eyes.

"What of your friends?" she asked.

"They have returned to London for the time being," he said. "We have no further performances until the holiday festivities, and my uncle had a house there where they can stay for a time. I owe it to my uncle to find out what happened here."

Kate nodded. She understood family obligations, even when family members weren't of perfect form, as Rob's uncle had not always been toward him. "How do they fare at Leighton now?"

"Well enough, I suppose. Lady Eaton wanted us to stay for a few more days and present more plays, but her husband refused her. So she took to her bed." Rob ruefully shook his head. "They are a strange household indeed. Lady Eaton seems most eager to confide in someone, anyone, but her husband keeps her locked away. They are certainly hiding a great deal."

Like a woman in a tower? Letters, papers, refugees from the queen? Kate looked up at him. "Did you find—"

Suddenly her words were cut off by a high, thin, whining noise through the air, like a flock of insects. She half turned to see what it was, and was driven back by a sudden blow to her shoulder. It felt as if someone had pushed her hard, and she stumbled, confused.

Then pain shot as a bolt of fire all through her body and she cried out. It was like nothing she had ever felt before, burning and freezing all at once, numbing. She fell to her knees and her hand flew up to her shoulder.

Her fingers found the wet, warm stickiness of blood. And the thin shaft of an arrow.

A thick cloud of tight pain closed around her mind.

"Kate!" she heard Rob shout. "God's blood, Kate, nay!"

She felt his arms close around her and lift her up before she could fall into the dirt, but then the darkness closed in and she didn't feel anything else.

It was the wrong woman.

The archer stared between the trees in astonishment. How could such a mistake have been made? The Lady Elizabeth wore that cloak so often, a fine red beacon on a gray day. But as the hood fell back, it was dark hair that tumbled free and not red.

Dark. How had the last piece of the puzzle slipped away so quickly? And why did it have to be *her?*

The figure watched in mounting anger and chagrin as the actor caught the girl in his arms. Her head fell back over his shoulder, her arms limp as if she was unconscious—or dead. He snatched a blanket from over his saddle and spread it on the ground before he laid her carefully down. He was much too busy with her to go chasing after the shooter.

The man certainly seemed to be good for something beyond spouting pretty verses. He drew out a dagger and rolled the girl to her side.

The arrow had gone straight through her left shoulder. The aim, then, was true, even though the real prey had used a decoy.

Yet another mark against the Boleyn whore's spawn. The girl would never have been hurt if Elizabeth hadn't sent her out in her own place.

The actor cut off the pointed arrow tip and swiftly lowered the girl onto her back. He grasped the feathered end and drew it out, slowly and smoothly, in one long tug. It came free, and the girl's back arched in a swift convulsion. He ripped off the hem of the pretty cloak and tied it around her in a makeshift bandage. It was quickly stained an even darker red.

So much blood. There had already been so much blood. And now there would have to be more.

The figure backed away from the view of the wounded girl and slipped into the woods.

CHAPTER 22

K ate. Kate, can you hear me?"
Kate heard the soft voice, but it seemed to come from a very long way away, like whispering in a dream or as words spoken through a tapestry. She tried to struggle up toward it, but her body felt as heavy as a stone. She couldn't even pry her eyes open. She started to let herself tumble back

into the comfortable darkness, but a cool hand grabbed onto hers and squeezed it tightly. A ring bit into her skin, jerking her to wakefulness.

She pried open her eyes, and for a moment she could see nothing but the canopy of a bed above her, dark red and full of shadows. Then a pale heart-shaped face swam into view, peering down at her with wide brown eyes. Red-gold hair, untidily pinned up, glowed like a torch.

"She is waking up," the face said with a smile, and Kate realized it was Princess Elizabeth. "Kate, can you hear me? Are you in much pain?"

"She shouldn't be," another voice said, one Kate recognized as Peg's. "We dosed her with Cora's syrup in wine after she thrashed about so much when we tried to clean the wound. Perhaps we should send for the doctor and have her bled, my lady."

"Nay!" Kate cried. She remembered the last time she was bled, the horror of the leeches. She couldn't bear that again. "No bleeding."

She tried to sit up, and pain shot down her side, making her whole body contract.

"Don't move around so, Kate," Elizabeth said. "You must be still or the wound will open again." She gently urged Kate to lie back down again and tucked the blankets around her. "Just be quiet now."

As the pain slowly ebbed away, Kate remembered all that had happened. Meeting Rob on the road. The arrow that flew out of the woods. The blood. The blackness. And now here she was, in her own chamber with no memory of how she got there.

She glanced down to see that she wore one of her old smocks with the left sleeve torn away to make room for a bulky bandage and a sling that bound her arm to her side. She could smell the feverfew and chamomile of a poultice, and the smoke from the fireplace. How long had she been there? Hours—or days?

"Rob," she whispered. Her mouth was dry and it was hard to force the words out. "Was he hurt?" She remembered the shock on his face as he leaned over her, and she knew for sure, for the first time, he could not have done these terrible things.

"Young Master Cartman?" Elizabeth said. "Not at all. He carried you all the way back to Hatfield when you were injured, and now he's waiting most impatiently in the kitchens. Do you remember what happened?"

An arm clad in gray wool appeared in front of Kate, holding a pottery goblet. She slowly turned her head to see Lady Pope. Her face was as pinched and disapproving as ever beneath her old-fashioned gable hood.

And Kate suddenly wondered what the Popes thought of the Greys and Protestant estates. They were vassals of Queen Mary, of course, given the task of guarding Elizabeth, but they had not been overtly hostile like Braceton or Souza. Kate realized their motives needed to be examined as closely as everyone else's. If Lord Braceton had been about to give a bad report of their guardianship to the queen . . .

"You should drink this, Mistress Haywood," Lady Pope said. "It will help the pain."

Kate did want to escape the pain that throbbed in her shoulder, but she didn't want to fall back into that sticky darkness again. She had to think, think.

She shook her head, and Lady Pope pressed the goblet closer. "Drink it, girl. You need to heal."

Kate turned away on the pillow. "Not now. My head is so cloudy. . . ."

"She will drink more later, Lady Pope," Elizabeth said firmly. She took the goblet away and put it down on the bedside table. "I will make sure she rests now."

Lady Pope gave a disapproving sniff, but she turned and bustled out of the room. As the door closed behind her, Elizabeth smiled.

"You should have taken a little more of her potion, Kate," she said. "Your face is so white. But so far there is no sign of infection."

"Was there no clue to who shot me?"

Elizabeth shook her head. "A search party was sent out as soon as Master Cartman stumbled into the hall, but it was too late. Anyone who was out there was long vanished. Only this was saved." She reached into the purse tied at her waist and drew out a small object.

As she held it up to the light, Kate saw it was a broken piece of an arrow. The purplish feathers of the fine fletching were iridescent in the firelight, just like the feather fragment she had once found caught on a shrub alongside the lane.

"These feathers are most distinctive. I don't think I've ever seen work quite like this before," Elizabeth said. "I will compare it to the arrow that killed Lord Braceton and his servant, but I'm sure it will be a match. Master Rob says he saw nothing on the road either."

"It was all so fast," Kate said. As her mind grew clearer, she remembered every detail of the scene. "We were just standing there talking, and then— so much pain."

"It's most fortunate Master Rob was there to bring you to us."

Kate nodded. It was indeed fortunate Rob had been there to help her. Or maybe he was there for some other, more nefarious purpose? She hated the suspicion that had infected her of late, which made her look at everyone as if they had hidden motives. Secrets.

"What do you remember from Leighton Abbey?"

Kate could feel the remnants of Cora's potion working through her blood, pulling her downward, but she knew she had to fight it away until she could tell Elizabeth what she knew. She quickly blurted to the princess about the veiled woman, about Lord Ambrose and his carelessly lost letter, about the plan to seize Protestant families' estates and hide the truth about the death of Lady Jane.

"It isn't much, I fear," Kate said ruefully, falling back to her pillows. "If I could have found the veiled woman—"

"Or perhaps she found you," Elizabeth murmured, tapping her fingertips on the bedpost. "Perhaps whoever she is followed you from Leighton and shot at you. It would be so much easier, would it not, if our murderer was this strange apparition and not someone we know? Not someone connected to us."

"But what if we do know her?" Kate cried, frustrated by all the unanswered questions flying through her mind. Every turn she made only seemed to create more puzzles. "She could be anyone at all."

Elizabeth nodded. "So she could. But it always seems to come back to the Greys, doesn't it? Damnable troublesome relations. I seem to be so rich in them."

The princess pushed herself up from the bed to pace across the small space of Kate's chamber.

"Families, we are told, are meant to be a comfort in this life. A loyal support. But mine is naught but a pack of wild tigers wherever I turn," Elizabeth said, and Kate had the sense she was no longer really there in the room, but in a chamber of her own mind, talking more to herself than to Kate.

"There is the queen, my sister, who hates me as no sister should," Elizabeth went on. "Indeed, she has never even seen me as a true sister, but as her enemy, as our mothers were enemies, even when I was a baby. My cousin Mary of Scotland, safe in France, just waiting for her chance to pounce here in England. And my cousins the Greys. They are never truly defeated, even when they seem most down. Jane is gone, poor girl, but her mother is ever there, my clever aunt Frances, and her two precious girls. Her undoubtedly legitimate Tudor girls."

She spun around to face Kate, her eyes glittering, but so still and calm. "We are a family that devours each other when we have the chance, Kate. I once had such affection for my brother, Edward, and he professed the same for me. We shared lessons and a faith, but he chose to disinherit me and raise Lady Jane and the Greys to the throne instead. And now they have something to do with all this trouble visited on my house. But what? Why now?"

Kate thought frantically back to every moment at Leighton, every word spoken, every glance, and still something eluded her. "I am sorry, Your Grace!" she cried. "If I could only have found the woman—"

"Oh, Kate, I am so sorry," Elizabeth said contritely, the chill clearing from her eyes. "You need your rest now. You have put yourself in such danger for me, and now I am putting more troubles on you. You should sleep, heal. You will remember more in the morning."

She hurried over to take up the abandoned goblet again and held it to Kate's lips. "Drink this."

"I've slept too much," Kate protested, even though her arm was throbbing with pain again. "I need to think."

"Nay, let me do the thinking right now. You rest. I'll stay here until you are asleep."

Kate took a few sips of the brew, and lay back against the bolsters. Slowly, the herbs spread their warmth through her veins, and her eyes fluttered closed. She felt the bedclothes being tucked closer around her, and the last thing she heard before sleep claimed her was the soft sound of the door closing.

CHAPTER 23

Kate faced a long corridor lined with closed doors and filled with flickering torchlight that cast grotesque shadows on the walls and ceiling. Dark tapestries hung everywhere, woven with snarling beasts that seemed to leap and snap in the light. The low hum of indistinct voices filled the air, whispered words and mirthless laughter that came out of nowhere.

She whirled around to try to escape, to run from that place, but a solid wall had sprung up behind her and she was trapped. She pounded on the wall until her hands bled, screaming and screaming, but the voices just laughed at her mockingly.

She ran down the corridor, flinging doors open as she went. Every one led only to more blank walls.

"Let me out!" she cried. There was something she had to do, was driven to do, and every moment trapped in that place meant time was slipping away. Faster and faster, like a slippery skein of silk in her hands, and soon she would lose it all.

Kate ran even faster, but the quicker she moved, the louder the voices grew. She heard footsteps clattering close behind her, though she could see no one there. She pushed open the very last door and stumbled into a chamber.

Here there was no blank wall. A block stood there, its dark hulk surrounded by blood-clotted straw. A headless body slumped beside it, the clothes saturated with red.

And the head that stared up at her with glassy eyes was her father's.

Kate screamed and spun away from the terrible sight, only to find her escape blocked once more.

The veiled woman stood in the doorway, the handle of the ax in her hand.

"Don't be afraid," the woman said, a disembodied voice from the depths of the veil. "I mean you no harm. . . ."

As the woman lifted the ax, Kate tried to run. She lost her footing and fell on the slippery straw. She was falling and falling, into the waiting black heart of an abyss. . . .

A hand caught her arm and jerked her back. Her eyes flew open, and she found herself not in the haunted chamber but in her own bed. Her heart thundered in her ears and she couldn't breathe, even once she saw she was safe.

Yet someone did hold on to her arm, a gloved grasp that was too real to be a nightmare.

Kate twisted around. Outlined by the firelight, standing right by her bed, was the veiled woman.

Kate tried to reach for the heavy goblet on the bedside table, reach for anything she could use as a weapon. The woman was surprisingly strong, though, and held her fast.

Kate opened her mouth to scream, and the woman cried in a hoarse voice, "Please! I mean you no harm; I vow it on my own mother's grave. I only want to help."

Her clasp loosened and Kate was able to pull free. She scrambled off the other side of the bed, ignoring the pain in her shoulder as she searched frantically for any sign of a weapon. "No harm? After you pushed me down and locked me in that tower at Leighton? After you crept into my room here? How did you even get past the guards?"

The woman stood very still, her gloved hands held out in a beseeching gesture. She wore all black still, and Kate could only just make out the faint pale outline of her face behind the opaque veil.

"I have learned how to go unnoticed," she said. "I move through the world like a ghost."

"A destructive ghost," Kate said. Something about the woman's very stillness was as eerie as any spirit. Kate reached for her shawl and wrapped it around her shoulders as she slowly backed toward the fireplace.

The woman shook her head, her veil rippling around her. "I never wanted to hurt anyone. I only wanted to be left alone in peace and quiet to remember. But every time I think I have a sanctuary, someone like *you* finds me."

"Someone like me?" Kate reached back to wrap her fingers around the handle of the fireplace poker. It was solid and heavy to the touch, and it made her feel a little safer. She'd wanted to talk to the veiled woman, and here she was right in front of her. She couldn't just let that go, not yet.

"Someone who thinks they know. Who won't let us rest." The woman's hoarse, rough voice quavered. "I have been so tired for so long! But you follow, follow—"

"I do not follow you. If anything, *you* follow *me*. You always appear where I am—as now, in my own chamber."

"I heard tell that you were hurt. I only wanted to explain that I had nothing to do with it."

How could she trust the word of such a woman? If she had nothing to do with it, who did? "But you did lock me in the tower at Leighton."

"Because I wanted to see no one else hurt!"

"Was that your chamber? The tower room?"

The woman sighed, her breath stirring the veil. "'Tis where I sleep, that's all. Lady Eaton and I were once friends. She gave me a place when I had nowhere else to hide."

Kate suddenly felt deeply weary, and she could no longer ignore the pain in her shoulder. She sat down in the chair by the fire, still clutching the poker. "When did you meet Lady Eaton?"

"When we both served the Greys. She was lady-in-waiting to the duchess, and I waited upon Lady Jane."

"The Greys," Kate whispered. Of course. "It always comes to them. Do you still work for them? Is that why Lord Braceton was killed?"

"I told you—I did nothing." She sounded most agitated now, her gloved hands twisting in her skirts. "But I fear I caused it."

"How?" Kate said, frustrated. "Was it the

Eatons? Or Master Payne, who they say preaches now at Leighton?"

"God has truly cursed me! When my husband died and I was left alone with my poor child. When they sent me to the Tower. I knew naught of any plans to rebel against Queen Mary! I only read with Lady Jane, walked with her in the gardens, looked after her gowns."

Kate sensed the woman was on the edge of tearful panic—and panicked people did wild things. Kate carefully rose to her feet, set aside the poker and held out her hand. She spoke quietly, calmly. "You were sent to the Tower?"

"I was caught there when Queen Mary over-threw the brief reign of my Lady Jane. But I was not allowed to serve her. I was locked in a small room, not given food or fresh air even though I could not answer their questions. That was why I sickened. Why—"

Suddenly, the woman threw back her veil, revealing her face. Surrounded by a cloud of faded blond hair, it must once have been beautiful, a finely drawn oval with a pretty nose and rosebud lips. But now it was ravaged with smallpox scars, deep lines and pits that marred the former beauty.

"I caught the pox there," she said. "They threw me out when I recovered, but of what use was freedom then? My child was lost to me. My Lady Jane was killed horribly. I had nowhere to go."

Kate's heart ached at the tale. So many losses,

so much pain. And still it went on and on. "But you did not take your revenge on Queen Mary? On the ones who did this to you?"

The woman shook her head frantically. "I could not. Just as I see in your eyes that *you* could not. You are too good, too kindhearted. So very loyal to your friends, as I once was. That is why I came to you tonight, even though I wanted only to hide."

Kate shook her head in confusion. "Why did you come to me?"

"You serve the Lady Elizabeth, as I once served Lady Jane. I could do nothing to save my lady, but I know you can help yours now."

That was all Kate wanted to do, but still she couldn't see what the woman meant. "How? Tell me exactly, and I will do all I can to help the princess."

The woman slowly sank to the floor, sitting amid the dark puddle of her skirts. "I could take no revenge. My heart would not harden enough to allow me. After all, I remember the days when Queen Mary was very kind to her cousins the Greys, when they visited her at Beaulieu and she sent Lady Jane a fine gown—which my lady foolishly rejected. Games of crowns bring everyone down in the end, and I know that. But my child—my child was born with a heart of stone. Only Lady Jane and her sisters could touch it. My child is cruel."

Kate took a step closer, engrossed in the tale. She reached out and gently touched the woman's scarred cheek.

The woman held on to Kate's wrist and looked up at her with tears in her eyes. Eyes of a distinctive violet-blue color, almond-shaped and framed with sooty lashes.

Shock flashed through Kate, as painful as the arrow shot. "Your child is Penelope?"

The woman's hand tightened on Kate's wrist so hard she could feel it all the way to her injured shoulder. "She is mad! Just as my own mother was. I feared it was so when she was born, but then she was so beautiful. I dared hope she would do better than my mother, who ended by being locked up. I thought Penelope would do better even than I did. She fared so well in the Grey household—she rose so high with them, they found her a husband. He was older than her, to be sure, but a fine match."

The husband who had not lived long. Who had been a soldier. Kate yanked her hand away and stumbled back from the woman. She was still so cold, stunned that Penelope had caused this insanity. "This husband—was he an archer then?"

"Aye, in the pay of the Duke of Suffolk. He went with the duke to fight the Scots and distinguished himself by his bravery in battle. He was so handsome, and seemed to love my

Penelope so much. Yet she could not be happy with him."

"I do see why she would kill Braceton, and why she went after Lord Ambrose," Kate said, struggling to sort through all the feelings tangled up inside her. "But why Ned and Master Cartman? Why would she go after me?"

The woman sobbed in earnest now, tears flowing down her pockmarked cheeks. She turned away from Kate, her hands covering her face. "Because she can no longer see reality. She sees only Lady Jane and what happened to her. She sees only her friends the Greys in disgrace. She won't speak to me. She won't—"

"Then why come to me now? Why not sooner? You were here at Hatfield before Ned died—I saw you. If I had known before—"

If she hadn't been so foolish. If she had only seen what was right in front of her. But she had been blinded by friendship.

"I thought I had talked her out of her anger," the woman said. "I convinced her she could not imperil her place here, that she was fortunate to be with the Lady Elizabeth and have a living after we lost our place with the Greys. I thought she was safe here, and she sent me back to the Eatons' with such protestations of affection, I wanted to believe it. But I was so very wrong."

"Why then did you run from me? I am Penelope's friend, too. I could have helped you."

"I let no one see me now, not—not like this. I promised my Penelope I would never show myself. Yet I was wrong. And now more people are dead. I cannot help her now, so I beg you to do it for me, Mistress Haywood."

A door slammed somewhere down the corridor, and the woman spun around. Her scarred face froze with panic.

"I must go," she gasped, snatching her veil down again.

"Nay," Kate cried. "There is still much I need to know. You cannot simply come here and tell me Penelope did these terrible things, and then run away again."

"I have to!" the woman sobbed. "She would kill me, too, if she knew I was here. It is all in God's hands now."

God's hands? No, indeed, for the woman had tossed it squarely at Kate. "Stay, I beg you! You must tell me . . ."

She lunged forward to grab for the woman's arm, but Kate was still slow from the potion she'd drunk, still spinning with confusion. The woman shoved her hard on her wounded shoulder. The pain was blinding, and sent Kate stumbling to her knees, stars shooting before her eyes. She curled into a ball as she gasped for breath.

By the time she could pull herself to the door and peer out into the dark corridor, the veiled woman was long gone. Kate stumbled to the door that led out to the garden, but it was empty too. Hatfield was deeply asleep and silent, like an enchanted castle in some country fairy story. Kate felt horribly alone, as if her chest was hollow where her heart should beat.

And the wind that rushed around her was freezing. Shivering, she carefully tiptoed back to her chamber and put on her slippers. She retrieved the fireplace poker where she'd dropped it on the floor and stirred at the dying embers of the fire.

Her gaze fell on the bloodstained red cloak draped carelessly over a stool, and she remembered she had been wearing it when she was shot. That she had the hood drawn up against the cold . . .

Princess Elizabeth had given her that cloak.

"No . . . no," she whispered. If Penelope was really the killer, surely she would not have shot at Elizabeth! Elizabeth had naught to do with Lady Jane's death; she was Jane's cousin, her coreligionist. There could be no reason to kill her.

But if Penelope was truly mad—and Kate had no reason to doubt the woman's word on that, as she seemed more than a little touched by insanity herself—she needn't have rational reasons. There was nothing rational about Ned's death.

Then again, perhaps it was not Penelope. There were more than enough anger and motives for revenge to spread across the whole county. Only the veiled woman accused Penelope, and she had already attacked Kate twice. Her word could not be trusted. The guilty could be the Eatons, or Master Payne, or anyone who hated Queen Mary.

Yet, even as Kate hoped it was not her friend who had done such things, something deep in her mind wouldn't let her quite deny it.

"I must find that cursed woman," she muttered. Grimacing with pain, she pushed herself to her feet and let her arm out of its sling. She wrapped her warmest shawl around her and slipped back out to the garden door. Maybe she could pick up the woman's trail.

But once again it was as if she truly was an apparition. There was no sign of anyone on the twisting pathways, no open doors or swinging gates. It seemed as if the woman knew Hatfield as well as she did Leighton Abbey, all the back entrances and hidden halls, and could slip away.

Hidden halls. Kate spun around to study the silent facade of the house, the way the chalky moonlight turned the intricate brickwork gray. Light burned in a few of the upstairs windows, and a shadow flickered behind the one that belonged to Princess Elizabeth.

Kate closed her eyes and let the chilly air flow over her as she tried to clear her mind of the pain and the residue of Lady Pope's herbal concoctions. She took herself back to the day she and Penelope had crept through the passageways to spy on Braceton. The way they had laughed together, scared and thrilled at the same time.

A flash of pain rippled through Kate at the hazy memory, and she clutched at her stomach. How could she have been so foolish as to think Penelope was her friend? That they were united in their service to Elizabeth and their hopes for the future? Kate had trusted Penelope, had never looked beyond the surface of their laughter and confidences to see what was truly there. Surely she should have seen it, in the flashes of coldness whenever Penelope spoke of her husband, her past. Kate should have known.

"Nay, there is no time for this now," she told herself sternly. She needed to find proof that it was indeed Penelope who had done this, proof both to take to Elizabeth and to know for herself. Without the veiled woman to repeat her story, Kate had to find something herself. But where to start?

She thought back again to that day in the passageways. Penelope knew her way around extraordinarily well, knew where every twist and turn lay. And there were boxes Penelope said she kept stored there, to make it easier to fetch and carry things through the house.

Those boxes were as good a place to begin the search as any.

Kate slipped back into the house and tiptoed into the kitchen, where she knew she could find one of the hidden doors. It was quiet there; everyone had gone to find their own beds before the day's tasks began all over again.

But one person remained. Rob was slumped in a cross-backed chair by the smoldering fire, his head resting on the high wooden back as he quietly snored. His doublet was unfastened, and there was a smear of dried blood where he'd lifted her against him on the road. Elizabeth had said he had carried her all the way home, after removing the arrow, which had saved her life.

For a moment, Kate thought about waking him and asking him to search with her. Yet as she gazed down at him, she saw the heavy lines of weariness on his face. He had already helped her so much.

And her heart could no longer trust so easily.

She reached for a blanket that had fallen to the floor and tucked it around him. Once she was sure he still slept, she took up a candle and flint and slipped into the passageway.

As the door slid closed behind her and the darkness gathered, she had a flash of panic and knew she had to turn back. To flee back to the light. But even as her senses clamored for her to run to safety, she knew she could not. Penelope had already killed. She had shot at Kate while Kate wore Princess Elizabeth's cloak. She had to be stopped, now, before anyone else was hurt.

Including Penelope herself.

Clutching the candleholder, Kate hurried ahead into the winding passages. She tried to remember the path she took that day with Penelope, where she saw the chests that Penelope pushed aside, but the corridors all looked the same, narrow and brick-walled, piled up with crates that didn't look at all like the ones she sought. Several times she turned around and switched directions, peeking through doorways to try to decipher where she was.

At last she found a slightly wider space that seemed familiar. When she pushed open the hidden door, she saw the foyer where she and Penelope had watched Elizabeth and Braceton argue. She remembered a small blue chest, decorated with vines.

The trunk was no longer there. Kate shoved the other crates and baskets aside, peered inside each one, but the painted chest was gone.

"Perhaps it had nothing to do with this at all," she whispered. She pushed her loosened hair back from her forehead, ignoring the pain in her shoulder as she studied the jumbled space. It could very possibly be just another storage chest, one carried away for a multitude of reasons.

Yet something told her it was not simply another box. When she closed her eyes she could see the flashing image of bright paint, the way Penelope touched it, much more carefully than she handled the others. It had surely been hers, and now it was gone.

Penelope would most likely be in the princess's chamber for a few more hours at least. Kate slipped out of the door into the foyer and hurried up the main staircase until she found the corridor at the top of the house where Elizabeth's ladies had their chambers.

Kate seldom went to Penelope's room. When they wanted a gossip, or to practice a new song, they sat before the fire in Kate's sitting room or walked in the gardens. But she knew where it was, at the very end of the hall with windows looking in two directions.

The corridor was silent, no laughter from maids staying up too late to whisper together. Penelope's door was unlatched and open an inch, as if she had departed in a hurry. Kate entered, pushed it closed behind her, and examined the small space.

The narrow bed was hastily made, bedclothes pulled crookedly over the bolster and skirts and sleeves piled atop them. Ribbons and combs were scattered across a dressing table, and muddy shoes were on the floor. Clumps of dirt littered the polished floorboards.

Lady Pope would have a fit if she could see such a mess, Kate thought as she picked her way through the jumble. And why were Penelope's good shoes caked in mud?

Her eye was caught by a painted miniature on a stand, tucked amid the clutter on the table. It depicted a woman in a fine blue velvet bodice that matched her startling blue eyes. A small smile curved the painted lips as she looked at a child cradled against her shoulder, a blond-curled beauty in white lace. Her mother, before the smallpox came? Before madness closed in around them?

Kate noticed a tiny set of initials at the bottom of the painting. MJ. Master John. She remembered the man, a fine artist who did portraits for the court of Queen Catherine Parr and then traveled to families connected to the queen to paint them as well. Including the Greys at Bradgate Manor. Penelope and her mother must have been close to the family indeed to have this miniature painted. And they must have worked for them a very long time.

She replaced the painting on the table and went back to studying the room. For a mere lady-in-waiting to a princess in exile, Penelope had many belongings, several baskets and chests, but they were all unpainted.

Finally, Kate found the one she sought, tucked under the bed where a truckle would usually be. She immediately recognized the blue paint, the curlicues of flowers. She drew it out and cautiously pried open the lid, which surprisingly wasn't locked.

Inside was a folded dark cloak spattered with mud at the hem. There were books—an English Bible like the one in the tower room at Leighton Abbey, Queen Catherine's volume of prayers, the Lady Jane pamphlet that had landed Kate's own father in trouble. And a long, plain wooden box that held arrows.

The purplish feathers gleamed in the candlelight, and Kate choked on a sudden, ragged sob. It was right there before her, the proof she had hoped against hope wouldn't be found. Had hoped didn't exist. But she could not deny it. There were the mates to the arrow shot at her, the arrows that had killed Braceton. Penelope's own mother said they hated the enemies of the Greys —and that madness had a hold on their family.

Yet perhaps Penelope hid them for someone? A lover or a friend? Maybe. Kate had the awful feeling, deep down in her heart, that was not the case.

She closed the trunk and pushed it back under the bed. Elizabeth would have to be told, and very soon, before the arrows could be moved again.

Suddenly the door swung quietly open, and Kate jumped up to find Penelope standing there. Penelope took in the sight of the intruder in her chamber with one glance of her cold, flat violet-blue eyes and smiled.

"Ah, Kate," she said softly. "I did truly hope you would not be here."

CHAPTER 24

Kate slowly rose to her feet. She kept the bed between herself and Penelope, even as she realized what a foolishly poor defense it was. In her rush to discover the truth, she had run right into the lion's den. Time seemed to slow down, the minutes inching forward in heightened awareness. The colors of the room brightened and sharpened. Every tiny sound, from the creak of the floorboards to the brush of the wind past the window, was magnified in her ears.

She thought she should feel frightened, but found she wasn't at all. A still, cold calm had lowered over her. When she looked at Penelope, she marveled that it was like looking at someone she had never seen before. All the time they had spent together waiting on the princess, laughing, worrying, seemed to be as nothing. A stranger stood before her.

A dangerous stranger.

Penelope's violet-blue eyes were steady and cold as she looked across the room at Kate. She closed the door softly behind her and made no other move. Kate was reminded of the times she had walked past the woods and felt the prickle of watchful eyes on her skin, like a rabbit under the speculative gaze of the hawk. She felt that now.

But she was tired of being the rabbit.

"You did this, Penelope?" she said, her voice strong. Even then, facing the icy coldness of Penelope, the certainty in her eyes, she dared hope there was some other answer. That her faith in people was not entirely misplaced. "Or are you helping your mother?"

A surprised laugh escaped Penelope's lips, and for an instant she looked like Kate's friend again. Then the icy mask slid back into place. "My mother? I fear she is weak. Her loyalty is such a frail thing. I have had to be strong for both of us."

Kate gestured to the arrows hidden under the bed, such beautiful, lethal things. "Strong enough to kill?"

"Oh, Kate. My sweet friend. Have you not learned yet? 'Tis kill or be killed in this world. We choose our side and we defend it however we must. My husband knew that as well, in a way my poor, mad mother never could. He died too soon, but at least he taught me his greatest skill before he left, and I have made use of it."

" 'Greatest skill'?"

"Archery, of course. He was a bowman in King Edward's army, and died fighting with the Duke of Suffolk against the Scots. A great waste, yet I daresay I have done much better without him. He had such—firm ideas of a woman's proper place."

"And where was that?" Kate asked. She had the

instinct that she needed to keep Penelope talking, distracted, until she found out all she could—and had a chance to make her escape.

"At home, of course, sewing his shirts, having his babies. Men are such deluded creatures, are they not? They never see that women are so much stronger than they. Cleverer."

"Is that how you lured Lord Braceton to his death? By being cleverer?"

Penelope laughed. She suddenly moved, striding across the chamber to unlatch the window and throw it open. Kate turned to watch her, keeping her closest attention on Penelope at every second. Cold air swept through the room.

"It was not hard to be smarter than the likes of him," Penelope said, leaning back against the edge of the window. "He was much like my husband. So sure of himself, always underestimating everyone around him. Always blustering his way through things he couldn't understand. He never even saw me, except as a pretty backside he could pinch in the corridor, a woman he could threaten into his bed if he wanted to. But I always knew who *he* was."

"One of the men who condemned Lady Jane Grey?" Kate said quietly.

Penelope's eyes widened. "So you *do* know. I wasn't sure how much you discovered at Leighton."

"I found out your mother served the Duchess of Suffolk."

"She more than served her—she was devoted to the duchess and her family. Devoted to their Protestant ideals. She went to the Tower for them, and was scarred by the smallpox, as well as scarred in her mind. It's the duchess who pays for her care at Leighton, even though she and Lady Eaton were once friends. The Eatons have also been cheated of their fortunes."

"And it was the duchess who found you a place here?"

"So she did. She has always been most kind to us. She is undeserving of the vile reputation her enemies have given her. It wasn't enough for them to kill her husband and daughter; they have to besmirch her name as well."

"And you repay the Greys by bringing chaos to Princess Elizabeth's house? Their own kinswoman?" Kate said, her anger burning even hotter.

"Kinswoman?" The icy facade of Penelope's beautiful face cracked and a spasm of fury twisted her mouth. "Elizabeth has never helped the Greys, and she never will, for she knows the throne should rightfully be theirs. They are legitimate where she is not, and Lady Katherine Grey should be the next queen. *That* is how I repay them. That is how I get my own life back at last."

And suddenly all the shattered pieces that had been floating through Kate's mind snapped together. These acts were not merely to avenge Lady Jane's death, but to remove Elizabeth to make way for the Greys to return to power.

Kate could understand Penelope's reasons. She and her mother had lost so much in their service to the Greys, had seen so much injustice done. Suffering could become twisted into something ugly and wrong. Seeing the men who had carried out the death of Lady Jane, the disgrace of her family, could surely drive someone to madness.

Yet there was one terrible thing Kate could not fathom. "What of Ned? He could have had nothing to do with this game of crowns. Yet you killed him as well."

A flicker of some emotion crossed Penelope's face, a swift crumpling of her brow, a flash in her eyes. But it vanished as quickly as it came, and she shrugged.

"I did not want to do that," Penelope said. "I heard from my mother of Braceton and his friends' scheme to seize Leighton Abbey, on the pretense that they were devout Catholics and servants of the queen and the Eatons were traitorous heretics." She gave a bitter laugh. "As if men like Braceton value their eternal souls over their earthly fortunes. I wanted him to see the hypocrisy of his words. I tried to kill him once, cleanly and quickly, but it didn't work, and I saw there was a reason for that. Killing such a man required something—dramatic. Something frightening and vivid. And Ned was so trusting and simple. He never would have been happy in this life. I did him a mercy, just as he did me a service for the greater good."

Kate had read of such things, of cruelty to the innocent, but now that she was face-to-face with it she feared she would be sick. It was so very appalling. Surely this was all some nightmare. But she knew it was very real. That evil was so close she could reach out and touch it. "And Master Cartman? Did he do you a service as well?"

"Of course. But he grew greedy in the end. The play was part of my plan to let Braceton see that someone knew what he had done, that someone would soon come after him. And it worked, did it not? You saw how furious he was. How frightened."

Kate *had* seen it, the raw terror that she now knew was realization on Braceton's part. The realization that someone knew the part he had played in Jane Grey's death and the official concealment of its true purpose, that someone unseen and ruthless was bent on revenge. All planned by Penelope, carefully, quietly. The consummate deception.

"But you also killed innocent people, Penelope, along with Lord Braceton," Kate whispered, her head still whirling with the terrible truth. These events had happened right under her nose, and yet she hadn't seen until it was too late.

"Innocent?" Penelope snapped. "Lady Jane was the innocent. She only wanted to be left alone with her studies. She never sought the crown, even though it was hers by right. She never would have risen against the queen. And I saw her die there in the Tower. I saw the blood. They left her body there for hours."

Kate shook her head, choking on a sob. "I saw Ned's blood! There on the holy altar. How does more blood, more death, make a wrong a right?"

"Oh, Kate. You are so innocent as well. Surely you have been in this world of the court long enough to see you must destroy your enemies before they destroy you? You must be strong, ruthless. The Lady Elizabeth knows that, and you must learn it if you stay in her service."

She never wanted to be strong like that. "Is that why you tried to kill me in the road?" Kate said.

"I did not try to kill *you*. I thought it was her—Elizabeth."

"And you were making room for Katherine Grey?"

"I told you, Kate. You must be strong; you must do a wrong sometimes to make something right. Queen Mary will soon be gone. Jane Dormer came to bring Elizabeth some of the royal jewels, which means even the queen knows the end is near. Katherine Grey should be the next queen. I had to act quickly. Too quickly, I see now. I never meant to hurt you. I swear it."

Kate stared at her, and for an instant she thought she saw the Penelope she once knew, or thought she knew. The friend who had shared this life in exile. But then it was gone, and the murderous stranger stood before her again.

And it made Kate ache with sorrow. With anger at the waste and cruelty of it all.

"I would gladly have let you kill me there on the road if it meant Princess Elizabeth lived," Kate said quietly. "She is the only hope any of us have."

A hard smile curved Penelope's lips. "Very noble of you, Kate. And foolish. You will learn, as I have had to do. You will do what you must to survive."

"And so I will. But I won't let you kill anyone else."

"You won't have to. Oh, Kate. Perhaps you will never believe me, but I am sorry. You have always been kind to everyone around you, even me. And I do not deserve it."

Penelope suddenly spun around, her right palm sliding up her left sleeve and emerging with a brightly polished dagger. Her eyes widened, and Kate knew that Penelope was about to kill her. Kate feinted to the right and then took a running step the other way, evading the flash of the blade as it slashed down. Sheer panic took over her mind, and all she knew was she had to escape.

Kate knocked a chest into Penelope's path,

making the other woman stumble. But Penelope leaped up again and scrambled after her. Kate screamed and screamed, the sound echoing through her own head. Penelope grabbed her arm, almost wrenching it out of its socket, and Kate scratched her down the side of the face. She heard Penelope shout, but she also heard something else—footsteps running up the stairs outside the chamber.

Penelope looked up, a frantic light in her eyes. Before Kate could fathom what Penelope was doing, Penelope spun around and clambered over the window ledge. In a flurry of silken skirts, she vanished into the night. In a mere second, there was a hideous thud—and complete silence.

Kate screamed in shock and ran to the window. She peered down to the cobblestone courtyard below and saw Penelope crumpled there, like a broken doll. Blood, darker than the night around them, seeped across the stones.

"Penelope, nay," Kate whispered. She couldn't breathe. It felt as if a great hand squeezed at her heart, twisting it, extinguishing it until she was no longer the girl she had been only moments before. The darkness of the blood enclosed her just as it had Penelope.

CHAPTER 25

"After all the stormy, tempestuous and blustering windy weather of Queen Mary was overblown, the darksome clouds of discomfort dispersed, the palpable fogs and mists of most intolerable misery consumed, and the dashing showers of persecution overpast; it pleased God to send England a calm and quiet season, a clear and lovely sunshine . . . and a world of blessings by Good Queen Elizabeth."

—Holinshed's Chronicles

November 17, 1558

A re you warm enough, Father? Here, you need another robe."

As Kate took a fur-trimmed blanket from the clothes chest, her father laughed and shook his head. "You must cease fussing, my Kate. I am well. I'm home now—am I not?—and not much worse for wear. I have a fine fire, and work to do. You needn't worry about me so much."

But Kate tucked the warm wrap around him anyway. It was true that in the days since her father had returned to Hatfield and the queen's officers had left, Matthew had been doing well.

Cora's good food had taken away his gaol thinness, and the princess's doctor had prescribed cordials to cure his cough. Yet his gout seemed to pain him more than ever, and she feared his eyes appeared more faded, more distant. He talked very little, losing himself even more in his music.

She wished she could lose herself thus as well. The notes and melodies that once carried her away from everything else were elusive now, jangling in her mind like mere noise. Dreams plagued her at night, visions of death and blood she couldn't be rid of.

"I *like* fussing over you, Father," she said. She went to stir at the embers of the fire. "It is so good to have you home again. Our rooms were much too lonely."

"And it is good to be home, for certes," he answered. "I fear I should have been here for you when—well, when everything happened. You should not have been alone and in such danger."

"I wasn't alone," Kate said. And indeed she had not been. From the moment Penelope died and Kate's screams woke the house, she had been surrounded by concerned people. Princess Elizabeth, Rob, Peg, all the household at Hatfield tucking her into bed, pressing possets on her. Yet in her heart she could only feel cold and hollow. "And I am assuredly not alone now that you have returned."

"I won't be here forever, Kate."

"Father!" she cried, appalled. "Nay . . ."

"You know it is true, my dear. I won't be here forever, and you are a lady now. You need a household of your own."

A household of her own? That seemed as distant as the stars. And Kate wasn't sure she wanted such a thing anyway. "Things are too uncertain right now to think of anything like that."

"But you have your mother's lovely face, and her talent too. You need to get out in the world, meet more people. What about your young lawyer friend?"

"Anthony? I have heard little of him lately. Master Hardy summoned him to London." And Anthony had only sent her a short note telling her of his journey, and of his happiness that she was not hurt. Nothing else since that strange, intimate moment between them at their last parting.

She told herself she didn't care about that, that he had his own career, his own life to lead. But she knew that wasn't entirely true.

"Well, there are plenty of young men out there. Once we are in London—"

"I think we have enough to consider right now, Father, without trying to marry me off," Kate said, mustering a laugh. "We have much work to do, with the Christmas season almost upon us. We all need a little cheer now."

"Aye, and hopefully we will have more

company by then. You need more to do than play nursemaid to me."

Kate gave a rueful smile. She sat back on her heels and watched the fire catch and roar higher and higher. "I think I have seen quite enough of the wider world for the time being, Father. I'm not sure I'm made of a courtier's cloth."

"My dear girl. You have seen too little of the world to be bitter about it now. There are many ways to serve a queen, you know. And I daresay fire building is not your best skill. It is so warm out today, we'll be roasted if you keep that up."

Suddenly there was a commotion in the corridor outside their sitting room, the sound of swift, light footsteps and the rustle of skirts.

Kate barely had time to rise to her feet before the door swung open and Elizabeth stood there. She was dressed in somber dark green, her red hair bound up in a gold knit caul. Kat Ashley, long the princess's governess and Mistress of Robes, separated from Elizabeth since Wyatt's Rebellion and her incarceration in the Tower, but now returned to Hatfield, hurried after her to wrap a shawl around her shoulders.

"Indeed it *is* a warm day, Kate," Elizabeth said. "We must not waste such a treasure after all the cold rain. Come walk with us in the garden."

"I thank you, Your Grace, but I really should stay with my father," Kate said.

"Nonsense," Matthew said heartily. "You need

exercise, my dear, and I need to get on with my work. I shall do very well here for a few hours."

Kate studied him uncertainly, but he did seem well settled in for the afternoon. And she would have to face Elizabeth sometime soon.

"Very well," she said. "But send Peg for me at once if you have any need of me."

"We will not go far," Elizabeth said.

Kate took up her cloak, her old dark brown one this time, as the fine red velvet one had been ruined with blood, and followed Elizabeth out to the gardens. In the foyer, just at the base of the grand staircase, Sir William Cecil, Elizabeth's surveyor and most trusted secretary, sat at a hastily arranged desk, busily writing out lists and documents. He had arrived just as Queen Mary's officers left, the greatest sign yet of vast changes to come.

Elizabeth led them briskly along the pathways, Kat Ashley and a few other ladies following, but the princess was much lighter of foot than they. She took Kate's hand and drew her along, and soon they were far ahead of the others, beyond the formal pathways and near a grove of old oak trees on the slope of a hill.

From there the red bricks of the house gleamed in the amber sunlight, warm and welcoming. A maid shook a rug out of an open window, and a dog barked. Everything looked so calm, so peaceful, as if nothing terrible had ever happened in such a beautiful place.

"Has your arm healed, Kate?" Elizabeth asked.

"Very well, Your Grace. Peg's poultices worked wonders. I think there will only be a small scar."

"Aye. 'Tis better to hide the scars inside, where others can't see them."

Elizabeth paused to lean back against a tree, narrowing her eyes as she stared off over the empty fields. She twisted her pearl-and-ruby ring around her finger. "Your father is right, you know. You cannot blame yourself for what happened."

Kate closed her eyes against the rush of pain. She had gone over and over those words in her own head and still she had no solution, no solace. "I should have seen it was Penelope all along. I let my feelings of friendship blind me."

"You did not. Mistress Bassett served me for many months, and she served my cousins before that. I never saw her true intentions, never even guessed them, and I am older than you and have a great deal more experience in courtly deceit. I have been playing this dangerous game since I was three. I didn't suspect her intentions. But I am only one person, Kate, as are you. A great change is coming very soon. I know that because Mistress Dormer was sent to me by my sister and brought me some of the royal jewels. And when this change does come, I will need many people around me to be my eyes and ears. People I can trust."

Kate shivered. She wanted so much to be one of

those so trusted, but how could she? She wasn't sure she could even trust herself. "People such as Cecil and Mistress Ashley?"

"Aye, of course them. They have been loyal to me since I was a child. But also you. I shall need you to come with me as well."

"But I failed you, Your Grace! I did not stop Penelope when I should have."

"You never failed me. In fact, you proved your worth. It is your great kindness I need now, Kate. Your sweetness and your steadfastness. Real kindness is rare in this world. You care about people, truly care about them, and that draws them close to you. It persuades them to confide in you, as no one ever would with a queen. And you can go places where I cannot, like kitchens and playhouses. Aye, I shall assuredly need you close to me."

Kate turned Elizabeth's words over in her mind, along with everything that had happened since Lord Braceton stormed into Hatfield. She remembered what Penelope had said, that Kate could never match the cruelty of those who sought to play games of crowns. But her heart was harder now, and her trust was cracked. She would surely never be so easily deceived again.

Though maybe Elizabeth was also right, and kindness could be an asset and a weapon in itself. Perhaps, with time, she *could* learn to use it to protect the people she loved.

Like in music, it took many disparate strands to make a coherent whole, to make a beautiful madrigal.

"I only know one thing now, Your Grace," she said. "I will serve you however you require, for as long as you need me."

Elizabeth gave a strangely sad smile. "My sweet Kate. I hope you shall never regret those words, for I shall certainly hold you to them."

One of the other ladies came dashing up the slope of the hill, the breeze threatening to sweep her cap from her head. "My lady! My lady, riders are approaching."

Elizabeth turned and shielded her eyes with her hand. Kate peered over her shoulder to see a large party of riders indeed, thundering through the gates, throwing up clouds of dirt. As they came closer, Kate could see that the leaders were men she recognized from court, the powerful earls of Pembroke and Arundel.

Elizabeth's face turned white and her hand trembled, but she stood very still as they galloped nearer. At the foot of the hill, Lord Arundel drew in his horse and slid to his feet. Out of breath, he climbed the hill to kneel before the unmoving Elizabeth.

"Your Majesty," he gasped. "I bring tidings from London."

He held up his hand, and on his gloved palm gleamed the coronation ring. The large ruby stone that never left a monarch's hand until he or she was dead. He did not need to say anything else.

"This is the Lord's doing," Elizabeth said, quietly but strongly. "And it is marvelous in our eyes."

Author's Note

I have been fascinated by the Tudors ever since I watched *Anne of the Thousand Days* on TV when I was about ten! Though I have to admit the gorgeous clothes were a big part of the attraction (and I still love the history of fashion), the big emotions and larger-than-life characters drew me in. I wanted to know more about them, so I ran to the library the day after I saw the movie and asked a very helpful librarian for anything they had about Tudor England. She gave me a large stack of books—and I haven't stopped reading about this extraordinary time ever since.

The one image that has always stuck with me most from *Anne* is that at the very end, of the little red-haired girl in a satin gown, looking up startled at the sound of the cannon announcing her mother's death. I was amazed to find out that little girl grew up to be Elizabeth I, a figure I had thought of up until then as being almost unreal and impossibly remote, wrapped in the dense symbolism of old, stiff portraits. Queen Elizabeth, and her vibrant, colorful, bawdy, dangerous times, sometimes seem more real to me than my own everyday life of grocery shopping, dog feeding, and yoga classes—and I'm hoping for the next time I get to travel to England!

With Kate Haywood, I get to immerse myself in Tudor times like I never have before, and I'm so excited about it. Kate, of course, is fictional, though she is somewhat based on the historical figure of Amelia (or Emilia) Lanier, who was a member of the famous musical Bassano family (and is one of the candidates to be Shakespeare's Dark Lady). Kate is the daughter of a court musician and loves music herself. It's her whole life—until Princess Elizabeth asks for her help in solving mysteries! Musicians, and performing artists of all sorts, were often in a perfect position to act as spies and mediators. They were generally well educated, mobile both physically and socially, and when they played at banquets and state occasions often overheard useful conversations. An intelligent, talented, and pretty (but not *too* pretty!) young lady like Kate would have much more freedom than most women in her strata.

And while Kate and her father (as well as her friends—the lawyer Anthony, the actor Rob Cartman, and the lady-in-waiting Penelope) are fictional, I had fun weaving real historical figures into my plot as well. Among the true characters are: Elizabeth's keeper-gaoler, Sir Thomas Pope (who actually was not very restrictive); the family of Nicholas Bacon at Gorhambury (who was later Elizabeth's Lord Keeper of the Privy Seal); the Count (later Duke) de Feria, Philip II of Spain's emissary (the dinner at Brocket Hall with Lady Clinton, Elizabeth's old friend "the fair Geraldine"—another true figure!—actually happened much the way I've written it, though I have had to fiddle with the timing a bit); and the count's English fiancée and Queen Mary's lady-in-waiting Jane Dormer (who lived a fascinating and very long life in her own right, though she makes only a quick appearance in this tale). I loved getting to spend more time with all these people.

I've also loved spending time in their homes and spaces! When I visited Hatfield many years ago, this story wasn't even in my mind, but since I always take lots of notes and photos at every historical site I visit (and am addicted to buying guidebooks!), I had lots of memories and materials to use for this book. Most of the house Elizabeth knew is gone now, except for Hatfield Old Palace, which gives a taste of what life must have been like for the young princess and her household.

(Also, if you happen to visit Hatfield, it's worth a look at the nearby churchyard, where Lady Caroline Lamb and her husband, Lord Melbourne, are buried! Along with the Tudors, I also love the Regency period.)

I also have to say that, though Queen Mary has to be a villain of sorts in this story, I've always felt sorry for her! She is one of the saddest, most misunderstood figures in English history, and I apologize to her for giving her such a vile servant as Lord Braceton.

I had so much fun visiting Elizabeth's world for *Murder at Hatfield House*, and can't wait to dip into it again for the next story (centered around the queen's glittering coronation—stalked by a serial killer!). I hope you enjoyed reading it. For more behind-the-book info, Tudor history sources, and lots of fun stuff, visit my Web site at amandacarmack.com!

Center Point Large Print
600 Brooks Road / PO Box 1
Thorndike ME 04986-0001 USA

(207) 568-3717

US & Canada:
1 800 929-9108
www.centerpointlargeprint.com